NINE TOMORROWS

NINE TOMORROWS

TALES OF THE NEAR FUTURE

ISAAC ASIMOV

THE SCIENCE FICTION BOOK CLUB
by arrangement with DENNIS DOBSON
London 1964

All of the characters in this book are fictitious, and any resemblance to actual persons; living or dead, is purely coincidental.

This Science Fiction Book Club edition was produced in 1964 for sale to its members only by the proprietors, Readers Union Ltd, at Aldine House, 10–13 Bedford Street, London W.C.2 and at Letchworth Garden City, Herts. Full details of membership may be obtained from our London address. The book has been reprinted by A. Wheaton & Co., Ltd., Exeter. It was first published by Dobson Books Ltd.

To Betty Shapian,
whose kindness and helpfulness
have been unfailing.

CONTENTS

CONTENTS

NINE TOMORROWS

I JUST MAKE THEM UP, SEE!

Oh, Dr. A.——
Oh, Dr. A.——
There is something (don't go 'way)
That I'd like to hear you say.
Though I'd rather die
Than try
To pry,
The fact, you'll find,
Is that my mind
Has evolved the jackpot question for today.

I intend no cheap derision,
So please answer with decision,
And, discarding all your petty cautious fears,
Tell the secret of your vision!
How on earth
Do you give birth
To those crazy and impossible ideas?

Is it indigestion
And a question
Of the nightmare that results?
Of your eyeballs whirling,
Twirling,
Fingers curling
And unfurling,
While your blood beats maddened chimes
As it keeps impassioned times
With your thick, uneven pulse?

Is it *that*, you think, or liquor
That brings on the wildness quicker?
For a teeny
Weeny
Dry martini
May be just your private genie;
Or perhaps those Tom and Jerries
You will find the very
Berries
For inducing
And unloosing
That weird gimmick or that kicker;
Or an awful
Combination
Of unlawful
Stimulation,
Marijuana plus tequila,
That will give you just that feel o'
Things a-clicking
And unsticking
As you start your cerebration
To the crazy syncopation
Of a brain a-tocking-ticking.

Surely *something*, Dr. A.,
Makes you fey
And quite *outré*.

Since I read you with devotion,
Won't you give me just a notion
Of that shrewdly pepped-up potion
Out of which emerge your plots?
That wild secret bubbly mixture
That has made you such a fixture
In most favored s. f. spots——

Now, Dr. A.,
Don't go away——

Oh, Dr. A.——

Oh, Dr. A.——

PROFESSION

GEORGE PLATEN could not conceal the longing in his voice. It was too much to suppress. He said, "Tomorrow's the first of May. Olympics!"

He rolled over on his stomach and peered over the foot of his bed at his roommate. Didn't *he* feel it, too? Didn't *this* make some impression on him?

George's face was thin and had grown a trifle thinner in the nearly year and a half that he had been at the House. His figure was slight but the look in his blue eyes was as intense as it had ever been, and right now there was a trapped look in the way his fingers curled against the bedspread.

George's roommate looked up briefly from his book and took the opportunity to adjust the light-level of the stretch of wall near his chair. His name was Hali Omani and he was a Nigerian by birth. His dark brown skin and massive features seemed made for calmness, and mention of the Olympics did not move him.

He said, "I know, George."

George owed much to Hali's patience and kindness when it was needed, but even patience and kindness could be overdone.

Was this a time to sit there like a statue built of some dark, warm wood?

George wondered if he himself would grow like that after ten years here and rejected the thought violently. No!

He said defiantly, "I think you've forgotten what May means."

The other said, "I remember very well what it means. It means nothing! You're the one who's forgotten that. May means nothing to you, George Platen, and," he added softly, "it means nothing to me, Hali Omani."

George said, "The ships are coming in for recruits. By June, thousands and thousands will leave with millions of men and women heading for any world you can name, and all that means nothing?"

"Less than nothing. What do you want me to do about it, anyway?" Omani ran his finger along a difficult passage in the book he was reading and his lips moved soundlessly.

George watched him. Damn it, he thought, yell, scream; you can do that much. Kick at me, do anything.

It was only that he wanted not to be so alone in his anger. He wanted not to be the only one so filled with resentment, not to be the only one dying a slow death.

It was better those first weeks when the Universe was a small shell of vague light and sound pressing down upon him. It was better before Omani had wavered into view and dragged him back to a life that wasn't worth living.

Omani! He was old! He was at least thirty. George thought: Will I be like that at thirty? Will I be like that in twelve years?

And because he was afraid he might be, he yelled at Omani, "Will you stop reading that fool book?"

Omani turned a page and read on a few words, then lifted his head with its skullcap of crisply curled hair and said, "What?"

"What good does it do you to read the book?" He stepped forward, snorted "More electronics," and slapped it out of Omani's hands.

Omani got up slowly and picked up the book. He smoothed a crumpled page without visible rancor. "Call it the satisfaction of curiosity," he said. "I understand a little of it today, perhaps a little more tomorrow. That's a victory in a way."

"A victory. What kind of a victory? Is that what satisfies you in life? To get to know enough to be a quarter of a Registered Electronician by the time you're sixty-five?"

"Perhaps by the time I'm thirty-five."

"And then who'll want you? Who'll use you? Where will you go?"

"No one. No one. Nowhere. I'll stay here and read other books."

"And that satisfies you? Tell me! You've dragged me to class. You've got me to reading and memorizing, too. For what? There's nothing in it that satisfies me."

"What good will it do you to deny yourself satisfaction?"

"It means I'll quit the whole farce. I'll do as I planned to do in the beginning before you dovey-lovied me out of it. I'm going to force them to—to——"

Omani put down his book. He let the other run down and then said, "To what, George?"

"To correct a miscarriage of justice. A frame-up. I'll get that Antonelli and force him to admit he—he——"

Omani shook his head. "Everyone who comes here insists it's a mistake. I thought you'd passed that stage."

"Don't call it a stage," said George violently. "In my case, it's a fact. I've told you——"

"You've told me, but in your heart you know no one made any mistake as far as you were concerned."

"Because no one will admit it? You think any of them would admit a mistake unless they were forced to? ——Well, I'll force them."

It was May that was doing this to George; it was Olympics month. He felt it bring the old wildness back and he couldn't stop it. He didn't want to stop it. He had been in danger of forgetting.

He said, "I was going to be a Computer Programmer and I *can* be one. I could be one today, regardless of what they say analysis shows." He pounded his mattress. "They're wrong. They *must* be."

"The analysts are never wrong."

"They *must* be. Do you doubt my intelligence?"

"Intelligence hasn't one thing to do with it. Haven't you been told that often enough? Can't you understand that?"

George rolled away, lay on his back, and stared somberly at the ceiling.

"What did you want to be, Hali?"

"I had no fixed plans. Hydroponicist would have suited me, I suppose."

"Did you think you could make it?"

"I wasn't sure."

George had never asked personal questions of Omani before. It struck him as queer, almost unnatural, that other people had had ambitions and ended here. Hydroponicist!

He said, "Did you think you'd make *this?*"

"No, but here I am just the same."

"And you're satisfied. Really, really satisfied. You're happy. You love it. You wouldn't be anywhere else."

Slowly, Omani got to his feet. Carefully, he began to unmake his bed. He said, "George, you're a hard case. You're knocking yourself out because you won't accept the facts about yourself. George, you're here in what you call the House, but I've never heard you give it its full title. Say it, George, say it. Then go to bed and sleep this off."

George gritted his teeth and showed them. He choked out, "No!"

"Then I will," said Omani, and he did. He shaped each syllable carefully.

George was bitterly ashamed at the sound of it. He turned his head away.

For most of the first eighteen years of his life, George Platen had headed firmly in one direction, that of Registered Computer Programmer. There were those in his crowd who spoke wisely of Spationautics, Refrigeration Technology, Transportation Control, and even Administration. But George held firm.

He argued relative merits as vigorously as any of them, and why not? Education Day loomed ahead of them and was the great fact of their existence. It approached steadily, as fixed and certain as the calendar—the first day of November of the year following one's eighteenth birthday.

After that day, there were other topics of conversation. One could discuss with others some detail of the profession, or the virtues of one's wife and children, or the fate of one's space-polo team, or one's experiences in the Olympics. Before Education Day, however, there was only one topic that unfailingly and unwearyingly held everyone's interest, and that was Education Day.

"What are you going for? Think you'll make it? Heck, that's no good. Look at the records; quota's been cut. Logistics now——"

Or Hypermechanics now—— Or Communications now—— Or Gravitics now——

Especially Gravitics at the moment. Everyone had been talking about Gravitics in the few years just before George's Education Day because of the development of the Gravitic power engine.

Any world within ten light-years of a dwarf star, everyone said, would give its eyeteeth for any kind of Registered Gravitics Engineer.

The thought of that never bothered George. Sure it would; all the eyeteeth it could scare up. But George had also heard what had happened before in a newly developed technique. Rationalization and simplification followed in a flood. New models each year; new types of gravitic engines; new principles. Then all those eyeteeth gentlemen would find themselves out of date and superseded by later models with later educations. The first group would then have to settle down to unskilled labor or ship out to some backwoods world that wasn't quite caught up yet.

Now Computer Programmers were in steady demand year after year, century after century. The demand never reached wild peaks; there was never a howling bull market for Programmers; but the demand climbed steadily as new worlds opened up and as older words grew more complex.

He had argued with Stubby Trevelyan about that constantly. As best friends, their arguments had to be constant and vitriolic and, of course, neither ever persuaded or was persuaded.

But then Trevelyan had had a father who was a Registered Metallurgist and had actually served on one of the Outworlds, and a grandfather who had also been a Registered Metallurgist. He himself was intent on becoming a Registered Metallurgist almost as a matter of family right and was firmly convinced that any other profession was a shade less than respectable.

"There'll always be metal," he said, "and there's an accomplishment in molding alloys to specification and watching structures grow.

Now what's a Programmer going to be doing. Sitting at a coder all day long, feeding some fool mile-long machine.

Even at sixteen, George had learned to be practical. He said simply, "There'll be a million Metallurgists put out along with you."

"Because it's good. A good profession. The best."

"But you get crowded out, Stubby. You can be way back in line. Any world can tape out its own Metallurgists, and the market for advanced Earth models isn't so big. And it's mostly the small worlds that want them. You know what per cent of the turnout of Registered Metallurgists get tabbed for worlds with a Grade A rating. I looked it up. It's just 13.3 per cent. That means you'll have seven chances in eight of being stuck in some world that just about has running water. You may even be stuck on Earth; 2.3 per cent are."

Trevelyan said belligerently, "There's no disgrace in staying on Earth. Earth needs technicians, too. Good ones." His grandfather had been an Earth-bound Metallurgist, and Trevelyan lifted his finger to his upper lip and dabbed at an as yet nonexistent mustache.

George knew about Trevelyan's grandfather and, considering the Earth-bound position of his own ancestry, was in no mood to sneer. He said diplomatically, "No intellectual disgrace. Of course not. But it's nice to get into a Grade A world, isn't it?

"Now you take Programmers. Only the Grade A worlds have the kind of computers that really need first-class Programmers so they're the only ones in the market. And Programmer tapes are complicated and hardly any one fits. They need more Programmers than their own population can supply. It's just a matter of statistics. There's one first-class Programmer per million, say. A world needs twenty and has a population of ten million, they have to come to Earth for five to fifteen Programmers. Right?

"And you know how many Registered Computer Programmers went to Grade A planets last year? I'll tell you. Every last one. If you're a Programmer, you're a picked man. Yes, sir."

Trevelyan frowned. "If only one in a million makes it, what makes you think *you*'ll make it?"

George said guardedly, "I'll make it."

He never dared tell anyone; not Trevelyan; not his parents; of exactly what he was doing that made him so confident. But he wasn't worried. He was simply confident (that was the worst of the memories he had in the hopeless days afterward). He was as blandly confident as the average eight-year-old kid approaching Reading Day—that childhood preview of Education Day.

Of course, Reading Day had been different. Partly, there was the simple fact of childhood. A boy of eight takes many extraordinary things in stride. One day you can't read and the next day you can. That's just the way things are. Like the sun shining.

And then not so much depended upon it. There were no recruiters just ahead, waiting and jostling for the lists and scores on the coming Olympics. A boy or girl who goes through the Reading Day is just someone who has ten more years of undifferentiated living upon Earth's crawling surface; just someone who returns to his family with one new ability.

By the time Education Day came, ten years later, George wasn't even sure of most of the details of his own Reading Day.

Most clearly of all, he remembered it to be a dismal September day with a mild rain falling. (September for Reading Day; November for Education Day; May for Olympics. They made nursery rhymes out of it.) George had dressed by the wall lights, with his parents far more excited than he himself was. His father was a Registered Pipe Fitter and had found his occupation on earth. This fact had always been a humiliation to him, although, of course, as anyone could see plainly, most of each generation must stay on Earth in the nature of things.

There had to be farmers and miners and even technicians on Earth. It was only the late-model, high-specialty professions that were in demand on the Outworlds, and only a few millions a year out of Earth's eight billion population could be exported. Every man and woman on Earth couldn't be among that group.

But every man and woman could hope that at least one of his children could be one, and Platen, Senior, was certainly no exception. It was obvious to him (and, to be sure, to others as well) that George was notably intelligent and quick-minded. He would be bound to do well and he would have to, as he was an only child. If George didn't end on an Outworld, they would have to wait for grandchildren before a next chance would come along, and that was too far in the future to be much consolation.

Reading Day would not prove much, of course, but it would be the only indication they would have before the big day itself. Every parent on Earth would be listening to the quality of reading when his child came home with it; listening for any particularly easy flow of words and building that into certain omens of the future. There were few families that didn't have at least one hopeful who, from Reading Day on, was the great hope because of the way he handled his trisyllabics.

Dimly, George was aware of the cause of his parents' tension, and if there was any anxiety in his young heart that drizzly morning, it was only the fear that his father's hopeful expression might fade out when he returned home with his reading.

The children met in the large assembly room of the town's Education hall. All over Earth, in millions of local halls, throughout that month, similar groups of children would be meeting. George felt depressed by the grayness of the room and by the other children, strained and stiff in unaccustomed finery.

Automatically, George did as all the rest of the children did. He found the small clique that represented the children on his floor of the apartment house and joined them.

Trevelyan, who lived immediately next door, still wore his hair childishly long and was years removed from the sideburns and thin, reddish mustache that he was to grow as soon as he was physiologically capable of it.

Trevelyan (to whom George was then known as Jaw-jee) said, "Bet you're scared."

"I am not," said George. Then, confidentially, "My folks got a hunk of printing up on the dresser in my room, and when I come home, I'm going to read it for them." (George's main suffering at the moment lay in the fact that he didn't quite know where to put his hands. He had been warned not to scratch his head or rub his ears or pick his nose or put his hands into his pockets. This eliminated almost every possibility.)

Trevelyan put *his* hands in his pockets and said, "My father isn't worried."

Trevelyan, Senior, had been a Metallurgist on Diporia for nearly seven years, which gave him a superior social status in his neighborhood even though he had retired and returned to Earth.

Earth discouraged these re-immigrants because of population problems, but a small trickle did return. For one thing the cost of living was lower on Earth, and what was a trifling annuity on Diporia, say, was a comfortable income on Earth. Besides, there were always men who found more satisfaction in displaying their success before the friends and scenes of their childhood than before all the rest of the Universe besides.

Trevelyan, Senior, further explained that if he stayed on Diporia, so would his children, and Diporia was a one-spaceship world. Back on Earth, his kids could end anywhere, even Novia.

Stubby Trevelyan had picked up that item early. Even before Reading Day, his conversation was based on the carelessly assumed fact that his ultimate home would be in Novia.

George, oppressed by thoughts of the other's future greatness and his own small-time contrast, was driven to belligerent defense at once.

"My father isn't worried either. He just wants to hear me read because he knows I'll be good. I suppose your father would just as soon not hear you because he knows you'll be all wrong."

"I will not be all wrong. Reading is *nothing*. On Novia, I'll *hire* people to read to me."

"Because *you* won't be able to read yourself, on account of you're *dumb!*"

"Then how come I'll be on Novia?"

And George, driven, made the great denial, "Who says you'll be on Novia? Bet you don't go anywhere."

Stubby Trevelyan reddened. "I won't be a Pipe Fitter like your old man."

"Take that back, you dumbhead."

"You take *that* back."

They stood nose to nose, not wanting to fight but relieved at having something familiar to do in this strange place. Furthermore, now that George had curled his hands into fists and lifted them before his face, the problem of what to do with his hands was, at least temporarily, solved. Other children gathered round excitedly.

But then it all ended when a woman's voice sounded loudly

over the public address system. There was instant silence every-
where. George dropped his fists and forgot Trevelyan.

"Children," said the voice, "we are going to call out your names.
As each child is called, he or she is to go to one of the men waiting
along the side walls. Do you see them? They are wearing red
uniforms so they will be easy to find. The girls will go to the right.
The boys will go to the left. Now look about and see which man in
red is nearest to you——"

George found his man at a glance and waited for his name to
be called off. He had not been introduced before this to the sophisti-
cations of the alphabet, and the length of time it took to reach
his own name grew disturbing.

The crowd of children thinned; little rivulets made their way to
each of the red-clad guides.

When the name "George Platen" was finally called, his sense
of relief was exceeded only by the feeling of pure gladness at
the fact that Stubby Trevelyan still stood in his place, uncalled.

George shouted back over his shoulder as he left, "Yay, Stubby,
maybe they don't want you."

That moment of gaiety quickly left. He was herded into a line
and directed down corridors in the company of strange children.
They all looked at one another, large-eyed and concerned, but beyond a snuffling, "Quitcher pushing" and "Hey, watch out" there
was no conversation.

They were handed little slips of paper which they were told
must remain with them. George stared at his curiously. Little
black marks of different shapes. He knew it to be printing but
how could anyone make words out of it? He couldn't imagine.

He was told to strip; he and four other boys who were all that
now remained together. All the new clothes came shucking off and
four eight-year-olds stood naked and small, shivering more out of
embarrassment than cold. Medical technicians came past, probing
them, testing them with odd instruments, pricking them for blood.
Each took the little cards and made additional marks on them with
little black rods that produced the marks, all neatly lined up, with
great speed. George stared at the new marks, but they were nc
more comprehensible than the old. The children were ordered back
into their clothes.

They sat on separate little chairs then and waited again. Names were called again and "George Platen" came third.

He moved into a large room, filled with frightening instruments with knobs and glassy panels in front. There was a desk in the very center, and behind it a man sat, his eyes on the papers piled before him.

He said, "George Platen?"

"Yes, sir," said George, in a shaky whisper. All this waiting and all this going here and there was making him nervous. He wished it were over.

The man behind the desk said, "I am Dr. Lloyed, George. How are you?"

The doctor didn't look up as he spoke. It was as though he had said those words over and over again and didn't have to look up any more.

"I'm all right."

"Are you afraid, George?"

"N—no, sir," said George, sounding afraid even in his own ears.

"That's good," said the doctor, "because there's nothing to be afraid of, you know. Let's see, George. It says here on your card that your father is named Peter and that he's a Registered Pipe Fitter and your mother is named Amy and is a Registered Home Technician. Is that right?"

"Y—yes, sir."

"And your birthday is February 13, and you had an ear infection about a year ago. Right?"

"Yes, sir."

"Do you know how I know all these things?"

"It's on the card, I think, sir."

"That's right." The doctor looked up at George for the first time and smiled. He showed even teeth and looked much younger than George's father. Some of George's nervousness vanished.

The doctor passed the card to George. "Do you know what all those things there mean, George?"

Although George knew he did not he was startled by the sudden request into looking at the card as though he might understand now through some sudden stroke of fate. But they were just marks as before and he passed the card back. "No, sir."

"Why not?"

George felt a sudden pang of suspicion concerning the sanity of this doctor. Didn't he know why not?

George said, "I can't read, sir."

"Would you like to read?"

"Yes, sir."

"Why, George?"

George stared, appalled. No one had ever asked him that. He had no answer. He said falteringly, "I don't know, sir."

"Printed information will direct you all through your life. There is so much you'll have to know even after Education Day. Cards like this one will tell you. Books will tell you. Television screens will tell you. Printing will tell you such useful things and such interesting things that not being able to read would be as bad as not being able to see. Do you understand?"

"Yes, sir."

"Are you afraid, George?"

"No, sir."

"Good. Now I'll tell you exactly what we'll do first. I'm going to put these wires on your forehead just over the corners of your eyes. They'll stick there but they won't hurt at all. Then, I'll turn on something that will make a buzz. It will sound funny and it may tickle you, but it won't hurt. Now if it does hurt, you tell me, and I'll turn it off right away, but it won't hurt. All right?"

George nodded and swallowed.

"Are you ready?"

George nodded. He closed his eyes while the doctor busied himself. His parents had explained this to him. They, too, had said it wouldn't hurt, but then there were always the older children. There were the ten- and twelve-year-olds who howled after the eight-year-olds waiting for Reading Day, "Watch out for the needle." There were the others who took you off in confidence and said, "They got to cut your head open. They use a sharp knife that big with a hook on it," and so on into horrifying details.

George had never believed them but he had had nightmares, and now he closed his eyes and felt pure terror.

He didn't feel the wires at his temple. The buzz was a distant thing, and there was the sound of his own blood in his ears, ringing hollowly as though it and he were in a large cave. Slowly he chanced opening his eyes.

The doctor had his back to him. From one of the instruments a strip of paper unwound and was covered with a thin, wavy purple line. The doctor tore off pieces and put them into a slot in another machine. He did it over and over again. Each time a little piece of film came out, which the doctor looked at. Finally, he turned toward George with a queer frown between his eyes.

The buzzing stopped.

George said breathlessly, "Is it over?"

The doctor said, "Yes," but he was still frowning.

"Can I read now?" asked George. He felt no different.

The doctor said, "What?" then smiled very suddenly and briefly. He said, "It works fine, George. You'll be reading in fifteen minutes. Now we're going to use another machine this time and it will take longer. I'm going to cover your whole head, and when I turn it on you won't be able to see or hear anything for a while, but it won't hurt. Just to make sure I'm going to give you a little switch to hold in your hand. If anything hurts, you press the little button and everything shuts off. All right?"

In later years, George was told that the little switch was strictly a dummy; that it was introduced solely for confidence. He never did know for sure, however, since he never pushed the button.

A large smoothly curved helmet with a rubbery inner lining was placed over his head and left there. Three or four little knobs seemed to grab at him and bite into his skull, but there was only a little pressure that faded. No pain.

The doctor's voice sounded dimly. "Everything all right, George?"

And then, with no real warning, a layer of thick felt closed down all about him. He was disembodied, there was no sensation, no universe, only himself and a distant murmur at the very ends of nothingness telling him something—telling him—telling him——

He strained to hear and understand but there was all that thick felt between.

Then the helmet was taken off his head, and the light was so bright that it hurt his eyes while the doctor's voice drummed at his ears.

The doctor said, "Here's your card, George. What does it say?"

George looked at his card again and gave out a strangled shout. The marks weren't just marks at all. They made up words. They were words just as clearly as though something were whispering them in his ears. He could *hear* them being whispered as he looked at them.

"What does it say, George?"

"It says—it says—'Platen, George. Born 13 February 6492 of Peter and Amy Platen in . . .' " He broke off.

"You can read, George," said the doctor. "It's all over."

"For good? I won't forget how?"

"Of course not." The doctor leaned over to shake hands gravely. "You will be taken home now."

It was days before George got over this new and great talent of his. He read for his father with such facility that Platen, Senior, wept and called relatives to tell the good news.

George walked about town, reading every scrap of printing he could find and wondering how it was that none of it had ever made sense to him before.

He tried to remember how it was not to be able to read and he couldn't. As far as his feeling about it was concerned, he had always been able to read. Always.

At eighteen, George was rather dark, of medium height, but thin enough to look taller. Trevelyan, who was scarcely an inch shorter, had a stockiness of build that made "Stubby" more than ever appropriate, but in this last year he had grown self-conscious. The nickname could no longer be used without reprisal. And since Trevelyan disapproved of his proper first name even more strongly, he was called Trevelyan or any decent variant of that. As though to prove his manhood further, he had most persistently grown a pair of sideburns and a bristly mustache.

He was sweating and nervous now, and George, who had himself grown out of "Jaw-jee" and into the curt monosyllabic gutturality of "George," was rather amused by that.

They were in the same large hall they had been in ten years before (and not since). It was as if a vague dream of the past had come to sudden reality. In the first few minutes George had been distinctly surprised at finding everything seem smaller and more cramped than his memory told him; then he made allowance for his own growth.

The crowd was smaller than it had been in childhood. It was exclusively male this time. The girls had another day assigned them.

Trevelyan leaned over to say, "Beats me the way they make you wait."

"Red tape," said George. "You can't avoid it."

Trevelyan said, "What makes *you* so damned tolerant about it?"

"I've got nothing to worry about."

"Oh, brother, you make me sick. I hope you end up Registered Manure Spreader just so I can see your face when you do." His somber eyes swept the crowd anxiously.

George looked about, too. It wasn't quite the system they used on the children. Matters went slower, and instructions had been given out at the start in print (an advantage over the pre-Readers). The names Platen and Trevelyan were well down the alphabet still, but this time the two knew it.

Young men came out of the education rooms, frowning and uncomfortable, picked up their clothes and belongings, then went off to analysis to learn the results.

Each, as he come out, would be surrounded by a clot of the thinning crowd. "How was it?" "How'd it feel?" "Whacha think ya made?" "Ya feel any different?"

Answers were vague and noncommittal.

George forced himself to remain out of those clots. You only raised your own blood pressure. Everyone said you stood the best chance if you remained calm. Even so, you could feel the palms of your hands grow cold. Funny that new tensions came with the years.

For instance, high-specialty professionals heading out for an Outworld were accompanied by a wife (or husband). It was important to keep the sex ratio in good balance on all worlds. And if you were going out to a Grade A world, what girl would refuse you? George had no specific girl in mind yet; he wanted none. Not now! Once he made Programmer; once he could add to his name, Registered Computer Programmer, he could take his pick, like a sultan in a harem. The thought excited him and he tried to put it away. Must stay calm.

Trevelyan muttered, "What's it all about anyway? First they say it works best if you're relaxed and at ease. Then they put you through this and make it impossible for you to be relaxed and at ease."

"Maybe that's the idea. They're separating the boys from the men to begin with. Take it easy, Trev."

"Shut up."

George's turn came. His name was not called. It appeared in glowing letters on the notice board.

He waved at Trevelyan. "Take it easy. Don't let it get you."

He was happy as he entered the testing chamber. Actually happy.

The man behind the desk said, "George Platen?"

For a fleeting instant there was a razor-sharp picture in George's mind of another man, ten years earlier, who had asked the same question, and it was almost as though this were the same man and he, George, had turned eight again as he had stepped across the threshold.

But the man looked up and, of course, the face matched that of the sudden memory not at all. The nose was bulbous, the hair thin and stringy, and the chin wattled as though its owner had once been grossly overweight and had reduced.

The man behind the desk looked annoyed. "Well?"

George came to Earth. "I'm George Platen, sir."

"Say so, then. I'm Dr. Zachary Antonelli, and we're going to be intimately acquainted in a moment."

He stared at small strips of film, holding them up to the light owlishly.

George winced inwardly. Very hazily, he remembered that other doctor (he had forgotten the name) staring at such film. Could these be the same? The other doctor had frowned and this one was looking at him now as though he were angry.

His happiness was already just about gone.

Dr. Antonelli spread the pages of a thickish file out before him now and put the films carefully to one side. "It says here you want to be a Computer Programmer."

"Yes, doctor."

"Still do?"

"Yes, sir."

"It's a responsible and exacting position. Do you feel up to it?"

"Yes, sir."

"Most pre-Educates don't put down any specific profession. I believe they are afraid of queering it."

"I think that's right, sir."

"Aren't you afraid of that?"

"I might as well be honest, sir."

Dr. Antonelli nodded, but without any noticeable lightening of his expression. "Why do you want to be a Programmer?"

"It's a responsible and exacting position as you said, sir. It's an important job and an exciting one. I like it and I think I can do it."

Dr. Antonelli put the papers away, and looked at George sourly. He said, "How do you know you like it? Because you think you'll be snapped up by some Grade A planet?"

George thought uneasily: He's trying to rattle you. Stay calm and stay frank.

He said, "I think a Programmer has a good chance, sir, but even if I were left on Earth, I know I'd like it." (That was true enough. I'm not lying, thought George.)

"All right, how do you know?"

He asked it as though he knew there was no decent answer and George almost smiled. He had one.

He said, "I've been reading about Programming, sir."

"You've been *what?*" Now the doctor looked genuinely astonished and George took pleasure in that.

"Reading about it, sir. I bought a book on the subject and I've been studying it."

"A book for Registered Programmers?"

"Yes, sir."

"But you couldn't understand it."

"Not at first. I got other books on mathematics and electronics. I made out all I could. I still don't know much, but I know enough to know I like it and to know I can make it." (Even his parents never found that secret cache of books or knew why he spent so much time in his own room or exactly what happened to the sleep he missed.)

The doctor pulled at the loose skin under his chin. "What was your idea in doing that, son?"

"I wanted to make sure I would be interested, sir."

"Surely you know that being interested means nothing. You could be devoured by a subject and if the physical make-up of your brain makes it more efficient for you to be something else, something else you will be. You know that, don't you?"

"I've been told that," said George cautiously.

"Well, believe it. It's true."

George said nothing.

Dr. Antonelli said, "Or do you believe that studying some subject will bend the brain cells in that direction, like that other theory that a pregnant woman need only listen to great music persistently to make a composer of her child. Do you believe that?"

George flushed. That had certainly been in his mind. By forcing his intellect constantly in the desired direction, he had felt sure that he would be getting a head start. Most of his confidence had rested on exactly that point.

"I never——" he began, and found no way of finishing.

"Well, it isn't true. Good Lord, youngster, your brain pattern is fixed at birth. It can be altered by a blow hard enough to damage the cells or by a burst blood vessel or by a tumor or by a major infection——each time, of course, for the worse. But it certainly can't be affected by your thinking special thoughts." He stared at George thoughtfully, then said, "Who told you to do this?"

George, now thoroughly disturbed, swallowed and said, "No one, doctor. My own idea."

"Who knew you were doing it after you started?"

"No one. Doctor, I meant to do no wrong."

"Who said anything about wrong? Useless is what I would say. Why did you keep it to yourself?"

"I—I thought they'd laugh at me." (He thought abruptly of a recent exchange with Trevelyan. George had very cautiously broached the thought, as of something merely circulating distantly in the very outermost reaches of his mind, concerning the possibility of learning something by ladling it into the mind by hand, so to speak, in bits and pieces. Trevelyan had hooted, "George, you'll be tanning your own shoes next and weaving your own shirts." He had been thankful then for his policy of secrecy.)

Dr. Antonelli shoved the bits of film he had first looked at from position to position in morose thought. Then he said, "Let's get you analyzed. This is getting me nowhere."

The wires went to George's temples. There was the buzzing. Again there came a sharp memory of ten years ago.

George's hands were clammy; his heart pounded. He should never have told the doctor about his secret reading.

It was his damned vanity, he told himself. He had wanted to show how enterprising he was, how full of initiative. Instead, he had showed himself superstitious and ignorant and aroused the hostility of the doctor. (He could tell the doctor hated him for a wise guy on the make.)

And now he had brought himself to such a state of nervousness, he was sure the analyzer would show nothing that made sense.

He wasn't aware of the moment when the wires were removed from his temples. The sight of the doctor, staring at him thoughtfully, blinked into his consciousness and that was that; the wires were gone. George dragged himself together with a tearing effort. He had quite given up his ambition to be a Programmer. In the space of ten minutes, it had all gone.

He said dismally, "I suppose no?"

"No what?"

"No Programmer?"

The doctor rubbed his nose and said, "You get your clothes and whatever belongs to you and go to room 15-C. Your files will be waiting for you there. So will my report."

George said in complete surprise. "Have I been Educated already? I thought this was just to———"

Dr. Antonelli stared down at his desk. "It will all be explained to you. You do as I say."

George felt something like panic. What was it they couldn't tell him? He wasn't fit for anything but Registered Laborer. They were going to prepare him for that; adjust him to it.

He was suddenly certain of it and he had to keep from screaming by main force.

He stumbled back to his place of waiting. Trevelyan was not there, a fact for which he would have been thankful if he had had enough self-possession to be meaningfully aware of his surroundings. Hardly anyone was left, in fact, and the few who were looked as though they might ask him questions were it not that they were too worn out by their tail-of-the-alphabet waiting to buck the fierce, hot look of anger and hate he cast at them.

What right had *they* to be technicians and he, himself, a Laborer? Laborer! He was *certain!*

He was led by a red-uniformed guide along the busy corridors lined with separate rooms each containing its groups, here two, there five: the Motor Mechanics, the Construction Engineers, the Agronomists—— There were hundreds of specialized Professions and most of them would be represented in this small town by one or two anyway.

He hated them all just then: the Statisticians, the Accountants, the lesser breeds and the higher. He hated them because they owned their smug knowledge now, knew their fate, while he himself, empty still, had to face some kind of further red tape.

He reached 15-C, was ushered in and left in an empty room. For one moment, his spirits bounded. Surely, if this were the Labor classification room, there would be dozens of youngsters present.

A door sucked into its recess on the other side of a waist-high partition and an elderly, white-haired man stepped out. He smiled and showed even teeth that were obviously false, but his face was still ruddy and unlined and his voice had vigor.

He said, "Good evening, George. Our own sector has only one of you this time, I see."

"Only one?" said George blankly.

"Thousands over the Earth, of course. Thousands. You're not alone."

George felt exasperated. He said, "I don't understand, sir. What's my classification? What's happening?"

"Easy, son. You're all right. It could happen to anyone." He held out his hand and George took it mechanically. It was warm and it pressed George's hand firmly. "Sit down, son. I'm Sam Ellenford."

George nodded impatiently. "I want to know what's going on, sir."

"Of course. To begin with, you can't be a Computer Programmer, George. You've guessed that, I think."

"Yes, I have," said George bitterly. "What will I be, then?"

"That's the hard part to explain, George." He paused, then said with careful distinctness, "Nothing."

"What!"

"Nothing!"

"But what does that mean? Why can't you assign me a profession?"

"We have no choice in the matter, George. It's the structure of your mind that decides that."

George went a sallow yellow. His eyes bulged. "There's something wrong with my mind?"

"There's *something* about it. As far as professional classification is concerned, I suppose you can call it wrong."

"But why?"

Ellenford shrugged. "I'm sure you know how Earth runs its Educational program, George. Practically any human being can absorb practically any body of knowledge, but each individual brain pattern is better suited to receiving some types of knowledge than others. We try to match mind to knowledge as well as we can within the limits of the quota requirements for each profession."

George nodded. "Yes, I know."

"Every once in a while, George, we come up against a young man whose mind is not suited to receiving a superimposed knowledge of any sort."

"You mean I can't be Educated?"

"That is what I mean."

"But that's crazy. I'm intelligent. I can understand——" He looked helplessly about as though trying to find some way of proving that he had a functioning brain.

"Don't misunderstand me, please," said Ellenford gravely. "You're intelligent. There's no question about that. You're even above average in intelligence. Unfortunately that has nothing to do with whether the mind ought to be allowed to accept superimposed knowledge or not. In fact, it is almost always the intelligent person who comes here."

"You mean I can't even be a Registered Laborer?" babbled George. Suddenly even that was better than the blank that faced him. "What's there to know to be a Laborer?"

"Don't underestimate the Laborer, young man. There are dozens of subclassifications and each variety has its own corpus of fairly detailed knowledge. Do you think there's no skill in knowing the proper manner of lifting a weight? Besides, for the Laborer, we must select not only minds suited to it, but bodies as well. You're not the type, George, to last long as a Laborer."

George was conscious of his slight build. He said, "But I've never heard of anyone without a profession."

"There aren't many," conceded Ellenford. "And we protect them."

"Protect them?" George felt confusion and fright grow higher inside him.

"You're a ward of the planet, George. From the time you walked through that door, we've been in charge of you." And he smiled.

It was a fond smile. To George it seemed the smile of ownership; the smile of a grown man for a helpless child.

He said, "You mean, I'm going to be in prison?"

"Of course not. You will simply be with others of your kind."

Your kind. The words made a kind of thunder in George's ear.

Ellenford said, "You need special treatment. We'll take care of you."

To George's own horror, he burst into tears. Ellenford walked to the other end of the room and faced away as though in thought.

George fought to reduce the agonized weeping to sobs and then to strangle those. He thought of his father and mother, of his friends, of Trevelyan, of his own shame——

He said rebelliously, "I learned to read."

"Everyone with a whole mind can do that. We've never found exceptions. It is at this stage that we discover—exceptions. And when you learned to read, George, we were concerned about your mind pattern. Certain peculiarities were reported even then by the doctor in charge."

"Can't you try Educating me? You haven't even tried. I'm willing to take the risk."

"The law forbids us to do that, George. But look, it will not be bad. We will explain matters to your family so they will not be hurt. At the place to which you'll be taken, you'll be allowed privileges. We'll get you books and you can learn what you will."

"Dab knowledge in by hand," said George bitterly. "Shred by shred. Then, when I die I'll know enough to be a Registered Junior Office Boy, Paper-Clip Division."

"Yet I understand you've already been studying books."

George froze. He was struck devastatingly by sudden understanding. "That's it . . ."

"What is?"

"That fellow Antonelli. He's knifing me."

"No, George. You're quite wrong."

"Don't tell me that." George was in an ecstasy of fury. "That lousy bastard is selling me out because he thought I was a little too wise for him. I read books and tried to get a head start toward programming. Well, what do you want to square things? Money? You won't get it. I'm getting out of here and when I finish broadcasting this——"

He was screaming.

Ellenford shook his head and touched a contact.

Two men entered on catfeet and got on either side of George. They pinned his arms to his sides. One of them used an air-spray hypodermic in the hollow of his right elbow and the hypnotic entered his vein and had an almost immediate effect.

His screams cut off and his head fell forward. His knees buckled and only the men on either side kept him erect as he slept.

They took care of George as they said they would; they were good to him and unfailingly kind—about the way, George thought, he himself would be to a sick kitten he had taken pity on.

They told him that he should sit up and take some interest in life; and then told him that most people who came there had the same attitude of despair at the beginning and that he would snap out of it.

He didn't even hear them.

Dr. Ellenford himself visited him to tell him that his parents had been informed that he was away on special assignment.

George muttered, "Do they know——"

Ellenford assured him at once, "We gave no details."

At first George had refused to eat. They fed him intravenously. They hid sharp objects and kept him under guard. Hali Omani came to be his roommate and his stolidity had a calming effect.

One day, out of sheer desperate boredom, George asked for a book. Omani, who himself read books constantly, looked up, smiling broadly. George almost withdrew the request then, rather than give any of them satisfaction, then thought: What do I care?

He didn't specify the book and Omani brought one on chemistry. It was in big print, with small words and many illustrations. It was for teen-agers. He threw the book violently against the wall.

That's what he would be always. A teen-ager all his life. A pre-Educate forever and special books would have to be written for him. He lay smoldering in bed, staring at the ceiling, and after an hour had passed, he got up sulkily, picked up the book, and began reading.

It took him a week to finish it and then he asked for another.

"Do you want me to take the first one back?" asked Omani.

George frowned. There were things in the book he had not understood, yet he was not so lost to shame as to say so.

But Omani said, "Come to think of it, you'd better keep it. Books are meant to be read and reread."

It was that same day that he finally yielded to Omani's invitation that he tour the place. He dogged at the Nigerian's feet and took in his surroundings with quick hostile glances.

The place was no prison certainly. There were no walls, no locked doors, no guards. But it was a prison in that the inmates had no place to go outside.

It was somehow good to see others like himself by the dozen. It was so easy to believe himself to be the only one in the world so— maimed.

He mumbled, "How many people here anyway?"

"Two hundred and five, George, and this isn't the only place of the sort in the world. There are thousands."

Men looked up as he passed, wherever he went; in the gymnasium, along the tennis courts; through the library (he had never in his life imagined books could exist in such numbers; they were stacked, actually stacked, along long shelves). They stared at him curiously and he returned the looks savagely. At least *they* were no better than he; no call for *them* to look at him as though he were some sort of curiosity.

Most of them were in their twenties. George said suddenly, "What happens to the older ones?"

Omani said, "This place specializes in the younger ones." Then, as though he suddenly recognized an implication in George's question that he had missed earlier, he shook his head gravely and said, "They're not put out of the way, if that's what you mean. There are other Houses for older ones."

"Who cares?" mumbled George, who felt he was sounding too interested and in danger of slipping into surrender.

"You might. As you grow older, you will find yourself in a House with occupants of both sexes."

That surprised George somehow. "Women, too?"

"Of course. Do you suppose women are immune to this sort of thing?"

George thought of that with more interest and excitement than he had felt for anything since before that day when—— He forced his thought away from that.

Omani stopped at the doorway of a room that contained a small closed-circuit television set and a desk computer. Five or six men sat about the television. Omani said, "This is a classroom."

George said, "What's that?"

"The young men in there are being educated. Not," he added, quickly, "in the usual way."

"You mean they're cramming it in bit by bit."

"That's right. This is the way everyone did it in ancient times."

This was what they kept telling him since he had come to the House but what of it? Suppose there had been a day when mankind had not known the diatherm-oven. Did that mean he should be satisfied to eat meat raw in a world where others ate it cooked?

He said, "Why do they want to go through that bit-by-bit stuff?"

"To pass the time, George, and because they're curious."

"What good does it do them?"

"It makes them happier."

George carried that thought to bed with him.

The next day he said to Omani ungraciously, "Can you get me into a classroom where I can find out something about programming?"

Omani replied heartily, "Sure."

It was slow and he resented it. Why should someone have to explain something and explain it again? Why should he have to read and reread a passage, then stare at a mathematical relationship and not understand it at once? That wasn't how other people had to be.

Over and over again, he gave up. Once he refused to attend classes for a week.

But always he returned. The official in charge, who assigned reading, conducted the television demonstrations, and even explained difficult passages and concepts, never commented on the matter.

George was finally given a regular task in the gardens and took his turn in the various kitchen and cleaning details. This was represented to him as being an advance, but he wasn't fooled. The place might have been far more mechanized than it was, but they deliberately made work for the young men in order to give them the illusion of worth-while occupation, of usefulness. George wasn't fooled.

They were even paid small sums of money out of which they could buy certain specified luxuries or which they could put aside for a problematical use in a problemical old age. George kept his money in an open jar, which he kept on a closet shelf. He had no idea how much he had accumulated. Nor did he care.

He made no real friends though he reached the stage where a civil good day was in order. He even stopped brooding (or almost stopped) on the miscarriage of justice that had placed him there. He would go weeks without dreaming of Antonelli, of his gross nose and wattled neck, of the leer with which he would push George into a boiling quicksand and hold him under, till he woke screaming with Omani bending over him in concern.

Omani said to him on a snowy day in February, "It's amazing how you're adjusting."

But that was February, the thirteenth to be exact, his nineteenth birthday. March came, then April, and with the approach of May he realized he hadn't adjusted at all.

The previous May had passed unregarded while George was still in his bed, drooping and ambitionless. This May was different.

All over Earth, George knew, Olympics would be taking place and young men would be competing, matching their skills against one another in the fight for a place on a new world. There would be the holiday atmosphere, the excitement, the news reports, the self-contained recruiting agents from the worlds beyond space, the glory of victory or the consolations of defeat.

How much of fiction dealt with these motifs; how much of his own boyhood excitement lay in following the events of Olympics from year to year; how many of his own plans——

George Platen could not conceal the longing in his voice. It was too much to suppress. He said, "Tomorrow's the first of May. Olympics!"

And that led to his first quarrel with Omani and to Omani's bitter enunciation of the exact name of the institution in which George found himself.

Omani gazed fixedly at George and said distinctly, "A House for the Feeble-minded."

George Platen flushed. Feeble-minded!

He rejected it desperately. He said in a monotone, "I'm leaving." He said it on impulse. His conscious mind learned it first from the statement as he uttered it.

Omani, who had returned to his book, looked up. "What?"

George knew what he was saying now. He said it fiercely, "I'm leaving."

"That's ridiculous. Sit down, George, calm yourself."

"Oh, no. I'm here on a frame-up, I tell you. This doctor, Antonelli, took a dislike to me. It's the sense of power these petty bureaucrats have. Cross them and they wipe out your life with a stylus mark on some card file."

"Are you back to that?"

"And staying there till it's all straightened out. I'm going to get to Antonelli somehow, break him, force the truth out of him." George was breathing heavily and he felt feverish. Olympics month was here and he couldn't let it pass. If he did, it would be the final surrender and he would be lost for all time.

Omani threw his legs over the side of his bed and stood up. He was nearly six feet tall and the expression on his face gave him the look of a concerned Saint Bernard. He put his arm about George's shoulder, "If I hurt your feeling——"

George shrugged him off. "You just said what you thought was the truth, and I'm going to prove it isn't the truth, that's all. Why not? The door's open. There aren't any locks. No one ever said I couldn't leave. I'll just walk out."

"All right, but where will you go?"

"To the nearest air terminal, then to the nearest Olympics center. I've got money." He seized the open jar that held the wages he had put away. Some of the coins jangled to the floor.

"That will last you a week maybe. Then what?"

"By then I'll have things settled."

"By then you'll come crawling back here," said Omani earnestly, "with all the progress you've made to do over again. You're mad, George."

"Feeble-minded is the word you used before."

"Well, I'm sorry I did. Stay here, will you?"

"Are you going to try to stop me?"

Omani compressed his full lips. "No, I guess I won't. This is your business. If the only way you can learn is to buck the world and come back with blood on your face, go ahead. ——Well, go ahead."

George was in the doorway now, looking back over his shoulder. "I'm going,"—he came back to pick up his pocket grooming set slowly—"I hope you don't object to my taking a few personal belongings."

Omani shrugged. He was in bed again reading, indifferent.

George lingered at the door again, but Omani didn't look up. George gritted his teeth, turned and walked rapidly down the empty corridor and out into the night-shrouded grounds.

He had expected to be stopped before leaving the grounds. He wasn't. He had stopped at an all-night diner to ask directions to an air terminal and expected the proprietor to call the police. That didn't happen. He summoned a skimmer to take him to the airport and the driver asked no questions.

Yet he felt no lift at that. He arrived at the airport sick at heart. He had not realized how the outer world would be. He was surrounded by professionals. The diner's proprietor had had his name inscribed on the plastic shell over the cash register. So and so, Registered Cook. The man in the skimmer had his license up, Registered Chauffeur. George felt the bareness of his name and experienced a kind of nakedness because of it; worse, he felt skinned. But no one challenged him. No one studied him suspiciously and demanded proof of professional rating.

George thought bitterly: Who would imagine any human being without one?

He bought a ticket to San Francisco on the 3 A.M. plane. No other plane for a sizable Olympics center was leaving before morning and he wanted to wait as little as possible. As it was, he sat huddled in the waiting room, watching for the police. They did not come.

He was in San Francisco before noon and the noise of the city struck him like a blow. This was the largest city he had ever seen and he had been used to silence and calm for a year and a half now.

Worse, it was Olympics month. He almost forgot his own predicament in his sudden awareness that some of the noise, excitement, confusion was due to that.

The Olympics boards were up at the airport for the benefit of the incoming travelers, and crowds jostled around each one. Each major profession had its own board. Each listed directions to the Olympics Hall where the contest for that day for that profession would be given; the individuals competing and their city of birth; the Outworld (if any) sponsoring it.

It was a completely stylized thing. George had read descriptions often enough in the newsprints and films, watched matches on television, and even witnessed a small Olympics in the Registered Butcher classification at the county seat. Even that, which had no conceivable Galactic implication (there was no Outworlder in attendance, of course) aroused excitement enough.

Partly, the excitement was caused simply by the fact of competition, partly by the spur of local pride (oh, when there was a home-town boy to cheer for, though he might be a complete stranger), and, of course, partly by betting. There was no way of stopping the last.

George found it difficult to approach the board. He found himself looking at the scurrying, avid onlookers in a new way.

There must have been a time when they themselves were Olympic material. What had *they* done? Nothing!

If they had been winners, they would be far out in the Galaxy somewhere, not stuck here on Earth. Whatever they were, their professions must have made them Earth-bait from the beginning; or else they had made themselves Earth-bait by inefficiency at whatever high-specialized professions they had had.

Now these failures stood about and speculated on the chances of newer and younger men. Vultures!

How he wished they were speculating on him.

He moved down the line of boards blankly, clinging to the outskirts of the groups about them. He had eaten breakfast on the strato and he wasn't hungry. He was afraid, though. He was in a big city during the confusion of the beginning of Olympics competition. That was protection, sure. The city was full of strangers. No one would question George. No one would care about George.

No one would care. Not even the House, thought George bitterly. They cared for him like a sick kitten, but if a sick kitten up and wanders off, well, too bad, what can you do?

And now that he was in San Francisco, what did he do? His thoughts struck blankly against a wall. See someone? Whom? How? Where would he even stay? The money he had left seemed pitiful.

The first shamefaced thought of going back came to him. He could go to the police—— He shook his head violently as though arguing with a material adversary.

A word caught his eye on one of the boards, gleaming there: *Metallurgist.* In smaller letters, *nonferrous.* At the bottom of a long list of names, in flowing script, *sponsored by Novia.*

It induced painful memories: himself arguing with Trevelyan, so certain that he himself would be a Programmer, so certain that a Programmer was superior to a Metallurgist, so certain that he was following the right course, so certain that he was clever——

So clever that he had to boast to that small-minded, vindictive Antonelli. He had been so sure of himself that moment when he had been called and had left the nervous Trevelyan standing there, so cocksure.

George cried out in a short, incoherent high-pitched gasp. Someone turned to look at him, then hurried on. People brushed past impatiently pushing him this way and that. He remained staring at the board, openmouthed.

It was as though the board had answered his thought. He was thinking "Trevelyan" so hard that it had seemed for a moment that of course the board would say "Trevelyan" back at him.

But that *was* Trevelyan, up there. And *Armand* Trevelyan (Stubby's hated first name; up in lights for everyone to see) and the right hometown. What's more, Trev had wanted Novia, aimed for Novia, insisted on Novia; and this competition was sponsored by Novia.

This had to be Trev; good old Trev. Almost without thinking, he noted the directions for getting to the place of competition and took his place in line for a skimmer.

Then he thought somberly: Trev made it! He wanted to be a Metallurgist, and he made it!

George felt colder, more alone than ever.

There was a line waiting to enter the hall. Apparently, Metallurgy Olympics was to be an exciting and closely fought one. At least, the illuminated sky sign above the hall said so, and the jostling crowd seemed to think so.

It would have been a rainy day, George thought, from the color of the sky, but San Francisco had drawn the shield across its breadth from bay to ocean. It was an expense to do so, of course, but all expenses were warranted where the comfort of Outworlders was concerned. They would be in town for the Olympics. They were heavy spenders. And for each recruit taken, there would be a fee both to Earth and to the local government from the planet sponsoring the Olympics. It paid to keep Outworlders in mind of a particular city as a pleasant place in which to spend Olympics time. San Francisco knew what it was doing.

George, lost in thought, was suddenly aware of a gentle pressure on his shoulder blade and a voice saying, "Are you in line here, young man?"

The line had moved up without George's having noticed the widening gap. He stepped forward hastily and muttered, "Sorry, sir."

There was the touch of two fingers on the elbow of his jacket and he looked about furtively.

The man behind him nodded cheerfully. He had iron-gray hair, and under his jacket he wore an old-fashioned sweater that buttoned down the front. He said, "I didn't mean to sound sarcastic."

"No offense."

"All right, then." He sounded cozily talkative. "I wasn't sure you might not simply be standing there, entangled with the line, so to speak, only by accident. I thought you might be a——"

"A what?" said George sharply.

"Why, a contestant, of course. You look young."

George turned away. He felt neither cozy nor talkative, and bitterly impatient with busybodies.

A thought struck him. Had an alarm been sent out for him? Was his description known, or his picture? Was Gray-hair behind him trying to get a good look at his face?

He hadn't seen any news reports. He craned his neck to see the moving strip of news headlines parading across one section of the city shield, somewhat lackluster against the gray of the cloudy afternoon sky. It was no use. He gave up at once. The headlines would never concern themselves with him. This was Olympics time and the only news worth headlining was the comparative scores of the winners and the trophies won by continents, nations, and cities.

It would go on like that for weeks, with scores calculated on a per capita basis and every city finding some way of calculating itself into a position of honor. His own town had once placed third in an Olympics covering Wiring Technician; third in the whole state. There was still a plaque saying so in Town Hall.

George hunched his head between his shoulders and shoved his hands in his pocket and decided that made him more noticeable. He relaxed and tried to look unconcerned, and felt no safer. He was in the lobby now, and no authoritative hand had yet been laid on his shoulder. He filed into the hall itself and moved as far forward as he could.

It was with an unpleasant shock that he noticed Gray-hair next to him. He looked away quickly and tried reasoning with himself. The man had been right behind him in line after all.

Gray-hair, beyond a brief and tentative smile, paid no attention to him and, besides, the Olympics was about to start. George rose in his seat to see if he could make out the position assigned to Trevelyan and at the moment that was all his concern.

The hall was moderate in size and shaped in the classical long oval, with the spectators in the two balconies running completely about the rim and the contestants in the linear trough down the center. The machines were set up, the progress boards above each bench were dark, except for the name and contest number of each man. The contestants themselves were on the scene, reading, talking together; one was checking his fingernails minutely. (It was, of course, considered bad form for any contestant to pay any attention to the problem before him until the instant of the starting signal.)

George studied the program sheet he found in the appropriate slot in the arm of his chair and found Trevelyan's name. His number was twelve and, to George's chagrin, that was at the wrong end of the hall. He could make out the figure of Contestant Twelve, standing with his hands in his pockets, back to his machine, and staring at the audience as though he were counting the house. George couldn't make out the face.

Still, that was Trev.

George sank back in his seat. He wondered if Trev would do well. He hoped, as a matter of conscious duty, that he would, and yet there was something within him that felt rebelliously resentful. George, professionless, here, watching. Trevelyan, Registered Metallurgist, Nonferrous, there, competing.

George wondered if Trevelyan had competed in his first year. Sometimes men did, if they felt particularly confident—or hurried.

It involved a certain risk. However efficient the Educative process, a preliminary year on Earth ("oiling the stiff knowledge," as the expression went) insured a higher score.

If Trevelyan was repeating, maybe he wasn't doing so well. George felt ashamed that the thought pleased him just a bit.

He looked about. The stands were almost full. This would be a well-attended Olympics, which meant greater strain on the contestants—or greater drive, perhaps, depending on the individual.

Why Olympics, he thought suddenly? He had never known. Why was bread called bread?

Once he had asked his father: "Why do they call it Olympics, Dad?"

And his father had said: "Olympics means competition."

George had said: "Is when Stubby and I fight an Olympics, Dad?"

Platen, Senior, had said: "No. Olympics is a special kind of competition and don't ask silly questions. You'll know all you have to know when you get Educated."

George, back in the present, sighed and crowded down into his seat.

All you have to know!

Funny that the memory should be so clear now. "When you get Educated." No one ever said, "*If* you get Educated."

He always had asked silly questions, it seemed to him now. It was as though his mind had some instinctive foreknowledge of its inability to be Educated and had gone about asking questions in order to pick up scraps here and there as best it could.

And at the House they encouraged him to do so because they agreed with his mind's instinct. It was the only way.

He sat up suddenly. What the devil was he doing? Falling for that lie? Was it because Trev was there before him, an Educee, competing in the Olympics that he himself was surrendering?

He *wasn't* feeble-minded! *No!*

And the shout of denial in his mind was echoed by the sudden clamor in the audience as everyone got to his feet.

The box seat in the very center of one long side of the oval was filling with an entourage wearing the colors of Novia, and the word "Novia" went up above them on the main board.

Novia was a Grade A world with a large population and a thoroughly developed civilization, perhaps the best in the Galaxy. It was the kind of world that every Earthman wanted to live in someday; or, failing that, to see his children live in. (George remembered Trevelyan's insistence on Novia as a goal—and there he was competing for it.)

The lights went out in that section of the ceiling above the audience and so did the wall lights. The central trough, in which the contestants waited, became floodlit.

Again George tried to make out Trevelyan. Too far.

The clear, polished voice of the announcer sounded. "Distinguished Novian sponsors. Ladies. Gentlemen. The Olympics competition for Metallurgist, Nonferrous, is about to begin. The contestants are——"

Carefully and conscientiously, he read off the list in the program. Names. Home towns. Educative years. Each name received its cheers, the San Franciscans among them receiving the loudest. When Trevelyan's name was reached, George surprised himself by shouting and waving madly. The gray-haired man next to him surprised him even more by cheering likewise.

George could not help but stare in astonishment and his neighbor leaned over to say (speaking loudly in order to be heard over the hubbub), "No one here from my home town; I'll root for yours. Someone you know?"

George shrank back. "No."

"I noticed you looking in that direction. Would you like to borrow my glasses?"

"No. Thank you." (Why didn't the old fool mind his own business?)

The announcer went on with other formal details concerning the serial number of the competition, the method of timing and scoring and so on. Finally, he approached the meat of the matter and the audience grew silent as it listened.

"Each contestant will be supplied with a bar of nonferrous alloy of unspecified composition. He will be required to sample and assay the bar, reporting all results correctly to four decimals in per cent. All will utilize for this purpose a Beeman Microspectrograph, Model FX-2, each of which is, at the moment, not in working order."

There was an appreciative shout from the audience.

"Each contestant will be required to analyze the fault of his machine and correct it. Tools and spare parts are supplied. The spare part necessary may not be present, in which case it must be asked for, and time of delivery thereof will be deducted from final time. Are all contestants ready?"

The board above Contestant Five flashed a frantic red signal. Contestant Five ran off the floor and returned a moment later. The audience laughed good-naturedly.

"Are all contestants ready?"

The boards remained blank.

"Any questions?"

Still blank.

"You may begin."

There was, of course, no way anyone in the audience could tell how any contestant was progressing except for whatever notations went up on the notice board. But then, that didn't matter. Except for what professional Metallurgists there might be in the audience, none would understand anything about the contest professionally in any case. What was important was who won, who was second, who was third. For those who had bets on the standings (illegal, but unpreventable) that was all-important. Everything else might go hang.

George watched as eagerly as the rest, glancing from one contestant to the next, observing how this one had removed the cover from his microspectrograph with deft strokes of a small instrument; how that one was peering into the face of the thing; how still a third was setting his alloy bar into its holder; and how a fourth adjusted a vernier with such small touches that he seemed momentarily frozen.

Trevelyan was as absorbed as the rest. George had no way of telling how he was doing.

The notice board over Contestant Seventeen flashed: Focus plate out of adjustment.

The audience cheered wildly.

Contestant Seventeen might be right and he might, of course, be wrong. If the latter, he would have to correct his diagnosis later and lose time. Or he might never correct his diagnosis and be unable to complete his analysis or, worse still, end with a completely wrong analysis.

Never mind. For the moment, the audience cheered.

Other boards lit up. George watched for Board Twelve. That came on finally: "Sample holder off-center. New clamp depresser needed."

An attendant went running to him with a new part. If Trevelyan was wrong, it would mean useless delay. Nor would the time elapsed in waiting for the part be deducted. George found himself holding his breath.

Results were beginning to go up on Board Seventeen, in gleaming letters: aluminum, 41.2649; magnesium, 22.1914; copper, 10.1001.

Here and there, other boards began sprouting figures.

The audience was in bedlam.

George wondered how the contestants could work in such pandemonium, then wondered if that were not even a good thing. A first-class technician should work best under pressure.

Seventeen rose from his place as his board went red-rimmed to signify completion. Four was only two seconds behind him. Another, then another.

Trevelyan was still working, the minor constituents of his alloy bar still unreported. With nearly all contestants standing, Trevelyan finally rose, also. Then, tailing off, Five rose, and received an ironic cheer.

It wasn't over. Official announcements were naturally delayed. Time elapsed was something, but accuracy was just as important. And not all diagnoses were of equal difficulty. A dozen factors had to be weighed.

Finally, the announcer's voice sounded, "Winner in the time of four minutes and twelve seconds, diagnosis correct, analysis correct within an average of zero point seven parts per hundred thousand, Contestant Number—*Seventeen,* Henry Anton Schmidt of——"

What followed was drowned in the screaming. Number Eight was next and then Four, whose good time was spoiled by a five part in ten thousand error in the niobium figure. Twelve was never mentioned. He was an also-ran.

George made his way through the crowd to the Contestant's Door and found a large clot of humanity ahead of him. There would be weeping relatives (joy or sorrow, depending) to greet them, newsmen to interview the top-scorers, or the home-town boys, autograph hounds, publicity seekers and the just plain curious. Girls, too, who might hope to catch the eye of a top-scorer, almost certainly headed for Novia (or perhaps a low-scorer who needed consolation and had the cash to afford it).

George hung back. He saw no one he knew. With San Francisco so far from home, it seemed pretty safe to assume that there would be no relatives to condole with Trev on the spot.

Contestants emerged, smiling weakly, nodding at shouts of approval. Policemen kept the crowds far enough away to allow a lane for walking. Each high-scorer drew a portion of the crowd off with him, like a magnet pushing through a mound of iron filings.

When Trevelyan walked out, scarcely anyone was left. (George felt somehow that he had delayed coming out until just that had come to pass.) There was a cigarette in his dour mouth and he turned, eyes downcast, to walk off.

It was the first hint of home George had had in what was almost a year and a half and seemed almost a decade and a half. He was almost amazed that Trevelyan hadn't aged, that he was the same Trev he had last seen.

George sprang forward. "*Trev!*"

Trevelyan spun about, astonished. He stared at George and then his hand shot out. "George Platen, *what* the devil——"

And almost as soon as the look of pleasure had crossed his face, it left. His hand dropped before George had quite the chance of seizing it.

"Were you in there?" A curt jerk of Trev's head indicated the hall.

"I was."

"To see me?"

"Yes."

"Didn't do so well, did I?" He dropped his cigarette and stepped on it, staring off to the street, where the emerging crowd was slowly eddying and finding its way into skimmers, while new lines were forming for the next scheduled Olympics.

Trevelyan said heavily, "So what? It's only the second time I missed. Novia can go shove after the deal I got today. There are planets that would jump at me fast enough—— But, listen, I haven't seen you since Education Day. Where did you go? Your folks said you were on special assignment but gave no details and you never wrote. You might have written."

"I should have," said George uneasily. "Anyway, I came to say I was sorry the way things went just now."

"Don't be," said Trevelyan. "I told you. Novia can go shove—— At that I should have known. They've been saying for weeks that the Beeman machine would be used. All the wise money was on Beeman machines. The damned Education tapes they ran through me were for Henslers and who uses Henslers? The worlds in the Goman Cluster if you want to call them worlds. Wasn't *that* a nice deal they gave me?"

"Can't you complain to——"

"Don't be a fool. They'll tell me my brain was built for Henslers. Go argue. *Everything* went wrong. I was the only one who had to send out for a piece of equipment. Notice that?"

"They deducted the time for that, though."

"Sure, but I lost time wondering if I could be right in my diagnosis when I noticed there wasn't any clamp depresser in the parts they had supplied. They don't deduct for that. If it had been a Hensler, I would have *known* I was right. How could I match up then? The top winner was a San Franciscan. So were three of the next four. And the fifth guy was from Los Angeles. They get big-city Educational tapes. The best available. Beeman spectrographs and all. How do I compete with them? I came all the way out here just to get a chance at a Novian-sponsored Olympics in my classification and I might just as well have stayed home. I knew it, I tell you, and that settles it. Novia isn't the only chunk of rock in space. Of all the damned——"

He wasn't speaking to George. He wasn't speaking to anyone. He was just uncorked and frothing. George realized that.

George said, "If you knew in advance that the Beemans were going to be used, couldn't you have studied up on them?"

"They weren't in my tapes, I tell you."

"You could have read—books."

The last word had tailed off under Trevelyan's suddenly sharp look.

Trevelyan said, "Are you trying to make a big laugh out of this? You think this is funny? How do you expect me to read some book and try to memorize enough to match someone else who *knows*."

"I thought——"

"You try it. You try——" Then, suddenly, "What's your profession, by the way?" He sounded thoroughly hostile.

"Well——"

"Come on, now. If you're going to be a wise guy with me, let's see what you've done. You're still on Earth, I notice, so you're not a Computer Programmer and your special assignment can't be much."

George said, "Listen, Trev, I'm late for an appointment." He backed away, trying to smile.

"No, you don't." Trevelyan reached out fiercely, catching hold of George's jacket. "You answer my question. Why are you afraid to tell me? What is it with you? Don't come here rubbing a bad showing in my face, George, unless you can take it, too. Do you hear me?"

He was shaking George in frenzy and they were struggling and swaying across the floor, when the Voice of Doom struck George's ear in the form of a policeman's outraged call.

"All right now. *All* right. Break it up."

George's heart turned to lead and lurched sickeningly. The policeman would be taking names, asking to see identity cards, and George lacked one. He would be questioned and his lack of profession would show at once; and before Trevelyan, too, who ached with the pain of the drubbing he had taken and would spread the news back home as a salve for his own hurt feelings.

George couldn't stand that. He broke away from Trevelyan and made to run, but the policeman's heavy hand was on his shoulder. "Hold on, there. Let's see your identity card."

Trevelyan was fumbling for his, saying harshly, "I'm Armand Trevelyan, Metallurgist, Nonferrous. I was just competing in the Olympics. You better find out about him, though, officer."

George faced the two, lips dry and throat thickened past speech.

Another voice sounded, quiet, well-mannered. "Officer. One moment."

The policeman stepped back. "Yes, sir?"

"This young man is my guest. What is the trouble?"

George looked about in wild surprise. It was the gray-haired man who had been sitting next to him. Gray-hair nodded benignly at George.

Guest? Was he mad?

The policeman was saying, "These two were creating a disturbance, sir."

"Any criminal charges? Any damages?"

"No, sir."

"Well, then, I'll be responsible." He presented a small card to the policeman's view and the latter stepped back at once.

Trevelyan began indignantly, "Hold on, now——" but the policeman turned on him.

"All right, now. Got any charges?"

"I just——"

"On your way. The rest of you—move on." A sizable crowd had gathered, which now, reluctantly, unknotted itself and raveled away.

George let himself be led to a skimmer but balked at entering.

He said, "Thank you, but I'm not your guest." (Could it be a ridiculous case of mistaken identity?)

But Gray-hair smiled and said, "You weren't but you are now. Let me introduce myself, I'm Ladislas Ingenescu, Registered Historian."

"But——"

"Come, you will come to no harm, I assure you. After all, I only wanted to spare you some trouble with a policeman."

"But why?"

"Do you want a reason? Well, then, say that we're honorary towns-mates, you and I. We both shouted for the same man, remember, and we townspeople must stick together, even if the tie is only honorary. Eh?"

And George, completely unsure of this man, Ingenescu, and of himself as well, found himself inside the skimmer. Before he could make up his mind that he ought to get off again, they were off the ground.

He thought confusedly: The man has some status. The policeman deferred to him.

He was almost forgetting that his real purpose here in San Francisco was not to find Trevelyan but to find some person with enough influence to force a reappraisal of his own capacity of Education.

It could be that Ingenescu was such a man. And right in George's lap.

Everything could be working out fine—fine. Yet it sounded hollow in his thought. He was uneasy.

During the short skimmer-hop, Ingenescu kept up an even flow of small-talk, pointing out the landmarks of the city, reminiscing about past Olympics he had seen. George, who paid just enough attention to make vague sounds during the pauses, watched the route of flight anxiously.

Would they head for one of the shield-openings and leave the city altogether?

No, they headed downward, and George sighed his relief softly. He felt safer in the city.

The skimmer landed at the roof-entry of a hotel and, as he alighted, Ingenescu said, "I hope you'll eat dinner with me in my room?"

George said, "Yes," and grinned unaffectedly. He was just beginning to realize the gap left within him by a missing lunch.

Ingenescu let George eat in silence. Night closed in and the wall lights went on automatically. (George thought: I've been on my own almost twenty-four hours.)

And then over the coffee, Ingenescu finally spoke again. He said, "You've been acting as though you think I intend you harm."

George reddened, put down his cup and tried to deny it, but the older man laughed and shook his head.

"It's so. I've been watching you closely since I first saw you and I think I know a great deal about you now."

George half rose in horror.

Ingenescu said, "But sit down. I only want to help you."

George sat down but his thoughts were in a whirl. If the old man knew who he was, why had he not left him to the policeman? On the other hand, why should he volunteer help?

Ingenescu said, "You want to know why I should want to help you? Oh, don't look alarmed. I can't read minds. It's just that my training enables me to judge the little reactions that give minds away, you see. Do you understand that?"

George shook his head.

Ingenescu said, "Consider my first sight of you. You were waiting in line to watch an Olympics, and your micro-reactions didn't match what you were doing. The expression of your face was wrong, the action of your hands was wrong. It meant that something, in general, was wrong, and the interesting thing was that, whatever it was, it was nothing common, nothing obvious. Perhaps, I thought, it was something of which your own conscious mind was unaware.

"I couldn't help but follow you, sit next to you. I followed you again when you left and eavesdropped on the conversation between your friend and yourself. After that, well, you were far too interesting an object of study—I'm sorry if that sounds cold-blooded—for me to allow you to be taken off by a policeman. ——Now tell me, what is it that troubles you?"

George was in an agony of indecision. If this was a trap, why should it be such an indirect, roundabout one? And he *had* to turn to someone. He had come to the city to find help and here was help being offered. Perhaps what was wrong was that it was being offered. It came too easy.

Ingenescu said, "Of course, what you tell me as a Social Scientist is a privileged communication. Do you know what that means?"

"No, sir."

"It means, it would be dishonorable for me to repeat what you say to anyone for any purpose. Moreover no one has the legal right to compel me to repeat it."

George said, with sudden suspicion, "I thought you were a Historian."

"So I am."

"Just now you said you were a Social Scientist."

Ingenescu broke into loud laughter and apologized for it when he could talk. "I'm sorry, young man, I shouldn't laugh, and I wasn't really laughing at you. I was laughing at Earth and it's emphasis on physical science, and the practical segments of it at that. I'll bet you can rattle off every subdivison of construction technology or mechanical engineering and yet you're a blank on social science."

"Well, then what *is* social science?"

"Social science studies groups of human beings and there are many high-specialized branches to it, just as there are to zoology, for instance. For instance, there are Culturists, who study the mechanics of cultures, their growth, development, and decay. Cultures," he added, forestalling a question, "are all the aspects of a way of life. For instance it includes the way we make our living, the things we enjoy and believe, what we consider good and bad and so on. Do you understand?"

"I think I do."

"An Economist—not an Economic Statistician, now, but an Economist—specializes in the study of the way a culture supplies the bodily needs of its individual members. A Psychologist specializes in the individual member of a society and how he is affected by the society. A Futurist specializes in planning the future course of a society, and a Historian—— That's where I come in, now."

"Yes, sir."

"A Historian specializes in the past development of our own society and of societies with other cultures."

George found himself interested. "Was it different in the past?"

"I should say it was. Until a thousand years ago, there was no Education; not what we call Education, at least."

George said, "I know. People learned in bits and pieces out of books."

"Why, how do you know this?"

"I've heard it said," said George cautiously. Then, "Is there any use in worrying about what's happened long ago? I mean, it's all done with, isn't it?"

"It's never done with, my boy. The past explains the present. For instance, why is our Educational system what it is?"

George stirred restlessly. The man kept bringing the subject back to that. He said snappishly, "Because it's best."

"Ah, but why is it best? Now you listen to me for one moment and I'll explain. Then you can tell me if there is any use in history. Even before interstellar travel was developed——" He broke off at the look of complete astonishment on George's face. "Well, did you think we always had it?"

"I never gave it any thought, sir."

"I'm sure you didn't. But there was a time, four or five thousand years ago when mankind was confined to the surface of Earth. Even then, his culture had grown quite technological and his numbers had increased to the point where any failure in technology would have meant mass starvation and disease. To maintain the technological level and advance it in the face of an increasing population, more and more technicians and scientists had to be trained, and yet, as science advanced, it took longer and longer to train them.

"As first interplanetary and then interstellar travel was developed, the problem grew more acute. In fact, actual colonization of extra-Solar planets was impossible for about fifteen hundred years because of a lack of properly trained men.

"The turning point came when the mechanics of the storage of knowledge within the brain was worked out. Once that had been done, it became possible to devise Educational tapes that would modify the mechanics in such a way as to place within the mind a body of knowledge ready-made so to speak. But you know about *that*.

"Once that was done, trained men could be turned out by the thousands and millions, and we could begin what someone has since called the "Filling of the Universe." There are now fifteen hundred inhabited planets in the Galaxy and there is no end in sight.

"Do you see all that is involved? Earth exports Education tapes for low-specialized professions and that keeps the Galactic culture unified. For instance, the Reading tapes insure a single language for all of us. ——Don't look so surprised, other languages are possible, and in the past were used. Hundreds of them.

"Earth also exports high-specialized professionals and keeps its own population at an endurable level. Since they are shipped out in a balanced sex ratio, they act as self-reproductive units and help increase the populations on the Outworlds where an increase is needed. Furthermore, tapes and men are paid for in material which we much need and on which our economy depends. *Now* do you understand why our Education is the best way?"

"Yes, sir."

"Does it help you to understand, knowing that without it, interstellar colonization was impossible for fifteen hundred years?"

"Yes, sir."

"Then you see the uses of history." The Historian smiled. "And now I wonder if you see why I'm interested in you?"

George snapped out of time and space back to reality. Ingenescu, apparently, didn't talk aimlessly. All this lecture had been a device to attack him from a new angle.

He said, once again withdrawn, hesitating, "Why?"

"Social Scientists work with societies and societies are made up of people."

"All right."

"But people aren't machines. The professionals in physical science work with machines. There is only a limited amount to know about a machine and the professionals know it all. Furthermore, all machines of a given sort are just about alike so that there is nothing to interest them in any given individual machine. But people, ah—— They are so complex and so different one from another that a Social Scientist never knows all there is to know or even a good part of what there is to know. To understand his own specialty, he must always be ready to study people; particularly unusual specimens."

"Like me," said George tonelessly.

"I shouldn't call you a specimen, I suppose, but you are unusual. You're worth studying, and if you will allow me that privilege then, in return, I will help you if you are in trouble and if I can."

There were pin wheels whirring in George's mind. ——All this talk about people and colonization made possible by Education. It was as though caked thought within him were being broken up and strewn about mercilessly.

He said, "Let me think," and clamped his hands over his ears.

He took them away and said to the Historian, "Will you do something for me, sir?"

"If I can," said the Historian amiably.

"And everything I say in this room is a privileged communication. You said so."

"And I meant it."

"Then get me an interview with an Outworld official, with—with a Novian."

Ingenescu looked startled. "Well, now——"

"You can do it," said George earnestly. "You're an important official. I saw the policeman's look when you put that card in front of his eyes. If you refuse, I—I won't let you study me."

It sounded a silly threat in George's own ears, one without force. On Ingenescu, however, it seemed to have a strong effect.

He said, "That's an impossible condition. A Novian in Olympics month——"

"All right, then, get me a Novian on the phone and I'll make my own arrangements for an interview."

"Do you think you can?"

"I know I can. Wait and see."

Ingenescu stared at George thoughtfully and then reached for the visiphone.

George waited, half drunk with this new outlook on the whole problem and the sense of power it brought. It couldn't miss. It *couldn't* miss. He would be a Novian yet. He would leave Earth in triumph despite Antonelli and the whole crew of fools at the House for the (he almost laughed aloud) Feeble-minded.

George watched eagerly as the visiplate lit up. It would open up a window into a room of Novians, a window into a small patch of Novia transplanted to Earth. In twenty-four hours, he had accomplished that much.

There was a burst of laughter as the plate unmisted and sharpened, but for the moment no single head could be seen but rather the fast passing of the shadows of men and women, this way and that. A voice was heard, clear-worded over a background of babble. "Ingenescu? He wants me?"

Then there he was, staring out of the plate. A Novian. A genuine Novian. (George had not an atom of doubt. There was something completely Outworldly about him. Nothing that could be completely defined, or even momentarily mistaken.)

He was swarthy in complexion with a dark wave of hair combed rigidly back from his forehead. He wore a thin black mustache and a pointed beard, just as dark, that scarcely reached below the lower limit of his narrow chin, but the rest of his face was so smooth that it looked as though it had been depilated permanently.

He was smiling. "Ladislas, this goes too far. We fully expect to be spied on, within reason, during our stay on Earth, but mind reading is out of bounds."

"Mind reading, Honorable?"

"Confess! You knew I was going to call you this evening. You knew I was only waiting to finish this drink." His hand moved up into view and his eye peered through a small glass of a faintly violet liqueur. "I can't offer you one, I'm afraid."

George, out of range of Ingenescu's transmitter could not be seen by the Novian. He was relieved at that. He wanted time to compose himself and he needed it badly. It was as though he were made up exclusively of restless fingers, drumming, drumming——

But he was right. He hadn't miscalculated. Ingenescu *was* important. The Novian called him by his first name.

Good! Things worked well. What George had lost on Antonelli, he would make up, with advantage, on Ingenescu. And someday, when he was on his own at last, and could come back to Earth as powerful a Novian as this one who could negligently joke with Ingenescu's first name and be addressed as "Honorable" in turn—when he came back, he would settle with Antonelli. He had a year and a half to pay back and he——

He all but lost his balance on the brink of the enticing daydream and snapped back in sudden anxious realization that he was losing the thread of what was going on.

The Novian was saying, "——doesn't hold water. Novia has a civilization as complicated and advanced as Earth's. We're not Zeston, after all. It's ridiculous that we have to come here for individual technicians."

Ingenescu said soothingly, "Only for new models. There is never any certainty that new models will be needed. To buy the Educa-

tional tapes would cost you the same price as a thousand technicians and how do you know you would need that many?"

The Novian tossed off what remained of his drink and laughed.
(It displeased George, somehow, that a Novian should be this
frivolous. He wondered uneasily if perhaps the Novian ought not
to have skipped that drink and even the one or two before that.)

The Novian said, "That's typical pious fraud, Ladislas. You know
we can make use of all the late models we can get. I collected five
Metallurgists this afternoon——"

"I know," said Ingenescu. "I was there."

"Watching me! Spying!" cried the Novian. "I'll tell you what it
is. The new-model Metallurgists I got differed from the previous
model only in knowing the use of Beeman Spectrographs. The
tapes couldn't be modified that much, not that much" (he held up
two fingers close together) "from last year's model. You introduce
the new models only to *make* us buy and spend and come here
hat in hand."

"We don't *make* you buy."

"No, but you sell late-model technicians to Landonum and so
we have to keep pace. It's a merry-go-round you have us on, you
pious Earthmen, but watch out, there may be an exit somewhere."
There was a sharp edge to his laugh, and it ended sooner than
it should have.

Ingenescu said, "In all honesty, I hope there is. Meanwhile, as
to the purpose of my call——"

"That's right, *you* called. Oh, well, I've said my say and I
suppose next year there'll be a new model of Metallurgist anyway
for us to spend goods on, probably with a new gimmick for niobium
assays and nothing else altered and the next year—— But go
on, what is it you want?"

"I have a young man here to whom I wish you to speak."

"Oh?" The Novian looked not completely pleased with that.
"Concerning what?"

"I can't say. He hasn't told me. For that matter he hasn't
even told me his name and profession."

The Novian frowned. "Then why take up my time?"

"He seems quite confident that you will be interested in what
he has to say."

"I dare say."

"And," said Ingenescu, "as a favor to me."

The Novian shrugged. "Put him on and tell him to make it short."

Ingenescu stepped aside and whispered to George, "Address him as 'Honorable.'"

George swallowed with difficulty. This was it.

George felt himself going moist with perspiration. The thought had come so recently, yet it was in him now so certainly. The beginnings of it had come when he had spoken to Trevelyan, then everything had fermented and billowed into shape while Ingenescu had prattled, and then the Novian's own remarks had seemed to nail it all into place.

George said, "Honorable, I've come to show you the exit from the merry-go-round." Deliberately, he adopted the Novian's own metaphor.

The Novian stared at him gravely. "What merry-go-round?"

"You yourself mentioned it, Honorable. The merry-go-round that Novia is on when you come to Earth to—to get technicians." (He couldn't keep his teeth from chattering; from excitement, not fear.)

The Novian said, "You're trying to say that you know a way by which we can avoid patronizing Earth's mental super-market. Is that it?"

"Yes, sir. You can control your own Educational system."

"Umm. Without tapes?"

"Y—yes, Honorable."

The Novian, without taking his eyes from George, called out, "Ingenescu, get into view."

The Historian moved to where he could be seen over George's shoulder.

The Novian said, "What is this? I don't seem to penetrate."

"I assure you solemnly," said Ingenescu, "that whatever this is it is being done on the young man's own initiative, Honorable. I have not inspired this. I have nothing to do with it."

"Well, then, what is the young man to you? Why do you call me on his behalf?"

Ingenescu said, "He is an object of study, Honorable. He has value to me and I humor him."

"What kind of value?"

"It's difficult to explain; a matter of my profession."

The Novian laughed shortly. "Well, to each his profession." He nodded to an invisible person or persons outside plate range. "There's a young man here, a protégé of Ingenescu or some such thing, who will explain to us how to Educate without tapes." He snapped his fingers, and another glass of pale liqueur appeared in his hand. "Well, young man?"

The faces on the plate were multiple now. Men and women, both, crammed in for a view of George, their faces molded into various shades of amusement and curiosity.

George tried to look disdainful. They were all, in their own ways, Novians as well as the Earthman, "studying" him as though he were a bug on a pin. Ingenescu was sitting in a corner, now, watching him owl-eyed.

Fools, he thought tensely, one and all. But they would have to understand. He would *make* them understand.

He said, "I was at the Metallurgist Olympics this afternoon."

"You, too?" said the Novian blandly. "It seems all Earth was there."

"No, Honorable, but I was. I had a friend who competed and who made out very badly because you were using the Beeman machines. His education had included only the Henslers, apparently an older model. You said the modification involved was slight." George held up two fingers close together in conscious mimicry of the other's previous gesture. "And my friend had known some time in advance that knowledge of the Beeman machines would be required."

"And what does that signify?"

"It was my friend's lifelong ambition to qualify for Novia. He already knew the Henslers. He had to know the Beemans to qualify and he knew that. To learn about the Beemans would have taken just a few more facts, a bit more data, a small amount of practice perhaps. With a life's ambition riding the scale, he might have managed this——"

"And where would he have obtained a tape for the additional

facts and data? Or has Education become a private matter for home study here on Earth?"

There was dutiful laughter from the faces in the background.

George said, "That's why he didn't learn, Honorable. He thought he needed a tape. He wouldn't even try without one, no matter what the prize. He refused to try without a tape."

"Refused, eh? Probably the type of fellow who would refuse to fly without a skimmer." More laughter and the Novian thawed into a smile and said, "The fellow is amusing. Go on. I'll give you another few moments."

George said tensely, "Don't think this is a joke. Tapes are actually bad. They teach too much; they're too painless. A man who learns that way doesn't know how to learn any other way. He's frozen into whatever position he's been taped. Now if a person *weren't* given tapes but were forced to learn by hand, so to speak, from the start; why, then he'd get the habit of learning, and continue to learn. Isn't that reasonable? Once he has the habit well developed he can be given just a small amount of tape-knowledge, perhaps, to fill in gaps or fix details. Then he can make further progress on his own. You can make Beeman Metallurgists out of your own Hensler Metallurgists in that way and not have to come to Earth for new models."

The Novian nodded and sipped at his drink. "And where does everyone get knowledge without tapes? From interstellar vacuum?"

"From books. By studying the instruments themselves. By *thinking.*"

"Books? How does one understand books without Education?"

"Books are in words. Words can be understood for the most part. Specialized words can be explained by the technicians you already have."

"What about reading? Will you allow reading tapes?"

"Reading tapes are all right, I suppose, but there's no reason you can't learn to read the old way, too. At least in part."

The Novian said, "So that you can develop good habits from the start?"

"Yes, yes," George said gleefully. The man was beginning to understand.

"And what about mathematics?"

"That's the easiest of all, sir—Honorable. Mathematics is different from other technical subjects. It starts with certain simple principles and proceeds by steps. You can start with nothing and learn. It's practically designed for that. Then, once you know the proper types of mathematics, other technical books become quite understandable. Especially if you start with easy ones."

"Are there easy books?"

"Definitely. Even if there weren't, the technicians you now have can try to write easy books. Some of them might be able to put some of their knowledge into words and symbols."

"Good Lord," said the Novian to the men clustered about him. "The young devil has an answer for everything."

"I have. I have," shouted George. "Ask me."

"Have you tried learning from books yourself? Or is this just theory with you?"

George turned to look quickly at Ingenescu, but the Historian was passive. There was no sign of anything but gentle interest in his face.

George said, "I have."

"And do you find it works?"

"Yes, Honorable," said George eagerly. "Take me with you to Novia. I can set up a program and direct——"

"Wait, I have a few more questions. How long would it take, do you suppose, for you to become a Metallurgist capable of handling a Beeman machine, supposing you started from nothing and did not use Educational tapes?"

George hesitated. "Well—years, perhaps."

"Two years? Five? Ten?"

"I can't say, Honorable."

"Well, there's a vital question to which you have no answer, have you? Shall we say five years? Does that sound reasonable to you?"

"I suppose so."

"All right. We have a technician studying metallurgy according to this method of yours for five years. He's no good to us during that time, you'll admit, but he must be fed and housed and paid all that time."

"But——"

"Let me finish. Then when he's done and can use the Beeman, five years have passed. Don't you suppose we'll have modified Beemans then which he *won't* be able to use?"

"But by then he'll be expert on learning. He could learn the new details necessary in a matter of days."

"So you say. And suppose this friend of yours, for instance, had studied up on Beemans on his own and managed to learn it; would he be as expert in its use as a competitor who had learned it off the tapes?"

"Maybe not——" began George.

"Ah," said the Novian.

"Wait, let *me* finish. Even if he doesn't know something as well, it's the ability to learn further that's important. He may be able to think up things, new things that no tape-Educated man would. You'll have a reservoir of original thinkers——"

"In your studying," said the Novian, "have you thought up any new things?"

"No, but I'm just one man and I haven't studied long——"

"Yes. ——Well, ladies, gentlemen, have we been sufficiently amused?"

"Wait," cried George, in sudden panic. "I want to arrange a personal interview. There are things I can't explain over the visiphone. There are details——"

The Novian looked past George. "Ingenescu! I think I have done you your favor. Now, really, I have a heavy schedule tomorrow. Be well!"

The screen went blank.

George's hands shot out toward the screen, as though in a wild impulse to shake life back into it. He cried out, "He didn't believe me. He didn't believe me."

Ingenescu said, "No, George. Did you really think he would?"

George scarcely heard him. "But why not? It's all true. It's all so much to his advantage. No risk. I and a few men to work with—— A dozen men training for years would cost less than one technician. ——He was drunk! Drunk! He didn't understand."

George looked about breathlessly. "How do I get to him? I've got to. This was wrong. Shouldn't have used the visiphone. I need time. Face to face. How do I——"

Ingenescu said, "He won't see you, George. And if he did, he wouldn't believe you."

"He will, I tell you. When he isn't drinking. He——" George turned squarely toward the Historian and his eyes widened. "Why do you call me George?"

"Isn't that your name? George Platen?"

"You know me?"

"All about you."

George was motionless except for the breath pumping his chest wall up and down.

Ingenescu said, "I want to help you, George. I told you that. I've been studying you and I want to help you."

George screamed, "I don't need help. I'm not feeble-minded. The whole world is, but I'm not." He whirled and dashed madly for the door.

He flung it open and two policemen roused themselves suddenly from their guard duty and seized him.

For all George's straining, he could feel the hypo-spray at the fleshy point just under the corner of his jaw, and that was it. The last thing he remembered was the face of Ingenescu, watching with gentle concern.

George opened his eyes to the whiteness of a ceiling. He remembered what had happened. He remembered it distantly as though it had happened to somebody else. He stared at the ceiling till the whiteness filled his eyes and washed his brain clean, leaving room, it seemed, for new thought and new ways of thinking.

He didn't know how long he lay there so, listening to the drift of his own thinking.

There was a voice in his ear. "Are you awake?"

And George heard his own moaning for the first time. Had he been moaning? He tried to turn his head.

The voice said, "Are you in pain, George?"

George whispered, "Funny. I was so anxious to leave Earth. I didn't understand."

"Do you know where you are?"

"Back in the—the House." George managed to turn. The voice belonged to Omani.

George said, "It's funny I didn't understand."

Omani smiled gently, "Sleep again——"

George slept.

And woke again. His mind was clear.

Omani sat at the bedside reading, but he put down the book as George's eyes opened.

George struggled to a sitting position. He said, "Hello."

"Are you hungry?"

"You bet." He stared at Omani curiously. "I was followed when I left, wasn't I?"

Omani nodded. "You were under observation at all times. We were going to maneuver you to Antonelli and let you discharge your aggressions. We felt that to be the only way you could make progress. Your emotions were clogging your advance."

George said, with a trace of embarrassment, "I was all wrong about him."

"It doesn't matter now. When you stopped to stare at the Metallurgy notice board at the airport, one of our agents reported back the list of names. You and I had talked about your past sufficiently so that I caught the significance of Trevelyan's name there. You asked for directions to the Olympics; there was the possibility that this might result in the kind of crisis we were hoping for; we sent Ladislas Ingenescu to the hall to meet you and take over."

"He's an important man in the government, isn't he?"

"Yes, he is."

"And you had him take over. It makes me sound important."

"You *are* important, George."

A thick stew had arrived, steaming, fragrant. George grinned wolfishly and pushed his sheets back to free his arms. Omani helped arrange the bed-table. For a while, George ate silently.

Then George said, "I woke up here once before just for a short time."

Omani said, "I know. I was here."

"Yes, I remember. You know, everything was changed. It was

as though I was too tired to feel emotion. I wasn't angry any more. I could just think. It was as though I had been drugged to wipe out emotion."

"You weren't," said Omani. "Just sedation. You had rested."

"Well, anyway, it was all clear to me, as though I had known it all the time but wouldn't listen to myself. I thought: What was it I had wanted Novia to let me do? I had wanted to go to Novia and take a batch of un-Educated youngsters and teach them out of books. I had wanted to establish a House for the Feeble-minded— like here—and Earth already has them—many of them."

Omani's white teeth gleamed as he smiled. "The Institute of Higher Studies is the correct name for places like this."

"Now I see it," said George, "so easily I am amazed at my blindness before. After all, who invents the new instrument models that require new-model technicians? Who invented the Beeman spectrographs, for instance? A man called Beeman, I suppose, but he couldn't have been tape-Educated or how could he have made the advance?"

"Exactly."

"Or who makes Educational tapes? Special tape-making technicians? Then who makes the tapes to train *them?* More advanced technicians? Then who makes the tapes—— You see what I mean. Somewhere there has to be an end. Somewhere there must be men and women with capacity for original thought."

"Yes, George."

George leaned back, stared over Omani's head, and for a moment there was the return of something like restlessness to his eyes.

"Why wasn't I told all this at the beginning?"

"Oh, if we could," said Omani, "the trouble it would save us. We can analyze a mind, George, and say this one will make an adequate architect and that one a good woodworker. We know of no way of detecting the capacity for original, creative thought. It is too subtle a thing. We have some rule-of-thumb methods that mark out individuals who may possibly or potentially have such a talent.

"On Reading Day, such individuals are reported. You were, for instance. Roughly speaking, the number so reported comes to one in ten thousand. By the time Education Day arrives, these individuals are checked again, and nine out of ten of them turn out to have been false alarms. Those who remain are sent to places like this."

George said, "Well, what's wrong with telling people that one out of—of a hundred thousand will end at places like these? Then it won't be such a shock to those who do."

"And those who don't? The ninety-nine thousand nine hundred and ninety-nine that don't? We can't have all those people considering themselves failures. They aim at the professions and one way or another they all make it. Everyone can place after his or her name: Registered something-or-other. In one fashion or another every individual has his or her place in society and this is necessary."

"But we?" said George. "The one in ten thousand exception?"

"You can't be told. That's exactly it. It's the final test. Even after we've thinned out the possibilities on Education Day, nine out of ten of those who come here are not quite the material of creative genius, and there's no way we can distinguish those nine from the tenth that we want by any form of machinery. The tenth one must tell us himself."

"How?"

"We bring you here to a House for the Feeble-minded and the man who won't accept that is the man we want. It's a method that can be cruel, but it works. It won't do to say to a man, 'You can create. Do so.' It is much safer to wait for a man to say, 'I can create, and I will do so whether you wish it or not.' There are ten thousand men like you, George, who support the advancing technology of fifteen hundred worlds. We can't allow ourselves to miss one recruit to that number or waste our efforts on one member who doesn't measure up."

George pushed his empty plate out of the way and lifted a cup of coffee to his lips.

"What about the people here who don't—measure up?"

"They are taped eventually and become our Social Scientists. Ingenescu is one. I am a Registered Psychologist. We are second echelon, so to speak."

74

George finished his coffee. He said, "I still wonder about one thing?"

"What is that?"

George threw aside the sheet and stood up. "Why do they call them Olympics?"

THE FEELING OF POWER

JEHAN SHUMAN was used to dealing with the men in authority on long-embattled Earth. He was only a civilian but he originated programming patterns that resulted in self-directing war computers of the highest sort. Generals consequently listened to him. Heads of congressional committees, too.

There was one of each in the special lounge of New Pentagon. General Weider was space-burnt and had a small mouth puckered almost into a cipher. Congressman Brant was smooth-cheeked and clear-eyed. He smoked Denebian tobacco with the air of one whose patriotism was so notorious, he could be allowed such liberties.

Shuman, tall, distinguished, and Programmer-first-class, faced them fearlessly.

He said, "This, gentlemen, is Myron Aub."

"The one with the unusual gift that you discovered quite by accident," said Congressman Brant placidly. "Ah." He inspected the little man with the egg-bald head with amiable curiosity.

The little man, in return, twisted the fingers of his hands anxiously. He had never been near such great men before. He was only an aging low-grade Technician who had long ago failed all tests designed to smoke out the gifted ones among mankind and had settled into the rut of unskilled labor. There was just this hobby of his that the great Programmer had found out about and was now making such a frightening fuss over.

General Weider said, "I find this atmosphere of mystery childish."

"You won't in a moment," said Shuman. "This is not something we can leak to the firstcomer. ——Aub!" There was something imperative about his manner of biting off that one-syllable name, but then he was a great Programmer speaking to a mere Technician. "Aub! How much is nine times seven?"

Aub hesitated a moment. His pale eyes glimmered with a feeble anxiety. "Sixty-three," he said.

Congressman Brant lifted his eyebrows. "Is that right?"

"Check it for yourself, Congressman."

The congressman took out his pocket computer, nudged the milled edges twice, looked at its face as it lay there in the palm of his hand, and put it back. He said, "Is this the gift you brought us here to demonstrate. An illusionist?"

"More than that, sir. Aub has memorized a few operations and with them he computes on paper."

"A paper computer?" said the general. He looked pained.

"No, sir," said Shuman patiently. "Not a paper computer. Simply a sheet of paper. General, would you be so kind as to suggest a number?"

"Seventeen," said the general.

"And you, Congressman?"

"Twenty-three."

"Good! Aub, multiply those numbers and please show the gentlemen your manner of doing it."

"Yes, Programmer," said Aub, ducking his head. He fished a small pad out of one shirt pocket and an artist's hairline stylus out of the other. His forehead corrugated as he made painstaking marks on the paper.

General Weider interrupted him sharply. "Let's see that."

Aub passed him the paper, and Weider said, "Well, it looks like the figure seventeen."

Congressman Brant nodded and said, "So it does, but I suppose anyone can copy figures off a computer. I think I could make a passable seventeen myself, even without practice."

"If you will let Aub continue, gentlemen," said Shuman without heat.

Aub continued, his hand trembling a little. Finally he said in a low voice, "The answer is three hundred and ninety-one."

Congressman Brant took out his computer a second time and flicked it, "By Godfrey, so it is. How did he guess?"

"No guess, Congressman," said Shuman. "He computed that result. He did it on this sheet of paper."

"Humbug," said the general impatiently. "A computer is one thing and marks on paper are another."

"Explain, Aub," said Shuman.

"Yes, Programmer. ——Well, gentlemen, I write down seventeen and just underneath it, I write twenty-three. Next, I say to myself: seven times three——"

The congressman interrupted smoothly, "Now, Aub, the problem is seventeen times twenty-three."

"Yes, I know," said the little Technician earnestly, "but I *start* by saying seven times three because that's the way it works. Now seven times three is twenty-one."

"And how do you know that?" asked the congressman.

"I just remember it. It's always twenty-one on the computer. I've checked it any number of times."

"That doesn't mean it always will be, though, does it?" said the congressman.

"Maybe not," stammered Aub. "I'm not a mathematician. But I always get the right answers, you see."

"Go on."

"Seven times three is twenty-one, so I write down twenty-one. Then one times three is three, so I write down a three under the two of twenty-one."

"Why under the two?" asked Congressman Brant at once.

"Because——" Aub looked helplessly at his superior for support. "It's difficult to explain."

Shuman said, "If you will accept his work for the moment, we can leave the details for the mathematicians."

Brant subsided.

Aub said, "Three plus two makes five, you see, so the twenty-one become a fifty-one. Now you let that go for a while and start fresh. You multiply seven and two, that's fourteen, and one and two, that's two. Put them down like this and it adds up to thirty-four. Now if you put the thirty-four under the fifty-one this way and add them, you get three hundred and ninety-one and that's the answer."

There was an instant's silence and then General Weider said, "I don't believe it. He goes through this rigmarole and makes up numbers and multiplies and adds them this way and that, but I don't believe it. It's too complicated to be anything but hornswoggling."

"Oh no, sir," said Aub in a sweat. "It only *seems* complicated because you're not used to it. Actually, the rules are quite simple and will work for any numbers."

"Any numbers, eh?" said the general. "Come then." He took out his own computer (a severely styled GI model) and struck it at random. Make a five seven three eight on the paper. That's five thousand seven hundred and thirty-eight."

"Yes, sir," said Aub, taking a new sheet of paper.

"Now," (more punching of his computer), "seven two three nine. Seven thousand two hundred and thirty-nine."

"Yes, sir."

"And now multiply those two."

"It will take some time," quavered Aub.

"Take the time," said the general.

"Go ahead, Aub," said Shuman crisply.

Aub set to work, bending low. He took another sheet of paper and another. The general took out his watch finally and stared at it. "Are you through with your magic-making, Technician?"

"I'm almost done, sir. ——Here it is, sir. Forty-one million five hundred and thirty-seven thousand, three hundred and eighty-two." He showed the scrawled figures of the result.

General Weider smiled bitterly. He pushed the multiplication contact on his computer and let the numbers whirl to a halt. And then he stared and said in a surprised squeak, "Great Galaxy, the fella's right."

The President of the Terrestrial Federation had grown haggard in office and, in private, he allowed a look of settled melancholy to appear on his sensitive features. The Denebian war, after its early start of vast movement and great popularity, had trickled down into a sordid matter of maneuver and countermaneuver, with discontent rising steadily on Earth. Possibly, it was rising on Deneb, too.

And now Congressman Brant, head of the important Committee on Military Appropriations was cheerfully and smoothly spending his half-hour appointment spouting nonsense.

"Computing without a computer," said the president impatiently, "is a contradiction in terms."

"Computing," said the congressman, "is only a system for handling data. A machine might do it, or the human brain might. Let me give you an example." And, using the new skills he had learned, he worked out sums and products until the president, despite himself, grew interested.

"Does this always work?"

"Every time, Mr. President. It is foolproof."

"Is it hard to learn?"

"It took me a week to get the real hang of it. I think you would do better."

"Well," said the president, considering, "it's an interesting parlor game, but what is the use of it?"

"What is the use of a newborn baby, Mr. President? At the moment there is no use, but don't you see that this points the way toward liberation from the machine. Consider, Mr. President," the congressman rose and his deep voice automatically took on some of the cadences he used in public debate, "that the Denebian war is a war of computer against computer. Their computers forge an impenetrable shield of counter-missiles against our missiles, and ours forge one against theirs. If we advance the efficiency of our computers, so do they theirs, and for five years a precarious and profitless balance has existed.

"Now we have in our hands a method for going beyond the computer, leapfrogging it, passing through it. We will combine the mechanics of computation with human thought; we will have the equivalent of intelligent computers; billions of them. I can't predict what the consequences will be in detail but they will be incalculable. And if Deneb beats us to the punch, they may be unimaginably catastrophic."

The president said, troubled, "What would you have me do?"

"Put the power of the administration behind the establishment of a secret project on human computation. Call it Project Number, if you like. I can vouch for my committee, but I will need the administration behind me."

"But how far can human computation go?"

"There is no limit. According to Programmer Shuman, who first introduced me to this discovery——"

"I've heard of Shuman, of course."

"Yes. Well, Dr. Shuman tells me that in theory there is nothing the computer can do that the human mind can not do. The computer merely takes a finite amount of data and performs a finite number of operations upon them. The human mind can duplicate the process."

The president considered that. He said, "If Shuman says this, I am inclined to believe him—in theory. But, in practice, how can anyone know how a computer works?"

Brant laughed genially. "Well, Mr. President, I asked the same question. It seems that at one time computers were designed directly by human beings. Those were simple computers, of course this being before the time of the rational use of computers to design more advanced computers had been established."

"Yes, yes. Go on."

"Technician Aub apparently had, as his hobby, the reconstruction of some of these ancient devices and in so doing he studied the details of their workings and found he could imitate them. The multiplication I just performed for you is an imitation of the workings of a computer."

"Amazing!"

The congressman coughed gently, "If I may make another point, Mr. President—— The further we can develop this thing, the more we can divert our Federal effort from computer production and computer maintenance. As the human brain takes over, more of our energy can be directed into peacetime pursuits and the impingement of war on the ordinary man will be less. This will be most advantageous for the party in power, of course."

"Ah," said the president, "I see your point. Well, sit down, Congressman, sit down. I want some time to think about this. ———But meanwhile, show me that multiplication trick again. Let's see if I can't catch the point of it."

Programmer Shuman did not try to hurry matters. Loesser was conservative, very conservative, and liked to deal with computers as his father and grandfather had. Still, he controlled the West European computer combine, and if he could be persuaded to join Project Number in full enthusiasm, a great deal would be accomplished.

But Loesser was holding back. He said, "I'm not sure I like the idea of relaxing our hold on computers. The human mind is a capricious thing. The computer will give the same answer to the same problem each time. What guarantee have we that the human mind will do the same?"

"The human mind, Computer Loesser, only manipulates facts. It doesn't matter whether the human mind or a machine does it. They are just tools."

"Yes, yes. I've gone over your ingenious demonstration that the mind can duplicate the computer but it seems to me a little in the air. I'll grant the theory but what reason have we for thinking that theory can be converted to practice?"

"I think we have reason, sir. After all, computers have not always existed. The cave men with their triremes, stone axes, and railroads had no computers."

"And possibly they did not compute."

"You know better than that. Even the building of a railroad or a ziggurat called for some computing, and that must have been without computers as we know them."

"Do you suggest they computed in the fashion you demonstrate?"

"Probably not. After all, this method—we call it 'graphitics,' by the way, from the old European word 'grapho' meaning 'to write'—is developed from the computers themselves so it cannot have antedated them. Still, the cave men must have had *some* method, eh?"

"Lost arts! If you're going to talk about lost arts———"

"No, no. I'm not a lost art enthusiast, though I don't say there may not be some. After all, man was eating grain before hydroponics, and if the primitives ate grain, they must have grown it in soil. What else could they have done?"

"I don't know, but I'll believe in soil-growing when I see someone grow grain in soil. And I'll believe in making fire by rubbing two pieces of flint together when I see that, too."

Shuman grew placative. "Well, let's stick to graphitics. It's just part of the process of etherealization. Transportation by means of bulky contrivances is giving way to direct mass-transference. Communications devices become less massive and more efficient constantly. For that matter, compare your pocket computer with the massive jobs of a thousand years ago. Why not, then, the last step of doing away with computers altogether? Come, sir, Project Number is a going concern; progress is already headlong. But we want your help. If patriotism doesn't move you, consider the intellectual adventure involved."

Loesser said skeptically, "What progress? What can you do beyond multiplication? Can you integrate a transcendental function?"

"In time, sir. In time. In the last month I have learned to handle division. I can determine, and correctly, integral quotients and decimal quotients."

"Decimal quotients? To how many places?"

Programmer Shuman tried to keep his tone casual. "Any number!"

Loesser's lower jaw dropped. "Without a computer?"

"Set me a problem."

"Divide twenty-seven by thirteen. Take it to six places."

Five minutes later, Shuman said, "Two point oh seven six nine two three."

Loesser checked it. "Well, now, that's amazing. Multiplication didn't impress me too much because it involved integers after all, and I thought trick manipulation might do it. But decimals——"

"And that is not all. There is a new development that is, so far, top secret and which, strictly speaking, I ought not to mention. Still—— We may have made a break-through on the square root front."

"Square roots?"

"It involves some tricky points and we haven't licked the bugs yet, but Technician Aub, the man who invented the science and who has an amazing intuition in connection with it, maintains he has the problem almost solved. And he is only a Technician. A man like yourself, a trained and talented mathematician ought to have no difficulty."

"Square roots," muttered Loesser, attracted.

"Cube roots, too. Are you with us?"

Loesser's hand thrust out suddenly, "Count me in."

General Weider stumped his way back and forth at the head of the room and addressed his listeners after the fashion of a savage teacher facing a group of recalcitrant students. It made no difference to the general that they were the civilian scientists heading Project Number. The general was the over-all head, and he so considered himself at every waking moment.

He said, "Now square roots are all fine. I can't do them myself and I don't understand the methods, but they're fine. Still, the Project will not be sidetracked into what some of you call the fundamentals. You can play with graphitics any way you want to after the war is over, but right now we have specific and very practical problems to solve."

In a far corner, Technician Aub listened with painful attention. He was no longer a Technician, of course, having been relieved of his duties and assigned to the project, with a fine-sounding title and good pay. But, of course, the social distinction remained and the highly placed scientific leaders could never bring themselves to admit him to their ranks on a footing of equality. Nor, to do Aub justice, did he, himself, wish it. He was as uncomfortable with them as they with him.

The general was saying, "Our goal is a simple one, gentlemen; the replacement of the computer. A ship that can navigate space without a computer on board can be constructed in one fifth the time and at one tenth the expense of a computer-laden ship. We could build fleets five times, ten times, as great as Deneb could if we could but eliminate the computer.

"And I see something even beyond this. It may be fantastic now; a mere dream; but in the future I see the manned missile!"

There was an instant murmur from the audience.

The general drove on. "At the present time, our chief bottle-neck is the fact that missiles are limited in intelligence. The computer controlling them can only be so large, and for that reason they can meet the changing nature of anti-missile defenses in an unsatisfactory way. Few missiles, if any, accomplish their goal and missile warfare is coming to a dead end; for the enemy, fortunately, as well as for ourselves.

"On the other hand, a missile with a man or two within, controlling flight by graphitics, would be lighter, more mobile, more intelligent. It would give us a lead that might well mean the margin of victory. Besides which, gentlemen, the exigencies of war compel us to remember one thing. A man is much more dispensable than a computer. Manned missiles could be launched in numbers and under circumstances that no good general would care to undertake as far as computer-directed missiles are concerned——"

He said much more but Technician Aub did not wait.

Technician Aub, in the privacy of his quarters, labored long over the note he was leaving behind. It read finally as follows:

"When I began the study of what is now called graphitics, it was no more than a hobby. I saw no more in it than an interesting amusement, an exercise of mind.

"When Project Number began, I thought that others were wiser than I; that graphitics might be put to practical use as a benefit to mankind, to aid in the production of really practical mass-transference devices perhaps. But now I see it is to be used only for death and destruction.

"I cannot face the responsibility involved in having invented graphitics."

He then deliberately turned the focus of a protein-depolarizer on himself and fell instantly and painlessly dead.

They stood over the grave of the little Technician while tribute was paid to the greatness of his discovery.

Programmer Shuman bowed his head along with the rest of them, but remained unmoved. The Technician had done his share and was no longer needed, after all. He might have started graphitics, but now that it had started, it would carry on by itself overwhelmingly, triumphantly, until manned missiles were possible with who knew what else.

Nine times seven, thought Shuman with deep satisfaction, is sixty-three, and I don't need a computer to tell me so. The computer is in my own head.

And it was amazing the feeling of power that gave him.

THE DYING NIGHT

Part 1

IT WAS ALMOST a class reunion, and though it was marked by joylessness, there was no reason as yet to think it would be marred by tragedy.

Edward Talliaferro, fresh from the Moon and without his gravity legs yet, met the other two in Stanley Kaunas's room. Kaunas rose to greet him in a subdued manner. Battersley Ryger merely sat and nodded.

Talliaferro lowered his large body carefully to the couch, very aware of its unusual weight. He grimaced a little, his plump lips twisting inside the rim of hair that surrounded his mouth on lip, chin, and cheek.

They had seen one another earlier that day under more formal conditions. Now for the first time they were alone, and Talliaferro said, "This is a kind of occasion. We're meeting for the first time in ten years. First time since graduation, in fact."

Ryger's nose twitched. It had been broken shortly before that same graduation and he had received his degree in astronomy with a bandage disfiguring his face. He said grumpily, "Anyone ordered champagne? Or something?"

Talliaferro said, "Come on! First big interplanetary astronomical convention in history is no place for glooming. And among friends, too!"

Kaunas said suddenly, "It's Earth. It doesn't feel right. I can't get used to it." He shook his head but his look of depression was not detachable. It remained.

Talliaferro said, "I know. I'm so heavy. It takes all the energy out of me. At that, you're better off than I am, Kaunas. Mercurian gravity is 0.4 normal. On the Moon, it's only 0.16." He interrupted Ryger's beginning of a sound by saying, "And on Ceres they use pseudo-grav fields adjusted to 0.8. You have no problems at all, Ryger."

The Cerian astronomer looked annoyed, "It's the open air. Going outside without a suit gets me."

"Right," agreed Kaunas, "and letting the sun beat down on you. Just letting it."

Talliaferro found himself insensibly drifting back in time. They had not changed much. Nor, he thought, had he himself. They were all ten years older, of course. Ryger had put on some weight and Kaunas's thin face had grown a bit leathery, but he would have recognized either if he had met him without warning.

He said, "I don't think it's Earth getting us. Let's face it."

Kaunas looked up sharply. He was a little fellow with quick, nervous movements of his hands. He habitually wore clothes that looked a shade too large for him.

He said, "Villiers! I know. I think about him sometimes." Then, with an air of desperation, "I got a letter from him."

Ryger sat upright, his olive complexion darkening further and said with energy, "You did? When?"

"A month ago."

Ryger turned to Talliaferro. "How about you?"

Talliaferro blinked placidly and nodded.

Ryger said, "He's gone crazy. He claims he's discovered a practical method of mass-transference through space. ——He told you two also? ——That's it, then. He was always a little bent. Now he's broken."

He rubbed his nose fiercely and Talliaferro thought of the day Villiers had broken it.

For ten years, Villiers had haunted them like the vague shadow of a guilt that wasn't really theirs. They had gone through their graduate work together, four picked and dedicated men being trained for a profession that had reached new heights in this age of interplanetary travel.

The Observatories were opening on the other worlds, surrounded by vacuum, unblurred by air.

There was the Lunar Observatory, from which Earth and the inner planets could be studied; a silent world in whose sky the home-planet hung suspended.

Mercury Observatory, closest to the sun, perched at Mercury's north pole, where the terminator moved scarcely at all, and the sun was fixed on the horizon and could be studied in the minutest detail.

Ceres Observatory, newest, most modern, with its range extending from Jupiter to the outermost galaxies.

There were disadvantages, of course. With interplanetary travel still difficult, leaves would be few, anything like normal life virtually impossible, but this was a lucky generation. Coming scientists would find the fields of knowledge well-reaped and, until the invention of an interstellar drive, no new horizon as capacious as this one would be opened.

Each of these lucky four, Talliaferro, Ryger, Kaunas, and Villiers, was to be in the position of a Galileo, who by owning the first real telescope, could not point it anywhere in the sky without making a major discovery.

But then Romero Villiers had fallen sick and it was rheumatic fever. Whose fault was that? His heart had been left leaking and limping.

He was the most brilliant of the four, the most hopeful, the most intense—and he could not even finish his schooling and get his doctorate.

Worse than that, he could never leave Earth; the acceleration of a spaceship's take-off would kill him.

Talliaferro was marked for the Moon, Ryger for Ceres, Kaunas for Mercury. Only Villiers stayed behind, a life-prisoner of Earth.

They had tried telling their sympathy and Villiers had rejected it with something approaching hate. He had railed at them and cursed them. When Ryger lost his temper and lifted his fist, Villiers had sprung at him, screaming, and had broken Ryger's nose.

Obviously Ryger hadn't forgotten that, as he caressed his nose gingerly with one finger.

Kaunas's forehead was an uncertain washboard of wrinkles. "He's at the Convention, you know. He's got a room in the hotel—405."

"*I* won't see him," said Ryger.

"He's coming up here. He said he wanted to see us. I thought——He said nine. He'll be here any minute."

"In that case," said Ryger, "if you don't mind, I'm leaving." He rose.

Talliaferro said, "Oh, wait a while. What's the harm in seeing him?"

"Because there's no point. He's mad."

"Even so. Let's not be petty about it. Are you afraid of him?"

"Afraid!" Ryger looked contemptuous.

"Nervous, then. What is there to be so nervous about?"

"I'm not nervous," said Ryger.

"Sure you are. We all feel guilty about him, and without real reason. Nothing that happened was our fault." But he was speaking defensively and he knew it.

And when, at that point, the door signal sounded, all three jumped and turned to stare uneasily at the barrier that stood between themselves and Villiers.

The door opened and Romero Villiers walked in. The others rose stiffly to greet him, then remained standing in embarrassment, without one hand being raised.

He stared them down sardonically.

He's changed, thought Talliaferro.

He had. He had shrunken in almost every dimension. A gathering stoop made him seem even shorter. The skin of his scalp glistened through thinning hair, the skin on the back of his hands was ridged crookedly with bluish veins. He looked ill. There seemed nothing to link him to the memory of the past except for his trick of shading his eyes with one hand when he stared intently and, when he spoke, the even, controlled baritone of his voice.

He said, "My friends! My space-trotting friends! We've lost touch."

Talliaferro said, "Hello, Villiers."

Villiers eyed him. "Are you well?"

"Well enough."

"And you two?"

Kaunas managed a weak smile and a murmur. Ryger snapped, "All right, Villiers. What's up?"

"Ryger, the angry man," said Villiers. "How's Ceres?"

"It was doing well when I left. How's Earth?"

"You can see for yourself," but Villiers tightened as he said that.

He went on, "I am hoping that the reason all three of you have come to the Convention is to hear my paper day after tomorrow."

"Your paper? What paper?" asked Talliaferro.

"I wrote you all about it. My method of mass-transference."

Ryger smiled with one corner of his mouth. "Yes, you did. You didn't say anything about a paper, though, and I don't recall that you're listed as one of the speakers. I would have noticed it if you had been."

"You're right. I'm not listed. Nor have I prepared an abstract for publication."

Villiers had flushed and Talliaferro said soothingly, "Take it easy, Villiers. You don't look well."

Villiers whirled on him, lips contorted. "My heart's holding out, thank you."

Kaunas said, "Listen, Villiers, if you're not listed or ab-stracted———"

"*You* listen. I've waited ten years. You have the jobs in space and I have to teach school on Earth, but I'm a better man than any of you or all of you."

"Granted———" began Talliaferro.

"And I don't want your condescension either. Mandel witnessed it. I suppose you've heard of Mandel. Well, he's chairman of the astronautics division at the Convention and I demonstrated mass-transference for him. It was a crude device and it burnt out after one use but—— Are you listening?"

"We're listening," said Ryger coldly, "for what that counts."

"He'll let me talk about it my way. You bet he will. No warning. No advertisement. I'm going to spring it at them like a bombshell. When I give them the fundamental relationships involved it will break up the Convention. They'll scatter to their home labs to check on me and build devices. And they'll find it works. I made a live mouse disappear at one spot in my lab and appear in another. Mandel witnessed it."

He stared at them, glaring first at one face, then at another. He said, "You don't believe me, do you?"

Ryger said, "If you don't want advertisement, why do you tell us?"

"You're different. You're my friends, my classmates. You went out into space and left me behind."

"That wasn't a matter of choice," objected Kaunas in a thin, high voice.

Villiers ignored that. He said, "So I want you to know *now*. What will work for a mouse will work for a human. What will move something ten feet across a lab will move it a million miles across space. I'll be on the Moon, *and* on Mercury, *and* on Ceres and anywhere I want to go. I'll match every one of you and more. And I'll have done more for astronomy just teaching school and thinking, than all of you with your observatories and telescopes and cameras and spaceships."

"Well," said Talliaferro, "I'm pleased. More power to you. May I see a copy of the paper?"

"Oh, no." Villiers' hands clenched close to his chest as though he were holding phantom sheets and shielding them from observation. "You wait like everyone else. There's only one copy and no one will see it till I'm ready. Not even Mandel."

"One copy," cried Talliaferro. "If you misplace it——"

"I won't. And if I do, it's all in my head."

"If you——" Talliaferro almost finished that sentence with "die" but stopped himself. Instead, he went on after an almost imperceptible pause, "——have any sense, you'll scan it at least. For safety's sake."

"No," said Villiers, shortly. "You'll hear me day after tomorrow. You'll see the human horizon expanded at one stroke as it never has been before."

Again he stared intently at each face. "Ten years," he said. "Good-by."

"He's mad," said Ryger explosively, staring at the door as though Villiers were still standing before it.

"Is he?" said Talliaferro thoughtfully. "I suppose he is, in a way. He hates us for irrational reasons. And, then, not even to scan his paper as a precaution——"

Talliaferro fingered his own small scanner as he said that. It was just a neutrally colored, undistinguished cylinder, somewhat thicker and somewhat shorter than an ordinary pencil. In recent years, it had become the hallmark of the scientist, much as the stethescope was that of the physician and the micro-computer that of the statistician. The scanner was worn in a jacket pocket, or clipped to a sleeve, or slipped behind the ear, or swung at the end of a string.

Talliaferro sometimes, in his more philosophical moments, wondered how it was in the days when research men had to make laborious notes of the literature or file away full-sized reprints. How unwieldy!

Now it was only necessary to scan anything printed or written to have a micro-negative which could be developed at leisure. Talliaferro had already recorded every abstract included in the program booklet of the Convention. The other two, he assumed with full confidence, had done likewise.

Talliaferro said, "Under the circumstances, refusal to scan is mad."

"Space!" said Ryger hotly. "There is no paper. There is no discovery. Scoring one on us would be worth any lie to him."

"But then what will he do day after tomorrow?" asked Kaunas.

"How do I know? He's a madman."

Talliaferro still played with his scanner and wondered idly if he ought to remove and develop some of the small slivers of film that lay stored away in its vitals. He decided against it. He said, "Don't underestimate Villiers. He's a brain."

"Ten years ago, maybe," said Ryger. "Now he's a nut. I propose we forget him."

He spoke loudly, as though to drive away Villiers and all that concerned him by the sheer force with which he discussed other things. He talked about Ceres and his work—the radio-plotting of the Milky Way with new radioscopes capable of the resolution of single stars.

Kaunas listened and nodded, then chimed in with information concerning the radio emissions of sunspots and his own paper, in press, on the association of proton storms with the gigantic hydrogen flares on the sun's surface.

Talliaferro contributed little. Lunar work was unglamorous in comparison. The latest information on long-scale weather forecasting through direct observation of terrestrial jet-streams would not compare with radioscopes and proton storms.

More than that, his thoughts could not leave Villiers. Villiers *was* the brain. They all knew it. Even Ryger, for all his bluster, must feel that if mass-transference were at all possible then Villiers was a logical discoverer.

The discussion of their own work amounted to no more than an uneasy admission that none of them had come to much. Talliaferro had followed the literature and knew. His own papers had been minor. The others had authored nothing of great importance.

None of them—face the fact—had developed into space-shakers. The colossal dreams of school days had not come true and that was that. They were competent routine workmen. No less. Unfortunately, no more. They knew that.

Villiers would have been more. They knew that, too. It was that knowledge, as well as guilt, which kept them antagonistic.

Talliaferro felt uneasily that Villiers, despite everything, was yet to *be* more. The others must be thinking so, too, and mediocrity could grow quickly unbearable. The mass-transference paper would come to pass and Villiers would be the great man after all, as he was always fated to be apparently, while his classmates, with all their advantages, would be forgotten. Their role would be no more than to applaud from the crowd.

He felt his own envy and chagrin and was ashamed of it, but felt it none the less.

Conversation died, and Kaunas said, his eyes turning away, "Listen, why don't we drop in on old Villiers?"

There was a false heartiness about it, a completely unconvincing effort at casualness. He added, "No use leaving bad feelings—unnecessarily——"

Talliaferro thought: He wants to make sure about the mass-transference. He's hoping it *is* only a madman's nightmare so he can sleep tonight.

But he was curious himself, so he made no objection, and even Ryger shrugged with ill grace and said, "Hell, why not?"

It was a little before eleven then.

Talliaferro was awakened by the insistent ringing of his door signal. He hitched himself to one elbow in the darkness and felt distinctly outraged. The soft glow of the ceiling indicator showed it to be not quite four in the morning.

He cried out, "Who is it?"

The ringing continued in short, insistent spurts.

Growling, Talliaferro slipped into his bathrobe. He opened the door and blinked in the corridor light. He recognized the man who faced him from the trimensionals he had seen often enough.

Nevertheless, the man said in an abrupt whisper, "My name is Hubert Mandel."

"Yes, sir," said Talliaferro. Mandel was one of the Names in astronomy, prominent enough to have an important executive position with the World Astronomical Bureau, active enough to be Chairman of the Astronautics section here at the Convention.

It suddenly struck Talliaferro that it was Mandel for whom Villiers claimed to have demonstrated mass-transference. The thought of Villiers was somehow a sobering one.

Mandel said, "You are Dr. Edward Talliaferro?"

"Yes, sir."

"Then dress and come with me. It is very important. It concerns a mutual acquaintance."

"Dr. Villiers?"

Mandel's eyes flickered a bit. His brows and lashes were so fair as to give those eyes a naked, unfringed appearance. His hair was silky-thin, his age about fifty.

He said, "Why Villiers?"

"He mentioned you last evening. I don't know any other mutual acquaintance."

Mandel nodded, waited for Talliaferro to finish slipping into his clothes, then turned and led the way. Ryger and Kaunas were waiting in a room one floor above Talliaferro's. Kaunas's eyes were red and troubled. Ryger was smoking a cigarette with impatient puffs.

Talliaferro said, "We're all here. Another reunion." It fell flat.

He took a seat and the three stared at one another. Ryger shrugged.

Mandel paced the floor, hands deep in his pockets. He said, "I apologize for any inconvenience, gentlemen, and I thank you for your co-operation. I would like more of it. Our friend, Romero Villiers, is dead. About an hour ago, his body was removed from the hotel. The medical judgment is heart failure."

There was a stunned silence. Ryger's cigarette hovered halfway to his lips, then sank slowly without completing its journey.

"Poor devil," said Talliaferro.

"Horrible," whispered Kaunas hoarsely. "He was——" His voice played out.

Ryger shook himself. "Well, he had a bad heart. There's nothing to be done."

"One little thing," corrected Mandel quietly. "Recovery."

"What does that mean?" asked Ryger sharply.

Mandel said, "When did you three see him last?"

Talliaferro spoke. "Last evening. It turned out to be a reunion. We all met for the first time in ten years. It wasn't a pleasant meeting, I'm sorry to say. Villiers felt he had cause for anger with us, and he was angry."

"That was—when?"

"About nine, the first time."

"The first time?"

"We saw him again later in the evening."

Kaunas looked troubled. "He had left angrily. We couldn't leave it at that. We had to try. It wasn't as if we hadn't all been friends at one time. So we went to his room and——"

Mandel pounced on that. "You were all in his room?"

"Yes," said Kaunas, surprised.

"About when?"

"Eleven, I think." He looked at the others. Talliaferro nodded.

"And how long did you stay?"

"Two minutes," put in Ryger. "He ordered us out as though we were after his paper." He paused as though expecting Mandel to ask what paper, but Mandel said nothing. He went on. "I think he kept it under his pillow. At least he lay across the pillow as he yelled at us to leave."

"He may have been dying then," said Kaunas, in a sick whisper.

"Not then," said Mandel shortly. "So you probably all left fingerprints."

"Probably," said Talliaferro. He was losing some of his automatic respect for Mandel and a sense of impatience was returning. It *was* four in the morning, Mandel or no. He said, "Now what's all this about?"

"Well, gentlemen," said Mandel, "there's more to Villiers' death than the fact of death. Villiers' paper, the only copy of it as far as I know, was stuffed into the cigarette flash-disposal unit and only scraps of it were left. I've never seen or read the paper, but I knew enough about the matter to be willing to swear in court if necessary that the remnants of unflashed paper in the disposal unit were of the paper he was planning to give at this Convention. ——You seem doubtful, Dr. Ryger."

Ryger smiled sourly. "Doubtful that he was going to give it. If you want my opinion, sir, he was mad. For ten years he was a prisoner of Earth and he fantasied mass-transference as escape. It was all that kept him alive probably. He rigged up some sort of fraudulent demonstration. I don't say it was deliberate fraud. He was probably madly sincere, and sincerely mad. Last evening was the climax. He came to our rooms—he hated us for having escaped Earth—and triumphed over us. It was what he had lived for for ten years. It may have shocked him back to some form of sanity. He knew he couldn't actually give the paper; there was nothing to give. So he burnt it and his heart gave out. It *is* too bad."

Mandel listened to the Cerian astronomer, wearing a look of sharp disapproval. He said, "Very glib, Dr. Ryger, but quite wrong. I am not as easily fooled by fraudulent demonstrations as you may believe. Now according to the registration data, which I have been forced to check rather hastily, you three were his classmates at college. Is that right?"

They nodded.

"Are there any other classmates of yours present at the Convention?"

"No," said Kaunas. "We were the only four qualifying for a doctorate in astronomy that year. At least he would have qualified except——"

"Yes, I understand," said Mandel. "Well, then, in that case one of you three visited Villiers in his room one last time at midnight."

There was a short silence. Then Ryger said coldly, "Not I." Kaunas, eyes wide, shook his head.

Talliaferro said, "What are you implying?"

"One of you came to him at midnight and insisted on seeing his paper. I don't know the motive. Conceivably, it was with the deliberate intention of forcing him into heart failure. When Villiers collapsed, the criminal, if I may call him so, was ready. He snatched the paper which, I might add, probably *was* kept under his pillow and scanned it. Then he destroyed the paper itself in the flash-disposal, but he was in a hurry and destruction wasn't complete."

Ryger interrupted. "How do you know all this? Were you a witness?"

"Almost," said Mandel. "Villiers was not quite dead at the moment of his first collapse. When the criminal left, he managed to reach the phone and call my room. He choked out a few phrases, enough to outline what had occurred. Unfortunately I was not in my room; a late conference kept me away. However, my recording attachment taped it. I always play the recording tape back whenever I return to my room or office. Bureaucratic habit. I called back. He was dead."

"Well, then," said Ryger, "who did he say did it?"

"He didn't. Or if he did, it was unintelligible. But one word rang out clearly. It was 'classmate.' "

Talliaferro detached his scanner from its place in his inner jacket pocket and held it out toward Mandel. Quietly he said, "If you would like to develop the film in my scanner, you are welcome to do so. You will not find Villiers' paper there."

At once, Kaunas did the same, and Ryger, with a scowl, joined.

Mandel took all three scanners and said dryly, "Presumably, whichever one of you has done this has already disposed of the piece of exposed film with the paper on it. However——"

Talliaferro raised his eyebrows. "You may search my person or my room."

But Ryger was still scowling, "Now wait a minute, wait one bloody minute. Are you the police?"

Mandel stared at him. "Do you *want* the police? Do you want a scandal and a murder charge? Do you want the Convention disrupted and the System press to make a holiday out of astronomy and astronomers? Villiers' death might well have been accidental. He *did* have a bad heart. Whichever one of you was there may well have acted on impulse. It may not have been a premeditated crime. If whoever it is will return the negative, we can avoid a great deal of trouble."

"Even for the criminal?" asked Talliaferro.

Mandel shrugged. "There may be trouble for him. I will not promise immunity. But whatever the trouble, it won't be public disgrace and life imprisonment, as it might be if the police are called in."

Silence.

Mandel said, "It is one of you three."

Silence.

Mandel went on, "I think I can see the original reasoning of the guilty person. The paper would be destroyed. Only we four knew of the mass-transference and only I had ever seen a demonstration. Moreover you had only his word, a madman's word perhaps, that I had seen it. With Villiers dead of heart failure and the paper gone, it would be easy to believe Dr. Ryger's theory that there was no mass-transference and never had been. A year or two might pass and our criminal, in possession of the mass-transference data, could reveal it little by little, rig experiments, publish careful papers, and end as the apparent discoverer with all that would imply in terms of money and renown. Even his own classmates would suspect nothing. At most they would believe that the long-past affair with Villiers had inspired him to begin investigations in the field. No more."

Mandel looked sharply from one face to another. "But none of that will work now. Any of the three of you who comes through with mass-transference is proclaiming himself the criminal. I've seen the demonstration; I know it is legitimate; I know that one of you possesses a record of the paper. The information is therefore useless to you. Give it up then."

Silence.

Mandel walked to the door and turned again, "I'd appreciate it if you would stay here till I return. I won't be long. I hope the guilty one will use the interval to consider. If he's afraid a confession will lose him his job, let him remember that a session with the police may lose him his liberty *and* cost him the Psychic Probe." He hefted the three scanners, looked grim and somewhat in need of sleep. "I'll develop these."

Kaunas tried to smile. "What if we make a break for it while you're gone?"

"Only one of you has reason to try," said Mandel. "I think I can rely on the two innocent ones to control the third, if only out of self-protection."

He left.

It was five in the morning. Ryger looked at his watch indignantly. "A hell of a thing. I want to sleep."

"We can curl up here," said Talliaferro philosophically. "Is anyone planning a confession?"

Kaunas looked away and Ryger's lip lifted.

"I didn't think so." Talliaferro closed his eyes, leaned his large head back against the chair and said in a tired voice, "Back on the Moon, they're in the slack season. We've got a two-week night and then it's busy, busy. Then there's two weeks of sun and there's nothing but calculations, correlations and bull-sessions. That's the hard time. I hate it. If there were more women, if I could arrange something permanent——"

In a whisper, Kaunas talked about the fact that it was still impossible to get the entire Sun above the horizon and in view of the telescope on Mercury. But with another two miles of track soon to be laid down for the Observatory—move the whole thing,

you know, tremendous forces involved, solar energy used directly—
it might be managed. It *would* be managed.

Even Ryger consented to talk of Ceres after listening to the low
murmur of the other voices. There was the problem there of the
two-hour rotation period, which meant the stars whipped across the
sky at an angular velocity twelve times that in Earth's sky. A net
of three light scopes, three radio scopes, three of everything, caught
the fields of study from one another as they whirled past.

"Could you use one of the poles?" asked Kaunas.

"You're thinking of Mercury and the Sun," said Ryger impatiently.
"Even at the poles, the sky would still twist, and half of it would
be forever hidden. Now if Ceres showed only one face to the
Sun, the way Mercury does, we could have a permanent night
sky with the stars rotating slowly once in three years."

The sky lightened and it dawned slowly.

Talliaferro was half asleep, but he kept hold of half-conscious-
ness firmly. He would not fall asleep and leave the others awake.
Each of the three, he thought, was wondering, "Who? Who?"—
except the guilty one, of course.

Talliaferro's eyes snapped open as Mandel entered again. The
sky, as seen from the window, had grown blue. Talliaferro was glad
the window was closed. The hotel was air-conditioned, of course,
but windows could be opened during the mild season of the year
by those Earthmen who fancied the illusion of fresh air. Talliaferro,
with Moon-vacuum on his mind, shuddered at the thought with
real discomfort.

Mandel said, "Have any of you anything to say?"

They looked at him steadily. Ryger shook his head.

Mandel said, "I have developed the film in your scanners,
gentlemen, and viewed the results." He tossed scanners and developed slivers of film on to the bed. "Nothing! ——You'll have
trouble sorting out the film, I'm afraid. For that I'm sorry. And
now there is still the question of the missing film."

"If any," said Ryger, and yawned prodigiously.

Mandel said, "I would suggest we come down to Villiers' room,
gentlemen."

Kaunas looked startled. "Why?"

Talliaferro said, "Is this psychology? Bring the criminal to the scene of the crime and remorse will wring a confession from him?"

Mandel said, "A less melodramatic reason is that I would like to have the two of you who are innocent help me find the missing film of Villiers' paper."

"Do you think it's there?" asked Ryger challengingly.

"Possibly. It's a beginning. We can then search each of your rooms. The symposium on Astronautics doesn't start till tomorrow at 10 A.M. We have till then."

"And after that?"

"It may have to be the police."

They stepped gingerly into Villiers' room. Ryger was red, Kaunas pale. Talliaferro tried to remain calm.

Last night they had seen it under artificial lighting with a scowling, disheveled Villiers clutching his pillow, staring them down, ordering them away. Now there was the scentless odor of death about it.

Mandel fiddled with the window-polarizer to let more light in, and adjusted it too far, so that the eastern Sun slipped in.

Kaunas threw his arm up to shade his eyes and screamed, "The Sun!" so that all the others froze.

Kaunas's face showed a kind of terror, as though it were his Mercurian sun that he had caught a blinding glimpse of.

Talliaferro thought of his own reaction to the possibility of open air and his teeth gritted. They were all bent crooked by their ten years away from Earth.

Kaunas ran to the window, fumbling for the polarizer, and then the breath came out of him in a huge gasp.

Mandel stepped to his side. "What's wrong?" and the other two joined them.

The city lay stretched below them and outward to the horizon in broken stone and brick, bathed in the rising sun, with the shadowed portions toward them. Talliaferro cast it all a furtive and uneasy glance.

Kaunas, his chest seemingly contracted past the point where he could cry out, stared at something much closer. There, on the outer window sill, one corner secured in a trifling imperfection, a crack in the cement, was an inch-long strip of milky-gray film, and on it were the early rays of the rising sun.

Mandel, with an angry, incoherent cry, threw up the window and snatched it away. He shielded it in one cupped hand, staring out of hot and reddened eyes.

He said, "Wait here!"

There was nothing to say. When Mandel left, they sat down and stared stupidly at one another.

Mandel was back in twenty minutes. He said quietly (in a voice that gave the impression, somehow, that it was quiet only because its owner had passed far beyond the raving stage), "The corner in the crack wasn't overexposed. I could make out a few words. It is Villiers' paper. The rest is ruined; nothing can be salvaged. It's gone."

"What next?" said Talliaferro.

Mandel shrugged wearily. "Right now, I don't care. Mass-transference is gone until someone as brilliant as Villiers works it out again. I shall work on it but I have no illusions as to my own capacity. With it gone, I suppose you three don't matter, guilty or not. What's the difference?" His whole body seemed to have loosened and sunk into despair.

But Talliaferro's voice grew hard. "Now, hold on. In your eyes, any of the three of us might be guilty. I, for instance. You are a big man in the field and you will never have a good word to say for me. The general idea may arise that I am incompetent or worse. I will not be ruined by the shadow of guilt. Now let's solve this thing."

"I am no detective," said Mandel wearily.

"Then call in the police, damn it."

Ryger said, "Wait a while, Tal. Are you implying that I'm guilty?"

"I'm saying that I'm innocent."

Kaunas raised his voice in fright. "It will mean the Psychic Probe for each of us. There may be mental damage——"

Mandel raised both arms high in the air. "Gentlemen! Gentlemen! Please! There is one thing we might do short of the police;

and you are right, Dr. Talliaferro, it would be unfair to the innocent to leave this matter here."

They turned to him in various stages of hostility. Ryger said, "What do you suggest?"

"I have a friend named Wendell Urth. You may have heard of him, or you may not, but perhaps I can arrange to see him tonight."

"What if you can?" demanded Talliaferro. "Where does that get us?"

"He's an odd man," said Mandel hesitantly, "very odd. And very brilliant in his way. He has helped the police before this and he may be able to help us now."

Part 2

Edward Talliaferro could not forbear staring at the room and its occupant with the greatest astonishment. It and he seemed to exist in isolation, and to be part of no recognizable world. The sounds of Earth were absent in this well-padded, windowless nest. The light and air of Earth had been blanked out in artificial illumination and conditioning.

It was a large room, dim and cluttered. They had picked their way across a littered floor to a couch from which book-films had been brusquely cleared and dumped to one side in a tangle.

The man who owned the room had a large, round face on a stumpy, round body. He moved quickly about on his short legs, jerking his head as he spoke until his thick glasses all but bounced off the thoroughly inconspicuous nubble that served as a nose. His thick-lidded, somewhat protuberant eyes gleamed in myopic good nature at them all, as he seated himself in his own chair-desk combination, lit directly by the one bright light in the room.

"So good of you to come, gentlemen. Pray excuse the condition of my room " He waved stubby fingers in a wide-sweeping gesture. "I am engaged in cataloguing the many objects of extraterrological interest I have accumulated. It is a tremendous job. For in-stance——"

He dodged out of his seat and burrowed in a heap of objects beside the desk till he came up with a smoky-gray object, semitranslucent and roughly cylindrical. "This," he said, "is a Callistan object that may be a relic of intelligent nonhuman entities. It is not decided. Not more than a dozen have been discovered and this is the most perfect single specimen I know of."

He tossed it to one side and Talliaferro jumped. The plump man stared in his direction and said, "It's not breakable." He sat down again, clasped his pudgy fingers tightly over his abdomen and let them pump slowly in and out as he breathed. "And now what can I do for you?"

Hubert Mandel had carried through the introductions and Talliaferro was considering deeply. Surely it was a man named Wendell Urth who had written a recent book entitled *Comparative Evolutionary Processes on Water-Oxygen Planets,* and surely this could not be the man.

He said, "Are you the author of *Comparative Evolutionary Processes,* Dr. Urth?"

A beatific smile spread across Urth's face, "You've read it?"

"Well, no, I haven't, but——"

Urth's expression grew instantly censorious. "Then you should. Right now. Here, I have a copy——"

He bounced out of his chair again and Mandel cried at once, "Now wait, Urth, first things first. This is serious."

He virtually forced Urth back into his chair and began speaking rapidly as though to prevent any further side issues from erupting. He told the whole story with admirable word-economy.

Urth reddened slowly as he listened. He seized his glasses and shoved them higher up on his nose. "Mass-transference!" he cried.

"I saw it with my own eyes," said Mandel.

"And you never told me."

"I was sworn to secrecy. The man was—peculiar. I explained that."

Urth pounded the desk. "How could you allow such a discovery to remain the property of an eccentric, Mandel? The knowledge should have been forced from him by Psychic Probe, if necessary."

"It would have killed him," protested Mandel.

But Urth was rocking back and forth with his hands clasped tightly to his cheeks. "Mass-transference. The only way a decent, civilized man should travel. The only possible way. The only conceivable way. If I had known. If I could have been there. But the hotel is nearly thirty miles away."

Ryger, who listened with an expression of annoyance on his face, interposed, "I understand there's a flitter line direct to Convention Hall. It could have gotten you there in ten minutes."

Urth stiffened and looked at Ryger strangely. His cheeks bulged. He jumped to his feet and scurried out of the room.

Ryger said, "What the devil?"

Mandel muttered, "Damn it. I should have warned you."

"About what?"

"Dr. Urth doesn't travel on any sort of conveyance. It's a phobia. He moves about only on foot."

Kaunas blinked about in the dimness. "But he's an extraterrologist, isn't he? An expert on life forms of other planets?"

Talliaferro had risen and now stood before a Galactic Lens on a pedestal. He stared at the inner gleam of the star systems. He had never seen a Lens so large or so elaborate.

Mandel said, "He's an extraterrologist, yes, but he's never visited any of the planets on which he is expert and he never will. In thirty years, I doubt if he's ever been more than a mile from this room."

Ryger laughed.

Mandel flushed angrily. "You may find it funny, but I'd appreciate your being careful what you say when Dr. Urth comes back."

Urth sidled in a moment later. "My apologies, gentlemen," he said in a whisper. "And now let us approach our problem. Perhaps one of you wishes to confess."

Talliaferro's lips quirked sourly. This plump, self-imprisoned extraterrologist was scarcely formidable enough to force a confession from anyone. Fortunately, there would be no need of his detective talents, if any, after all.

Talliaferro said, "Dr. Urth, are you connected with the police?"

A certain smugness seemed to suffuse Urth's ruddy face. "I have no official connection, Dr. Talliaferro, but my unofficial relationships are very good indeed."

"In that case, I will give you some information which you can carry to the police."

Urth drew in his abdomen and hitched at his shirttail. It came free, and slowly he polished his glasses with it. When he was quite through and had perched them precariously on his nose once more, he said, "And what is that?"

"I will tell you who was present when Villiers died and who scanned his paper."

"You have solved the mystery?"

"I've thought about it all day. I think I've solved it." Talliaferro rather enjoyed the sensation he was creating.

"Well, then?"

Talliaferro took a deep breath. This was not going to be easy to do, though he had been planning it for hours. "The guilty man," he said, "is obviously Dr. Hubert Mandel."

Mandel stared at Talliaferro in sudden, hard-breathing indignation. "Look here, Doctor," he began, loudly, "if you have any basis for such a ridiculous——"

Urth's tenor voice soared above the interruption. "Let him talk, Hubert, let us hear him. You suspected him and there is no law that forbids him to suspect you."

Mandel fell angrily silent.

Talliaferro, not allowing his voice to falter, said, "It is more than just suspicion, Dr. Urth. The evidence is perfectly plain. Four of us knew about mass-transference, but only one of us, Dr. Mandel, had actually seen a demonstration. He *knew* it to be a fact. He *knew* a paper on the subject existed. We three knew only that Villiers was more or less unbalanced. Oh, we might have thought there was just a chance. We visited him at eleven, I think, just to check on that, though none of us actually said so—but he just acted crazier than ever."

"Check special knowledge and motive then on Dr. Mandel's side. Now, Dr. Urth, picture something else. Whoever it was who confronted Villiers at midnight, saw him collapse, and scanned his paper (let's keep him anonymous for a moment) must have been terribly startled to see Villiers apparently come to life again and to hear him talking into the telephone. Our criminal, in the panic of the moment, realized one thing: he must get rid of the one piece of incriminating material evidence.

"He had to get rid of the undeveloped film of the paper and

he had to do it in such a way that it would be safe from discovery so that he might pick it up once more if he remained unsuspected. The outer window sill was ideal. Quickly he threw up Villiers' window, placed the strip of film outside, and left. Now, even if Villiers survived or if his telephoning brought results, it would be merely Villiers' word against his own and it would be easy to show that Villiers was unbalanced."

Talliaferro paused in something like triumph. This would be irrefutable.

Wendell Urth blinked at him and wiggled the thumbs of his clasped hands so that they slapped against his ample shirt front. He said, "And the significance of all that?"

"The significance is that the window was thrown open and the film placed in open air. Now Ryger has lived for ten years on Ceres, Kaunas on Mercury, I on the Moon—barring short leaves and not many of them. We commented to one another several times yesterday on the difficulty of growing acclimated to Earth.

"Our work-worlds are each airless objects. We never go out in the open without a suit. To expose ourselves to unenclosed space is unthinkable. None of us could have opened the window without a severe inner struggle. Dr. Mandel, however, has lived on Earth exclusively. Opening a window to him is only a matter of a bit of muscular exertion. He could do it. We couldn't. Ergo, he did it."

Talliaferro sat back and smiled a bit.

"Space, that's it!" cried Ryger, with enthusiasm.

"That's not it at all," roared Mandel, half rising as though tempted to throw himself at Talliaferro. "I deny the whole miserable fabrication. What about the record I have of Villiers' phone call? He used the word 'classmate.' The entire tape makes it obvious——"

"He was a dying man," said Talliaferro. "Much of what he said you admitted was incomprehensible. I ask you, Dr. Mandel, without having heard the tape, if it isn't true that Villiers' voice is distorted past recognition."

"Well——" said Mandel in confusion.

"I'm sure it is. There is no reason to suppose, then, that you might not have rigged up the tape in advance, complete with the damning word 'classmates.' "

Mandel said, "Good Lord, how would I know there were classmates at the Convention? How would I know they knew about the mass-transference?"

"Villiers might have told you. I presume he did."

"Now, look," said Mandel, "you three saw Villiers alive at eleven. The medical examiner, seeing Villiers' body shortly after 3 A.M. declared he had been dead at least two hours. That was certain. The time of death, therefore, was between 11 P.M. and 1 A.M. I was at a late conference last night. I can prove my whereabouts, miles from the hotel, between 10:00 and 2:00 by a dozen witnesses no one of whom anyone can possibly question. Is that enough for you?"

Talliaferro paused a moment. Then he went on stubbornly, "Even so. Suppose you got back to the hotel by 2:30. You went to Villiers' room to discuss his talk. You found the door open, or you had a duplicate key. Anyway, you found him dead. You seized the opportunity to scan the paper——"

"And if he were already dead, and couldn't make phone calls, why should I hide the film?"

"To remove suspicion. You may have a second copy of the film safe in your possession. For that matter, we have only your own word that the paper itself was destroyed."

"Enough. Enough," cried Urth. "It is an interesting hypothesis, Dr. Talliaferro, but it falls to the ground of its own weight."

Talliaferro frowned. "That's your opinion, perhaps——"

"It would be anyone's opinion. Anyone, that is, with the power of human thought. Don't you see that Hubert Mandel did too much to be the criminal?"

"No," said Talliaferro.

Wendell Urth smiled benignly. "As a scientist, Dr. Talliaferro, you undoubtedly know better than to fall in love with your own theories to the exclusion of facts or reasoning. Do me the pleasure of behaving similarly as a detective.

"Consider that if Dr. Mandel had brought about the death of Villiers and faked an alibi, or if he had found Villiers dead and taken advantage of that, how little he would really have had to do! Why scan the paper or even pretend that anyone had done so? He could simply have taken the paper. Who else knew of its existence? Nobody, really. There is no reason to think Villiers told anyone else about it. Villiers was pathologically secretive. There would have been every reason to think that he told no one.

"No one knew Villiers was giving a talk, except Dr. Mandel. It wasn't announced. No abstract was published. Dr. Mandel could have walked off with the paper in perfect confidence.

"Even if he had discovered that Villiers had talked to his classmates about the matter, what of it? What evidence would his classmates have except the word of one whom they are themselves half willing to consider a madman.

"By announcing instead that Villiers' paper had been destroyed, by declaring his death to be not entirely natural, by searching for a scanned copy of the film—in short by everything Dr. Mandel has done—he has aroused a suspicion that only he could possibly have aroused when he need only have remained quiet to have committed a perfect crime. If he were the criminal, he would be more stupid, more colossally obtuse than anyone I have ever known. And Dr. Mandel, after all, is none of that."

Talliaferro thought hard but found nothing to say.

Ryger said, "Then who did do it?"

"One of you three. That's obvious."

"But which?"

"Oh, that's obvious, too. I knew which of you was guilty the moment Dr. Mandel had completed his description of events."

Talliaferro stared at the plump extraterrologist with distaste. The bluff did not frighten him, but it was affecting the other two. Ryger's lips were thrust out and Kaunas's lower jaw had relaxed moronically. They looked like fish, both of them.

He said, "Which one, then? Tell us."

Urth blinked. "First, I want to make it perfectly plain that the important thing is mass-transference. It can still be recovered."

Mandel, scowling still, said querulously, "What the devil are you talking about, Urth?"

"The man who scanned the paper probably looked at what he was scanning. I doubt that he had the time or presence of mind to read it, and if he did, I doubt if he could remember it—consciously. However, there is the Psychic Probe. If he even glanced at the paper, what impinged on his retina could be Probed."

There was an uneasy stir.

Urth said at once, "No need to be afraid of the Probe. Proper handling is safe, particularly if a man offers himself voluntarily. When damage is done, it is usually because of unnecessary resistance, a kind of mental tearing, you know. So if the guilty man will voluntarily confess, place himself in my hands——"

Talliaferro laughed. The sudden noise rang out sharply in the dim quiet of the room. The psychology was so transparent and artless.

Wendell Urth looked almost bewildered at the reaction and stared earnestly at Talliaferro over his glasses. He said, "I have enough influence with the police to keep the Probing entirely confidential."

Ryger said savagely, "I didn't do it."

Kaunas shook his head.

Talliaferro disdained any answer.

Urth sighed. "Then I will have to point out the guilty man. It will be traumatic. It will make things harder." He tightened the grip on his belly and his fingers twitched. "Dr. Talliaferro pointed out that the film was hidden on the outer window sill so that it might remain safe from discovery and from harm. I agree with him."

"Thank you," said Talliaferro dryly.

"However, why should anyone think that an outer window sill is a particularly safe hiding place? The police would certainly look there. Even in the absence of the police it was discovered. Who would tend to consider anything outside a building as particularly safe? Obviously, some person who has lived a long time on an airless world and has had it drilled into him that no one goes outside an enclosed place without detailed precautions.

"To someone on the Moon, for instance, anything hidden outside a Lunar Dome would be comparatively safe. Men venture out only rarely and then only on specific business. So he would overcome the hardship of opening a window and exposing himself to what he would subconsciously consider a vacuum for the sake of a safe hiding place. The reflex thought, 'Outside an inhabited structure is safe,' would do the trick."

Talliaferro said between clenched teeth, "Why do you mention the moon, Dr. Urth?"

Urth said blandly, "Only as an example. What I've said so far applies to all three of you. But now comes the crucial point, the matter of the dying night."

Talliaferro frowned. "You mean the night Villiers died?"

"I mean any night. See here, even granted that an outer window sill was a safe hiding place, which of you would be mad enough to consider it a safe hiding place *for a piece of unexposed film?* Scanner film isn't very sensitive, to be sure, and is made to be developed under all sorts of hit-and-miss conditions. Diffuse night-time illumination wouldn't seriously affect it, but diffuse daylight would ruin it in a few minutes, and direct sunlight would ruin it at once. Everyone knows that."

Mandel said, "Go ahead, Urth. What is this leading to?"

"You're trying to rush me," said Urth, with a massive pout. "I want you to see this clearly. The criminal wanted, above all, to keep the film safe. It was his only record of something of supreme value to himself and to the world. Why would he put it where it would inevitably be ruined by the morning sun? ——Only because he did not expect the morning sun ever to come. He thought the night, so to speak, was immortal.

"But nights *aren't* immortal. On Earth, they die and give way to daytime. Even the six-month polar night is a dying night eventually. The nights on Ceres last only two hours; the nights on the Moon last two weeks. They are dying nights, too, and Drs. Talliaferro and Ryger know that day must always come."

Kaunas was on his feet. "But wait——"

Wendell Urth faced him full. "No longer any need to wait, Dr. Kaunas. Mercury is the only sizable object in the Solar System that turns only one face to the sun. Even taking libration into account, fully three-eighths of its surface is true dark-side and never sees the sun. The Polar Observatory is at the rim of that dark-side. For ten years, you have grown used to the fact that nights are immortal, that a surface in darkness remains eternally in darkness, and so you entrusted unexposed film to Earth's night, forgetting in your excitement that nights must die——"

Kaunas stumbled forward. "Wait——"

Urth was inexorable. "I am told that when Mandel adjusted the polarizer in Villiers' room, you screamed at the sunlight. Was that your ingrained fear of Mercurian sun, or your sudden realization of what sunlight meant to your plans? You rushed forward. Was that to adjust the polarizer or to stare at the ruined film?"

Kaunas fell to his knees. "I didn't mean it. I wanted to speak to him, only to speak to him, and he screamed and collapsed. I thought he was dead and the paper was under his pillow and it all just followed. One thing led on to another and before I knew it, I couldn't get out of it anymore. But I meant none of it. I swear it."

They had formed a semicircle about him and Wendell Urth stared at the moaning Kaunas with pity in his eyes.

An ambulance had come and gone. Talliaferro finally brought himself to say stiffly to Mandel, "I hope, sir, there will be no hard feelings for anything said here."

And Mandel had answered, as stiffly, "I think we had all better forget as much as possible of what has happened during the last twenty-four hours."

They were standing in the doorway, ready to leave, and Wendell Urth ducked his smiling head, and said, "There's the question of my fee, you know."

Mandel looked startled.

"Not money," said Urth at once. "But when the first mass-transference setup for humans is established, I want a trip arranged for me."

Mandel continued to look anxious. "Now, wait. Trips through outer space are a long way off."

Urth shook his head rapidly. "Not outer space. Not at all. I would like to step across to Lower Falls, New Hampshire."

"All right. But why?"

Urth looked up. To Talliaferro's outright surprise, the extra-terrologist's face wore an expression compounded of shyness and eagerness.

Urth said, "I once—quite a long time ago—knew a girl there. It's been many years—but I sometimes wonder——"

I'M IN MARSPORT WITHOUT HILDA

IT WORKED ITSELF OUT, to begin with, like a dream. I didn't have
to make any arrangements. I didn't have to touch it. I just watched
things work out. ——Maybe that's when I should have first smelled
catastrophe.

It began with my usual month's layoff between assignments. A
month on and a month off is the right and proper routine for the
Galactic Service. I reached Marsport for the usual three-day lay-
over before the short hop to Earth.

Ordinarily, Hilda, God bless her, as sweet a wife as any man
ever had, would be there waiting for me and we'd have a nice
sedate time of it—a nice little interlude for the two of us. The
only trouble with that is that Marsport is the rowdiest spot in the
System, and a nice little interlude isn't exactly what fits in. Only,
how do I explain that to Hilda, hey?

Well, *this* time, my mother-in-law, God *bless* her (for a change)
got sick just two days before I reached Marsport, and the night
before landing, I got a spacegram from Hilda saying she would
stay on Earth with her mother and wouldn't meet me this one
time.

Copyright 1957, by Fantasy House, Inc. (first appeared in Venture Science
Fiction, November 1957).

I 'grammed back my loving regrets and my feverish anxiety concerning her mother and when I landed, there I was——

I was in Marsport without Hilda!

That was still nothing, you understand. It was the frame of the picture, the bones of the woman. Now there was the matter of the lines and coloring inside the frame; the skin and flesh outside the bones.

So I called up Flora (Flora of certain rare episodes in the past) and for the purpose I sued a video booth. ——Damn the expense; full speed ahead.

I was giving myself ten to one odds she'd be out, she'd be busy with her videophone disconnected, she'd be dead, even.

But she was in, with her videophone connected, and Great Galaxy, was she anything but dead.

She looked better than ever. Age cannot wither, as somebody or other once said, nor custom stale her infinite variety.

Was she glad to see me? She squealed, "Max! It's been years."

"I know, Flora, but this is it, if you're available. Because guess what! I'm in Marsport without Hilda."

She squealed again, "Isn't that *nice!* Then come on over."

I goggled a bit. This was too much. "You mean you *are* available?" You have to understand that Flora was never available without plenty of notice. Well, she was that kind of knockout.

She said, "Oh, I've got some quibbling little arrangement, Max, but I'll take care of that. You come on over."

"I'll come," I said happily.

Flora was the kind of girl—— Well, I tell you, she had her rooms under Martian gravity, 0.4 Earth-normal. The gadget to free her of Marsport's pseudo-grav field was expensive of course, but if you've ever held a girl in your arms at 0.4 gees, you need no explanation. If you haven't, explanations will do no good. I'm also sorry for you.

Talk about floating on clouds.

I closed connections, and only the prospect of seeing it all in the flesh could have made me wipe out the image with such alacrity. I stepped out of the booth.

And at that point, that precise point, that very split-instant of time, the first whiff of catastrophe nudged itself up to me.

That first whiff was the bald head of that lousy Rog Crinton of the Mars offices, gleaming over a headful of pale blue eyes, pale yellow complexion, and pale brown mustache. I didn't bother getting on all fours and beating my forehead against the ground because my vacation had started the minute I had gotten off the ship.

So I said with only normal politeness, "What do you want and I'm in a hurry. I've got an appointment."

He said, "You've got an appointment with me. I was waiting for you at the unloading desk."

I said, "I didn't see you——"

He said, "You didn't see anything."

He was right at that, for, come to think of it, if he was at the unloading desk, he must have been spinning ever since because I went past that desk like Halley's Comet skimming the Solar Corona.

I said, "All right. What do you want?"

"I've got a little job for you."

I laughed. "It's my month off, friend."

He said, "Red emergency alert, friend."

Which meant, no vacation, just like that. I couldn't believe it. I said, "Nuts, Rog. Have a heart. I got an emergency alert of my own."

"Nothing like this."

"Rog," I yelled, "can't you get someone else? Anyone else?"

"You're the only Class A agent on Mars."

"Send to Earth, then. They stack agents like micro-pile units at Headquarters."

"This has got to be done before 11 P.M. What's the matter? You haven't got three hours?"

I grabbed my head. The boy just didn't *know*. I said, "Let me make a call, will you?"

I stepped back into the booth, glared at him, and said, "Private!"

Flora shone on the screen again, like a mirage on an asteroid. She said, "Something wrong, Max? Don't say something's wrong. I canceled my other engagement."

I said, "Flora, baby, I'll be there. I'll *be* there. But something's come up."

She asked the natural question in a hurt tone of voice and I said, *"No.* Not another girl. With you in the same town they don't make any other girls. Females, maybe. Not girls. Baby! Honey!" (I had a wild impulse but hugging 'vision screen is no pastime for a grown man.) "It's business. Just hold on. It won't take long."

She said, "All right," but she said it kind of like it was just enough not all right so that I got the shivers.

I stepped out of the booth and said, "All right, Rog, what kind of mess have you cooked up for me?"

We went into the spaceport bar and got us an insulated booth. He said, "The *Antares Giant* is coming in from Sirius in exactly half an hour; at 8 P.M. local time."

"Okay."

"Three men will get out, among others, and will wait for the *Space Eater* coming in from Earth at 11 P.M. and leaving for Capella some time thereafter. The three men will get on the *Space Eater* and will then be out of our jurisdiction."

"So."

"So between 8:00 and 11:00, they will be in a special waiting room and you will be with them. I have a trimensional image of each for you so you'll know which they are and which is which. You have between 8:00 and 11:00 to decide which one of the three is carrying contraband."

"What kind of contraband?"

"The worst kind. Altered Spaceoline."

"Altered Spaceoline?"

He had thrown me. I knew what Spaceoline was. If you've been on a space-hop you know, too. And in case you're Earth-bound yourself the bare fact is that everyone needs it on the first space-trip; almost everybody needs it for the first dozen trips; lots need it every trip. Without it, there is vertigo associated with free fall, screaming terrors, semi-permanent psychoses. With it, there is nothing; no one minds a thing. And it isn't habit-forming; it has no adverse side-effects. Spaceoline is ideal, essential, unsubstitutable. When in doubt, take Spaceoline.

Rog said, "That's right, altered Spaceoline. It can be changed chemically by a very simple reaction that can be conducted in anyone's basement into a drug that will give one giant-size charge and become your baby-blue habit the first time. It is on a par with the most dangerous alkaloids we know."

"And we just found out about it?"

"No. The Service has known about it for years, and we've kept others from knowing by squashing every discovery flat. Only now the discovery has gone too far."

"In what way?"

"One of the men who will be stopping over at this spaceport is carrying some of the altered Spaceoline on his person. Chemists in the Capellan system, which is outside the Federation, will analyze it and set up ways of synthesizing more. After that, it's either fight the worst drug menace we've ever seen or suppress the matter by suppressing the source."

"You mean Spaceoline."

"Right. And if we suppress Spaceoline, we suppress space-travel."

I decided to put my finger on the point. "Which one of the three has it?"

Rog smiled nastily, "If we knew, would we need you? You're to find out which of the three."

"You're calling on me for a lousy frisk job."

"Touch the wrong one at the risk of a haircut down to the larynx. Every one of the three is a big man on his own planet. One is Edward Harponaster; one is Joaquin Lipsky; and one is Andiamo Ferrucci. Well?"

He was right. I'd heard of every one of them. Chances are you have, too; and not one was touchable without proof in advance, as you know. I said, "Would one of them touch a dirty deal like——"

"There are trillions involved," said Rog, "which means any one of the three would. And one of them *is*, because Jack Hawk got that far before he was killed——"

"Jack Hawk's *dead?*" For a minute, I forgot about the Galactic drug menace. For a minute, I nearly forgot about Flora.

"Right, and one of those guys arranged the killing. Now you find out which. You put the finger on the right one before 11:00 and there's a promotion, a raise in pay, a pay-back for poor Jack Hawk, and a rescue of the Galaxy. You put the finger on the wrong one and there'll be a nasty interstellar situation and you'll be out on your ear and also on every black list from here to Antares and back."

I said, "Suppose I don't finger anybody?"

"That would be like fingering the wrong one as far as the Service is concerned."

"I've got to finger someone but only the right one or my head's handed to me."

"In thin slices. You're beginning to understand me, Max."

In a long lifetime of looking ugly, Rog Crinton had never looked uglier. The only comfort I got out of staring at him was the realization that he was married, too, and that he lived with his wife at Marsport all year round. And does he deserve that. Maybe I'm hard on him, but he *deserves* it.

I put in a quick call to Flora, as soon as Rog was out of sight. She said, "Well?"

I said, "Baby, honey, it's something I can't talk about, but I've got to do it, see? Now you hang on, I'll get it over with if I have to swim the Grand Canal to the icecap in my underwear, see? If I have to claw Phobos out of the sky. If I have to cut myself in pieces and mail myself parcel post."

"Gee," she said, "if I thought I was going to have to wait——"

I winced. She just wasn't the type to respond to poetry. Actually, she was a simple creature of action—— But after all, if I was going to be drifting through low-gravity in a sea of jasmine perfume with Flora, poetry-response is not the type of qualification I would consider most indispensable.

I said urgently, "Just hold on, Flora. I won't be any time at all. I'll make it up to you."

I was annoyed, sure, but I wasn't worried as yet. Rog hadn't more than left me when I figured out exactly how I was going to tell the guilty man from the others.

It was easy. I should have called Rog back and told him, but there's no law against wanting egg in your beer and oxygen in your air. It would take me five minutes and then off I would go to Flora; a little late, maybe, but with a promotion, a raise, and a slobbering kiss from the Service on each cheek.

You see, it's like this. Big industrialists don't go space-hopping much; they use trans-video reception. When they do go to some ultra-high interstellar conference, as these three were probably going, they take Spaceoline. For one thing, they don't have enough hops under their belt to risk doing without. For another, Spaceoline is the expensive way of doing it and industrialists do things the expensive way. I know their psychology.

Now that would hold for two of them. The one who carried contraband, however, couldn't risk Spaceoline—even to prevent space-sickness. Under Spaceoline influence, he could throw the drug away; or give it away; or talk gibberish about it. He would *have* to stay in control of himself.

It was as simple as that, so I waited.

The *Antares Giant* was on time and I waited with my leg muscles tense for a quick take-off as soon as I collared the murdering drug-toting rat and sped the two eminent captains of industry on their way.

They brought in Lipsky first. He had thick, ruddy lips, rounded jowls, very dark eyebrows, and graying hair. He just looked at me and sat down. Nothing. He was under Spaceoline.

I said, "Good evening, sir."

He said, in a dreamy voice, "Surrealismus of Panamy hearts in three-quarter time for a cup of coffeedom of speech."

That was Spaceoline all the way. The buttons in the human mind were set free-swing. Each syllable suggests the next in free association.

Andiamo Ferrucci came in next. Black mustache, long and waxed, olive complexion, pock-marked face. He took a seat in another chair, facing us.

I said, "Nice trip?"

He said, "Trip the light fantastic tock the clock is crowings on the bird."

Lipsky said, "Bird to the wise guyed book to all places every body."

I grinned. That left Harponaster. I had my needle gun neatly palmed out of sight and the magnetic coil ready to grip him.

And then Harponaster came in. He was thin, leathery, near-bald and rather younger than he seemed in his trimensional image. And he was Spaceolined to the gills.

I said, "Damn!"

Harponaster said, "Damyankee note speech to his last time I saw wood you say so."

Ferrucci said, "Sow the seed the territory under dispute do well to come along long road to a nightingale."

Lipsky said, "Gay lords hopping pong balls."

I stared from one to the other as the nonsense ran down in shorter and shorter spurts and then silence.

I got the picture, all right. One of them was faking. He had thought ahead and realized that omitting the Spaceoline would be a giveaway. He might have bribed an official into injecting saline or dodged it some other way.

One of them must be faking. It wasn't hard to fake the thing. Comedians on sub-etheric had a Spaceoline skit regularly. *You*'ve heard them.

I stared at them and got the first prickle at the base of my skull that said: What if you *don't* finger the right one?

It was 8:30 and there was my job, my reputation, my head growing rickety upon my neck to be considered. I saved it all for later and thought of Flora. She wasn't going to wait for me forever. For that matter, chances were she wouldn't wait for half an hour.

I wondered. Could the faker keep up free association if nudged gently onto dangerous territory?

I said, "The floor's covered with a nice solid rug" and ran the last two words together to make it "soli drug."

Lipsky said, "Drug from underneath the dough re mi fa sol to be saved."

Ferrucci said, "Saved and a haircut above the common herd something about younicorny as a harmonican the cheek by razor and shine."

Harponaster said, "Shiner wind nor snow use trying to by four ever and effervescence and sensibilityter totter."

Lipsky said, "Totters and rags."

Ferrucci said, "Ragsactly."

Harponaster said, "Actlymation."

A few grunts and they ran down.

I tried again and I didn't forget to be careful. They would remember everything I said afterward and what I said had to be harmless. I said, "This is a darned good space-line."

Ferrucci said, "Lines and tigers through the prairie dogs do bark
of the bough-wough———"

I interrupted, looking at Harponaster, "A darned good space-
line."

"Line the bed and rest a little black sheepishion of wrong the
clothes of a perfect day."

I interrupted again, glaring at Lipsky, "Good space-line."

"Liron is hot chocolate ain't gonna be the same on you vee and
double the stakes and potatoes and heel."

Some one else said, "Heel the sicknecessaryd and write will
wincetance."

"Tance with mealtime."

"I'm comingle."

"Inglish."

"Ishter seals."

"Eels."

I tried a few more times and got nowhere. The faker, whichever
he was, had practiced or had natural talents at talking free association. He was disconnecting his brain and letting the words come
out any old way. And he must be inspired by knowing exactly
what I was after. If "drug" hadn't given it away, "space-line"
three times repeated must have. I was safe with the other two, but *he*
would know.

———And he was having fun with me. All three were saying
phrases that might have pointed to a deep inner guilt ("sol to be
saved," "little black sheepishion of wrong," "drug from underneath," and so on). Two were saying such things helplessly, randomly. The third was amusing himself.

So how did I find the third? I was in a feverish thrill of hatred
against him and my fingers twitched. The rat was subverting the
Galaxy. More than that, he had killed my colleague and friend.
More than that, he was keeping me from Flora.

I could go up to each of them and start searching. The two
who were really under Spaceoline would make no move to stop

me. They could feel no emotion, no fear, no anxiety, no hate, no passion, no desire for self-defense. And if one made the slightest gesture of resistance I would have my man.

But the innocent ones would remember afterward. They would remember a personal search while under Spaceoline.

I sighed. If I tried it, I would get the criminal all right but later I would be the nearest thing to chopped liver any man had ever been. There would be a shake-up in the Service, a big stink the width of the Galaxy, and in the excitement and disorganization, the secret of altered Spaceoline would get out anyway and so what the hell.

Of course, the one I wanted might be the first one I touched. One chance out of three. I'd have one out and only God can make a three.

Nuts, something had started them going while I was muttering to myself and Spaceoline is contagioust a gigolo my, oh——

I stared desperately at my watch and my line of sight focused on 9:15.

Where the devil was time going to?

Oh, my; oh, nuts; oh, Flora!

I had no choice. I made my way to the booth for another quick call to Flora. Just a quick one, you understand, to keep things alive; assuming they weren't dead already.

I kept saying to myself: She won't answer.

I tried to prepare myself for that. There were other girls, there were other——

What's the use, there were no other girls.

If Hilda had been in Marsport, I never would have had Flora on my mind in the first place and it wouldn't have mattered. *But I was in Marsport without Hilda* and I had made a date with Flora.

The signal was signaling and signaling and I didn't dare break off.

Answer! Answer!

She answered. She said, "It's *you!*"

"Of course, sweetheart, who else would it be?"

"Lots of people. Someone who would *come.*"

"There's just this little detail of business, honey."

"What business? Plastons for who?"

I almost corrected her grammar but I was too busy wondering what this plastons kick was.

Then I remembered. I told her once I was a plaston salesman. That was the time I brought her a plaston nightgown that was a honey.

I said, "Look. Just give me another half hour——"

Her eyes grew moist. "I'm sitting here all by myself."

"I'll make it up to you." To show you how desperate I was getting, I was definitely beginning to think along paths that could lead only to jewelry even though a sizable dent in the bankbook would show up to Hilda's piercing eye like the Horsehead Nebula interrupting the Milky Way. But then I was desperate.

She said, "I had a perfectly good date and I broke it off."

I protested, "You said it was a quibbling little arrangement."

That was a mistake. I knew it the minute I said it.

She shrieked, *"Quibbling little arrangement!"* (It was what she had said. It was what she had said. But having the truth on your side just makes it worse in arguing with a woman. Don't I know?) "You call a man who's promised me an estate on Earth——"

She went on and on about that estate on Earth. There wasn't a gal in Marsport who wasn't wangling for an estate on Earth, and you could count the number who got one on the sixth finger of either hand.

I tried to stop her. No use.

She finally said, "And here I am all alone, with *nobody*," and broke off contact.

Well, she was right. I felt like the lowest heel in the Galaxy.

I went back into the reception room. A flunky outside the door saluted me in.

I stared at the three industrialists and speculated on the order in which I would slowly choke each to death if I could but receive choking orders. Harponaster first, maybe. He had a thin, stringy neck that the fingers could go round neatly and a sharp Adam's apple against which the thumbs could find purchase.

It cheered me up infinitesimally, to the point where I muttered,

"Boy!" just out of sheer longing, though it was no boy I was longing for.

It started them off at once. Ferrucci said, "Boyl the watern the spout you goateeming rain over us, God savior pennies——"

Harponaster of the scrawny neck added, "Nies and nephew don't like orporalley cat."

Lipsky said, "Cattle corral go down off a ductilitease drunk."

"Drunkle aunterior passagewayt a while."

"While beasts oh pray."

"Prayties grow."

"Grow way."

"Waiter."

"Terble."

"Ble."

Then nothing.

They stared at me. I stared at them. They were empty of emotion (or two were) and I was empty of ideas. And time passed.

I stared at them some more and thought about Flora. It occurred to me that I had nothing to lose that I had not already lost. I might as well talk about her.

I said, "Gentlemen, there is a girl in this town whose name I will not mention for fear of compromising her. Let me describe her to you, gentlemen."

And I did. If I say so myself, the last two hours had honed me to such a fine force-field edge that the description of Flora took on a kind of poetry that seemed to be coming from some wellspring of masculine force deep in the subbasement of my unconscious.

And they sat frozen, almost as though they were listening, and hardly ever interrupting. People under Spaceoline have a kind of politeness about them. They won't speak when someone else is speaking. That's why they take turns.

I kept it up with a kind of heartfelt sadness in my voice until the loud-speaker announced in stirring tones the arrival of the *Space Eater*.

That was that. I said in a loud voice, "Rise, gentlemen."

"Not you, you murderer," and my magnetic coil was on Ferrucci's wrist before he could breathe twice.

Ferrucci fought like a demon. He was under no Spaceoline influence. They found the altered Spaceoline in thin flesh-colored plastic pads hugging the inner surface of his thighs. You couldn't see it at all; you could only feel it, and even then it took a knife to make sure.

Afterward, Rog Crinton, grinning and half insane with relief, held me by the lapel with a death grip. "How did you do it? What gave it away?"

I said, trying to pull loose, "One of them was faking a Spaceoline jag. I was sure of it. So I told them," (I grew cautious—none of his business as to the details, you know) ". . . uh, about a girl, see, and two of them never reacted, so they were Spaceolined. But Ferrucci's breathing speeded up and the beads of sweat came out on his forehead. I gave a pretty dramatic rendition, and he reacted, so he was under no Spaceoline. Now will you let me go?"

He let go and I almost fell over backward.

I was set to take off. My feet were pawing at the ground without any instruction from me—but then I turned back.

"Hey, Rog," I said, "can you sign me a chit for a thousand credits without its going on the record—for services rendered to the Service?"

That's when I realized he was half insane with relief and very temporary gratitude, because he said, "Sure, Max, sure. Ten thousand credits if you want."

"I *want*," I said, grabbing him for a change. "I want. I want."

He filled out an official Service chit for ten thousand credits; good as cash anywhere in half the Galaxy. He was actually grinning as he gave it to me and you can bet I was grinning as I took it.

How *he* intended accounting for it was his affair; the point was that *I* wouldn't have to account for it to Hilda.

I stood in the booth, one last time, signaling Flora. I didn't dare let matters go till I reached her place. The additional half hour might just give her time to get someone else, if she hadn't already.

Make her answer. Make her answer. Make her——

She answered, but she was in formal clothes. She was going out and I had obviously caught her by two minutes.

"I am going out," she announced. "*Some* men can be decent. And I do not wish to see you in the henceforward. I do not wish ever to find my eyes upon you. You will do me a great favor, Mister Whoeveryouare, if you unhand my signal combination and never pollute it with——"

I wasn't saying anything. I was just standing there holding my breath and also holding the chit up where she could see it. Just standing there. Just holding.

Sure enough, at the word "pollute" she came in for a closer look. She wasn't much on education, that girl, but she could read "ten thousand credits" faster than any college graduate in the Solar System.

She said, "Max! For me?"

"All for you, baby," I said, "I told you I had a little business to do. I wanted to surprise you."

"Oh, Max, that's sweet of you. I didn't really mind. I was joking. Now you come right here to me." She took off her coat.

"What about your date?" I said.

"I *said* I was joking," she said.

"I'm coming," I said faintly.

"With every single one of those credits now," she said roguishly.

"With every single one," I said.

I broke contact, stepped out of the booth, and now, finally, I was set—set——

I heard my name called. "Max! Max!" Someone was running toward me. "Rog Crinton said I would find you here. Mamma's all right after all, so I got special passage on the *Space Eater* and what's this about ten thousand credits?"

I didn't turn. I said, "Hello, Hilda."

And then I turned and did the hardest thing I ever succeeded in doing in all my good-for-nothing, space-hopping life.

I managed to smile.

THE GENTLE VULTURES

FOR FIFTEEN YEARS NOW, the Hurrians had maintained their base on the other side of the Moon.

It was unprecedented; unheard of. No Hurrian had dreamed it possible to be delayed so long. The decontamination squads had been ready; ready and waiting for fifteen years; ready to swoop down through the radioactive clouds and save what might be saved for the remnant of survivors. ——In return, of course, for fair payment.

But fifteen times the planet had revolved about its Sun. During each revolution, the satellite had rotated not quite thirteen times about the primary. And in all that time the nuclear war had not come.

Nuclear bombs were exploded by the large-primate intelligences at various points on the planet's surface. The planet's stratosphere had grown amazingly warm with radioactive refuse. But still no war.

Devi-en hoped ardently that he would be replaced. He was the fourth Captain-in-charge of this colonizing expedition (if it could still be called so after fifteen years of suspended animation) and he was quite content that there should be a fifth. Now that the home world was sending an Arch-administrator to make a personal survey of the situation, his replacement might come soon. Good!

He stood on the surface of the Moon, encased in his space-suit, and thought of home, of Hurria. His long, thin arms moved restlessly with the thought, as though aching (through millions of years of instinct) for the ancestral trees. He stood only three feet high. What could be seen of him through the glass-fronted head plate was a black and wrinkled face with the fleshy, mobile nose dead-centered. The little tuft of fine beard was a pure white in contrast. In the rear of the suit, just below center, was the bulge within which the short and stubby Hurrian tail might rest comfortably.

Devi-en took his appearance for granted, of course, but was well aware of the difference between the Hurrians and all the other intelligences in the Galaxy. The Hurrians alone were so small; they alone were tailed; they alone were vegetarians—they alone had escaped the inevitable nuclear war that had ruined every other known intelligent species.

He stood on the walled plain that extended for so many miles that the raised and circular rim (which on Hurria would have been called a crater, if it were smaller) was invisible beyond the horizon. Against the southern edge of the rim, where there was always some protection against the direct rays of the Sun, a city had grown. It had begun as a temporary camp, of course, but with the years, women had been brought in, and children had been born in it. Now there were schools and elaborate hydroponics establishments, large water reservoirs, all that went with a city on an airless world.

It was ridiculous! All because one planet had nuclear weapons and would not fight a nuclear war.

The Arch-administrator, who would be arriving soon, would undoubtedly ask, almost at once, the same question that Devi-en had asked himself a wearisome number of times.

Why had there not been a nuclear war?

Devi-en watched the hulking Mauvs preparing the ground now for the landing, smoothing out the unevennesses and laying down the ceramic bed designed to absorb the hyperatomic field-thrusts with minimum discomfort to the passengers within the ship.

Even in their space-suits, the Mauvs seemed to exude power, but it was the power of muscle only. Beyond them was the little figure of a Hurrian giving orders, and the docile Mauvs obeyed. Naturally.

The Mauvian race, of all the large-primate intelligences, paid their fees in the most unusual coin, a quota of themselves, rather than of material goods. It was a surprisingly useful tribute, better than steel, aluminum, or fine drugs in many ways.

Devi-en's receiver stuttered to life. "The ship is sighted, sir," came the report. "It will be landing within the hour."

"Very good," said Devi-en. Have my car made ready to take me to the ship as soon as landing is initiated."

He did not feel that it was very good at all.

The Arch-administrator came, flanked by a personal retinue of five Mauvs. They entered the city with him, one on each side, three following. They helped him off with his space-suit, then removed their own.

Their thinly haired bodies, their large, coarse-featured faces, their broad noses and flat cheekbones were repulsive but not frightening. Though twice the height of the Hurrians and more than twice the breadth, there was a blankness about their eyes, something completely submissive about the way they stood, with their thick-sinewed necks slightly bent, their bulging arms hanging listlessly.

The Arch-administrator dismissed them and they trooped out. He did not really need their protection, of course, but his position required a retinue of five and that was that.

No business was discussed during the meal or during the almost endless ritual of welcome. At a time that might have been more appropriate for sleeping, the Arch-administrator passed small fingers through his tuft of beard and said, "How much longer must we wait for this planet, Captain?"

He was visibly advancing in age. The hair on his upper arms was grizzled and the tufts at the elbows were almost as white as his beard.

"I cannot say, your Height," said Devi-en humbly. "They have not followed the path."

"That is obvious. The point is, *why* have they not followed the path? It is clear to the Council that your reports promise more than they deliver. You talk of theories but you give no details. Now we are tired of all this back on Hurria. If you know of anything you have not told us, now is the time to talk of it."

"The matter, your Height, is hard to prove. We have had no experience of spying on a people over such an extended period. Until recently, we weren't watching for the right things. Each year we kept expecting the nuclear war the year after and it is only in my time as Captain that we have taken to studying the people more intensively. It is at least one benefit of the long waiting time that we have learned some of their principal languages."

"Indeed? Without even landing on their planet?"

Devi-en explained. "A number of radio messages were recorded by those of our ships that penetrated the planetary atmosphere on observation missions, particularly in the early years. I set our linguistics computers to work on them, and for the last year I have been attempting to make sense out of it all."

The Arch-administrator stared. His bearing was such that any outright exclamation of surprise would have been superfluous. "And have you learned anything of interest?"

"I may have, your Height, but what I have worked out is so strange and the underpinning of actual evidence is so uncertain that I dared not speak of it officially in my reports."

The Arch-administrator understood. He said, stiffly, "Would you object to explaining your views unofficially—to me?"

"I would be glad to," said Devi-en at once. "The inhabitants of this planet are, of course, large-primate in nature. And they are competitive."

The other blew out his breath in a kind of relief and passed his tongue quickly over his nose. "I had the queer notion," he muttered, "that they might *not* be competitive and that that might—— But go on, go on."

"They *are* competitive," Devi-en assured him. "Much more so than one would expect on the average."

"Then why doesn't everything else follow?"

"Up to a point it does, your Height. After the usual long incubation period, they began to mechanize; and after that, the usual large-primate killings became truly destructive warfare. At the conclusion of the most recent large-scale war, nuclear weapons were developed and the war ended at once."

The Arch-administrator nodded. "And then?"

Devi-en said, "What should have happened was that a nuclear war ought to have begun shortly afterward and in the course of the war, nuclear weapons would have developed quickly in destructiveness, have been used nevertheless in typical large-primate fashion, and have quickly reduced the population to starving remnants in a ruined world."

"Of course, but that didn't happen. Why not?"

Devi-en said, "There is one point. I believe these people, once mechanization started, developed at an unusually high rate."

"And if so?" said the other. "Does that matter? They reached nuclear weapons the more quickly."

"True. But after the most recent general war, they continued to develop nuclear weapons at an unusual rate. That's the trouble. The deadly potential had increased before the nuclear war had a chance to start and now it has reached a point where even large-primate intelligences dare not risk a war."

The Arch-administrator opened his small black eyes wide. "But that is impossible. I don't care how technically talented these creatures are. Military science advances rapidly only during a war."

"Perhaps that is not true in the case of these particular creatures. But even if it were, it seems they *are* having a war; not a real war, but a war."

"Not a real war, but a war," repeated the Arch-administrator blankly. "What does that mean?"

"I'm not sure." Devi-en wiggled his nose in exasperation. "This is where my attempts to draw logic out of the scattered material we have picked up is least satisfactory. This planet has something called a Cold War. Whatever it is, it drives them furiously onward in research and yet it does not involve complete nuclear destruction."

The Arch-administrator said, "Impossible!"

Devi-en said, "There is the planet. Here we are. We have been waiting fifteen years."

The Arch-administrator's long arms came up and crossed over his head and down again to the opposite shoulders. "Then there *is* only one thing to do. The Council has considered the possibilty that the planet may have achieved a stalemate, a kind of uneasy peace that balances just short of a nuclear war. Something of the sort you describe, though no one suggested the actual reasons you advance. But it's something we can't allow."

"No, your Height?"

"No," he seemed almost in pain. "The longer the stalemate continues, the greater the possibility that large-primate individuals may discover the methods of interstellar travel. They will leak out into the Galaxy, in full competitive strength. You see?"

"Then?"

The Arch-administrator hunched his head deeper into his arms, as though not wishing to hear what he himself must say. His voice was a little muffled. "If they are balanced precariously, we must push them a little, Captain. We must push them."

Devi-en's stomach churned and he suddenly tasted his dinner once more in the back of his throat. "Push them, your Height?" He didn't want to understand.

But the Arch-administrator put it bluntly, "We must help them start their nuclear war." He looked as miserably sick as Devi-en felt. He whispered, "We must!"

Devi-en could scarcely speak. He said, in a whisper, "But how could such a thing be done, your Height?"

"I don't know how. ——And do not look at *me* so. It is not my decision. It is the decision of the Council. Surely you understand what would happen to the Galaxy if a large-primate intelligence were to enter space in full strength without having been tamed by nuclear war."

Devi-en shuddered at the thought. All that competitiveness loosed on the Galaxy. He persisted though. "But *how* does one start a nuclear war? How is it done?"

"I don't know, I tell you. But there must be some way; perhaps a——a message we might send or a——a crucial rainstorm we might start by cloud-seeding. We could manage a great deal with their weather conditions——"

"How would that start a nuclear war?" said Devi-en, unimpressed.

"Maybe it wouldn't. I mention such a thing only as a possible example. But large-primates would know. After all, they are the ones who *do* start nuclear wars in actual fact. It is in their brain-pattern to know. That is the decision the Council came to."

Devi-en felt the soft noise his tail made as it thumped slowly against the chair. He tried to stop it and failed. "What decision, your Height?"

"To trap a large-primate from the planet's surface. To kidnap one."

"A *wild* one?"

"It's the only kind that exists at the moment on the planet. Of course, a wild one."

"And what do you expect him to tell us?"

"That doesn't matter, Captain. As long as he says enough about anything, mentalic analysis will give us the answer."

Devi-en withdrew his head as far as he could into the space between his shoulder blades. The skin just under his armpits quivered with repulsion. A wild large-primate being! He tried to picture one, untouched by the stunning aftermath of nuclear war, unaltered by the civilizing influence of Hurrian eugenic breeding.

The Arch-administrator made no attempt to hide the fact that he shared the repulsion, but he said, "You will have to lead the trapping expedition, Captain. It is for the good of the Galaxy."

Devi-en had seen the planet a number of times before but each time a ship swung about the Moon and placed the world in his line of sight a wave of unbearable homesickness swept him.

It was a beautiful planet, so like Hurria itself in dimensions and characteristics but wilder and grander. The sight of it, after the desolation of the Moon, was like a blow.

How many other planets like it were on Hurrian master listings at this moment, he wondered. How many other planets were there concerning which meticulous observers had reported seasonal changes in appearance that could be interpreted only as being caused by artificial cultivation of food plants? How many times in the future would a day come when the radioactivity in the stratosphere of one of these planets would begin to climb; when colonizing squadrons would have to be sent out at once?

———As they were to this planet.

It was almost pathetic, the confidence with which the Hurrians had proceeded at first. Devi-en could have laughed as he read through those initial reports, if he weren't trapped in this project himself now. The Hurrian scoutships had moved close to the planet to gather geographical information, to locate population centers. They were sighted, of course, but what did it matter? Any time, now, they thought, the final explosion.

Any time——— But useless years passed and the scoutships wondered if they ought not to be cautious. They moved back.

Devi-en's ship was cautious now. The crew was on edge because of the unpleasantness of the mission; not all Devi-en's assurances that there was no harm intended to the large-primate could quite calm them. Even so, they could not hurry matters. It had to be over a fairly deserted and uncultivated tract of uneven ground that they hovered. They stayed at a height of ten miles for days, while the crew became edgier and only the ever-stolid Mauvs maintained calm.

Then the scope showed them a creature, alone on the uneven ground, a long staff in one hand, a pack across the upper portion of his back.

They lowered silently, supersonically. Devi-en himself, skin crawling, was at the controls.

The creature was heard to say two definite things before he was taken, and they were the first comments recorded for use in mentalic computing.

The first, when the large-primate caught sight of the ship almost upon him, was picked up by the direction telemike. It was, "My God! A flying saucer!"

Devi-en understood the second phrase. That was a term for the Hurrian ships that had grown common among the large-primates those first careless years.

The second remark was made when the wild creature was brought into the ship, struggling with amazing strength, but helpless in the iron grip of the unperturbed Mauvs.

Devi-en, panting, with his fleshy nose quivering slightly, advanced to receive him, and the creature (whose unpleasantly hairless face had become oily with some sort of fluid secretion) yelled, "Holy Toledo, a *monkey!*"

Again, Devi-en understood the second part. It was the word for little-primate in one of the chief languages of the planet.

The wild creature was almost impossible to handle. He required infinite patience before he could be spoken to reasonably. At first, there was nothing but a series of crises. The creature realized almost at once that he was being taken off Earth, and what Devi-en thought might prove an exciting experience for him, proved nothing of the sort. He talked instead of his offspring and of a large-primate female.

(They have wives and children, thought Devi-en, compassionately, and, in their way, love them, for all they are large-primate.)

Then he had to be made to understand that the Mauvs who kept him under guard and who restrained him when his violence made that necessary would not hurt him, that he was not to be damaged in any way.

(Devi-en was sickened at the thought that one intelligent being might be damaged by another. It was very difficult to discuss the subject, even if only to admit the possibility long enough to deny it. The creature from the planet treated the very hesitation with great suspicion. It was the way the large-primates were.)

On the fifth day, when out of sheer exhaustion, perhaps, the creature remained quiet over a fairly extended period, they talked in Devi-en's private quarters, and suddenly he grew angry again when the Hurrian first explained, matter-of-factly, that they were waiting for a nuclear war.

"Waiting!" cried the creature. "What makes you so sure there will be one?"

Devi-en wasn't sure, of course, but he said, "There is always a nuclear war. It is our purpose to help you afterward."

"Help us *afterward.*" His words grew incoherent. He waved his arms violently, and the Mauvs who flanked him had to restrain him gently once again and lead him away.

Devi-en sighed. The creature's remarks were building in quantity and perhaps mentalics could do something with them. His own unaided mind could make nothing of them.

And meanwhile the creature was not thriving. His body was almost completely hairless, a fact that long-distance observation had not revealed owing to the artificial skins worn by them. This was either for warmth or because of an instinctive repulsion even on the part of these particular large-primates themselves for hairless skin. (It might be an interesting subject to take up. Mentalics computation could make as much out of one set of remarks as another.)

Strangely enough, the creature's face had begun to sprout hair; more, in fact, than the Hurrian face had, and of a darker color.

But still, the central fact was that he was not thriving. He had grown thinner because he was eating poorly, and if he was kept too long, his health might suffer. Devi-en had no wish to feel responsible for that.

On the next day, the large-primate seemed quite calm. He talked almost eagerly, bringing the subject around to nuclear warfare almost at once. (It had a terrible attraction for the large-primate mind, Devi-en thought.)

The creature said, "You said nuclear wars always happen? Does that mean there are other people than yours and mine—and theirs?" He indicated the near-by Mauvs.

"There are thousands of intelligent species, living on thousands of worlds. Many thousands," said Devi-en.

"And they all have nuclear wars?"

"All who have reached a certain stage of technology. All but us. We were different. We lacked competitiveness. We had the co-operative instinct."

"You mean you know that nuclear wars will happen and you do nothing about it?"

"We *do*," said Devi-en, pained. "Of course, we do. We try to help. In the early history of my people, when we first developed space-travel, we did not understand large-primates. They repelled our attempts at friendship and we stopped trying. Then we found worlds in radioactive ruins. Finally, we found one world actually in the process of a nuclear war. We were horrified, but could do nothing. Slowly, we learned. We are ready, now, at every world we discover to be at the nuclear stage. We are ready with decontamination equipment and eugenic analyzers."

"What are eugenic analyzers?"

Devi-en had manufactured the phrase by analogy with what he knew of the wild one's langu_ge. Now he said carefully, "We direct matings and sterilizations to remove, as far as possible, the competitive element in the remnant of the survivors."

For a moment, he thought the creature would grow violent again.

Instead, the other said in a monotone, "You make them docile, you mean, like these things?" Once again he indicated the Mauvs.

"No. No. These are different. We simply make it possible for the remnants to be content with a peaceful, nonexpanding, non-aggressive society under our guidance. Without this, they destroyed themselves, you see, and without it, they would destroy themselves again."

"What do you get out of it?"

Devi-en stared at the creature dubiously. Was it really necessary to explain the basic pleasure of life? He said, "Don't you enjoy helping someone?"

"Come on. Besides that. What's in it for you?"

"Of course, there are contributions to Hurria."

"Ha."

"Payment for saving a species is only fair," protested Devi-en, "and there are expenses to be covered. The contribution is not much and is adjusted to the nature of the world. It may be an annual supply of wood from a forested world; manganese salts from another. The world of these Mauvs is poor in physical resources and they themselves offered to supply us with a number of individuals to use as personal assistants. They are extremely powerful even for large-primates and we treat them painlessly with anticerebral drugs——"

"To make zombies out of them!"

Devi-en guessed at the meaning of the noun and said indignantly, "Not at all. Merely to make them content with their role as personal servant and forgetful of their homes. We would not want them to be unhappy. They are intelligent beings!"

"And what would you do with Earth if we had a war?"

"We have had fifteen years to decide that," said Devi-en. "Your world is very rich in iron and has developed a fine steel technology. Steel, I think, would be your contribution." He sighed, "But the contribution would not make up for our expense in this case, I think. We have overwaited now by ten years at least."

The large-primate said, "How many races do you tax in this way?"

"I do not know the exact number. Certainly more than a thousand."

"Then you're the little landlords of the Galaxy, are you? A thousand worlds destroy themselves in order to contribute to your welfare. You're something else, too, you know." The wild one's voice was rising, growing shrill. "You're vultures."

"Vultures?" said Devi-en, trying to place the word.

"Carrion-eaters. Birds that wait for some poor creature to die of thirst in the desert and then come down to eat the body."

Devi-en felt himself turn faint and sick at the picture conjured up for him. He said weakly, "No, no, we *help* the species."

"You wait for the war to happen like vultures. If you want to help, *prevent* the war. Don't save the remnants. Save them all."

Devi-en's tail twitched with sudden excitement. "How do we prevent a war? Will you tell me that?" (What was prevention of war but the reverse of bringing about a war? Learn one process and surely the other would be obvious.)

But the wild one faltered. He said finally, "Get down there. Explain the situation."

Devi-en felt keen disappointment. That didn't help. Besides——
He said, "Land among you? Quite impossible." His skin quivered in half a dozen places at the thought of mingling with the wild ones in their untamed billions.

Perhaps the sick look on Devi-en's face was so pronounced and unmistakable that the wild one could recognize it for what it was even across the barrier of species. He tried to fling himself at the Hurrian and had to be caught virtually in mid-air by one of the Mauvs, who held him immobile with an effortless constriction of biceps.

The wild one screamed. "No. Just sit here and wait! Vulture! Vulture! *Vulture!*"

It was days before Devi-en could bring himself to see the wild one again. He was almost brought to disrespect of the Arch-administrator when the latter insisted that he lacked sufficient data for a complete analysis of the mental make-up of these wild ones.

Devi-en said boldly, "Surely, there is enough to give some solution to our question."

The Arch-administrator's nose quivered and his pink tongue passed over it meditatively. "A solution of a kind, perhaps. I can't trust this solution. We are facing a very unusual species. We know that already. We can't afford to make mistakes. ——One thing, at least. We have happened upon a highly intelligent one. Unless— unless he is at his race's norm." The Arch-administrator seemed upset at that thought.

Devi-en said, "The creature brought up the horrible picture of that—that bird—that——"

"Vulture," said the Arch-administrator.

"It put our entire mission into such a distorted light. I have not been able to eat properly since, or sleep. In fact, I am afraid I will have to ask to be relieved——"

"Not before we have completed what we have set out to do," said the Arch-administrator firmly. "Do you think I enjoy the picture of—of carrion-eat—— You *must* collect more data."

Devi-en nodded finally. He understood, of course. The Arch-administrator was no more anxious to cause a nuclear war than any Hurrian would be. He was putting off the moment of decision as long as possible.

Devi-en settled himself for one more interview with the wild one. It turned out to be a completely unbearable one, and the last.

The wild one had a bruise across his cheek as though he had been resisting the Mauvs again. In fact, it was certain he had. He had done so numerous times before, and the Mauvs, despite their most earnest attempts to do no harm, could not help but bruise him on occasion. One would expect the wild one to see how intensely they tried not to hurt him and to quiet his behavior as a result. Instead, it was as though the conviction of safety spurred him on to additional resistance.

(These large-primate species were vicious, vicious, thought Devi-en sadly.)

For over an hour, the interview hovered over useless small talk and then the wild one said with sudden belligerence, "How long did you say you things have been here?"

"Fifteen of your years," said Devi-en.

"That figures. The first flying saucers were sighted just after World War II. How much longer before the nuclear war?"

With automatic truth, Devi-en said, "We wish we knew," and stopped suddenly.

The wild one said, "I thought nuclear war was inevitable. Last time you said you overstayed ten years. You expected the war ten years ago, didn't you?"

Devi-en said, "I can't discuss this subject."

"No?" The wild one was screaming. "What are you going to do about it? How long will you wait? Why not nudge it a little? Don't just wait, vulture. Start one."

Devi-en jumped to his feet. "What are you saying?"

"Why else are you waiting, you dirty———" He choked on a completely incomprehensible expletive, then continued, breathlessly, "Isn't that what vultures do when some poor miserable animal, or man, maybe, is taking too long to die? They can't wait. They come swirling down and peck out his eyes. They wait till he's helpless and just hurry him along the last step."

Devi-en ordered him away quickly and retired to his sleeping room, where he was sick for hours. Nor did he sleep then or that night. The word "vulture" screamed in his ears and that final picture danced before his eyes.

Devi-en said firmly, "Your Height, I can speak with the wild one no more. If you need still more data, I cannot help you."

The Arch-administrator looked haggard. "I know. This vulture business—— Very difficult to take. Yet you notice the thought didn't affect him. Large-primates are immune to such things, hardened, calloused. It is part of their way of thinking. Horrible."

"I can get you no more data."

"It's all right. I understand. ——Besides, each additional item only strengthens the preliminary answer; the answer I thought was

only provisional; that I hoped earnestly was only provisional."
He buried his head in his grizzled arms. "We have a way to start
their nuclear war for them."

"Oh? What need be done?"

"It is something very direct, very simple. It is something I could
never have thought of. Nor you."

"What is it, your Height?" He felt an anticipatory dread.

"What keeps them at peace now is that neither of two nearly
equal sides dares take the responsibility of starting a war. If one
side did, however, the other—well, let's be blunt about it—would
retaliate in full."

Devi-en nodded.

The Arch-administrator went on. "If a single nuclear bomb
fell on the territory of either of the two sides, the victims would
at once assume the other side had launched it. They would feel
they could not wait for further attacks. Retaliation in full would
follow within hours; the other side would retaliate in its turn.
Within weeks it would be over."

"But how do we make one of them drop that first bomb?"

"We don't, Captain. That is the point. We drop the first bomb
ourselves."

"What?" Devi-en swayed.

"That is it. Compute a large-primate's mind and that answer
thrusts itself at you."

"But how can we?"

"We assemble a bomb. That is easy enough. We send it down
by ship and drop it over some inhabited locality———"

"Inhabited?"

The Arch-administrator looked away and said uneasily, "The
effect is lost otherwise."

"I see," said Devi-en. He was picturing vultures; he couldn't
help it. He visualized them as large, scaled bird (like the small
harmless flying creatures on Hurria, but immensely large), with
rubber-skinned wings and long razor-bills, circling down, pecking
at dying eyes.

His hands covered his eyes. He said shakily, "Who will pilot
the ship? Who will launch the bomb?"

The Arch-administrator's voice was no stronger than Devi-en's. "I don't know."

"I won't," said Devi-en. "I can't. There is no Hurrian who can, at any price."

The Arch-administrator rocked back and forth miserably. "Perhaps the Mauvs could be given orders——"

"Who could give them such orders?"

The Arch-administrator sighed heavily. "I will call the Council. They may have all the data. Perhaps they will suggest something."

So after a little over fifteen years, the Hurrians were dismantling their base on the other side of the Moon.

Nothing had been accomplished. The large-primates of the planet had not had their nuclear war; they might never have.

And despite all the future horror that might bring, Devi-en was in an agony of happiness. There was no point in thinking of the future. For the present, he was getting away from this most horrible of horrible worlds.

He watched the Moon fall away and shrink to a spot of light, along with the planet, and the Sun of the system itself, till the whole thing was lost among the constellations.

It was only then that he could feel anything but relief. It was only then that he felt a first tiny twinge of it-might-have-been.

He said to the Arch-administrator, "It might all have been well if we had been more patient. They might yet have blundered into nuclear war."

The Arch-administrator said, "Somehow I doubt it. The mentalic analysis of——"

He stopped and Devi-en understood. The wild one had been replaced on his planet with minimal harm. The events of the past weeks had beeen blanked out of his mind. He had been placed near a small, inhabited locality not far from the spot where he had been first found. His fellows would assume he had been lost. They would blame his loss of weight, his bruises, his amnesia upon the hardships he had undergone.

But the harm done *by* him——

If only they had not brought him up to the Moon in the first place. They might have reconciled themselves to the thought of starting a war. They might somehow have thought of dropping a bomb; and worked out some indirect, long-distance system for doing so.

It had been the wild one's word-picture of the vulture that had stopped it all. It had ruined Devi-en and the Arch-administrator. When all data was sent back to Hurria, the effect on the Council itself had been notable. The order to dismantle the Base had come quickly.

Devi-en said, "I will never take part in colonization again."

The Arch-administrator said mournfully, "None of us may ever have to. The wild ones of that planet will emerge and with large-primates and large-primate thinking loose in the Galaxy, it will mean the end of—of——"

Devi-en's nose twitched. The end of everything; of all the good Hurria had done in the Galaxy; all the good it might have continued to do in the future.

He said, "We ought to have dropped——" and did not finish.

What was the use of saying that? They couldn't have dropped the bomb for all the Galaxy. If they could have, they would have been large-primate themselves in their manner of thinking, and there are worse things than merely the end of everything.

Devi-en thought of the vultures.

ALL THE TROUBLES OF THE WORLD

THE GREATEST INDUSTRY on Earth centered about Multivac—Multivac, the giant computer that had grown in fifty years until its various ramifications had filled Washington, D.C. to the suburbs and had reached out tendrils into every city and town on Earth.

An army of civil servants fed it data constantly and another army correlated and interpreted the answers it gave. A corps of engineers patrolled its interior while mines and factories consumed themselves in keeping its reserve stocks of replacement parts ever complete, ever accurate, ever satisfactory in every way.

Multivac directed Earth's economy and helped Earth's science. Most important of all, it was the central clearing house of all known facts about each individual Earthman.

And each day it was part of Multivac's duties to take the four billion sets of facts about individual human beings that filled its vitals and extrapolate them for an additional day of time. Every Corrections Department on Earth received the data appropriate to its own area of jurisdiction, and the over-all data was presented in one large piece to the Central Board of Corrections in Washington, D.C.

Bernard Gulliman was in the fourth week of his year term as Chairman of the Central Board of Corrections and had grown casual enough to accept the morning report without being frightened by it. As usual, it was a sheaf of papers some six inches thick. He knew by now, he was not expected to read it. (No human could.) Still, it was amusing to glance through it.

There was the usual list of predictable crimes: frauds of all sorts, larcenies, riots, manslaughters, arsons.

He looked for one particular heading and felt a slight shock at finding it there at all, then another one at seeing two entries. Not one, but two. *Two* first-degree murders. He had not seen two in one day in all his term as Chairman so far.

He punched the knob of the two-way intercom and waited for the smooth face of his co-ordinator to appear on the screen.

"Ali," said Gulliman. "There are two first-degrees this day. Is there any unusual problem?"

"No, sir." The dark-complexioned face with its sharp, black eyes seemed restless. "Both cases are quite low probability."

"I know that," said Gulliman. "I observed that neither probability is higher than 15 per cent. Just the same, Multivac has a reputation to maintain. It has virtually wiped out crime, and the public judges that by its record on first-degree murder which is, of course, the most spectacular crime."

Ali Othman nodded. "Yes, sir. I quite realize that."

"You also realize, I hope," Gulliman said, "that I don't want a single consummated case of it during my term. If any other crime slips through, I may allow excuses. If a first-degree murder slips through, I'll have your hide. Understand?"

"Yes, sir. The complete analyses of the two potential murders are already at the district offices involved. The potential criminals and victims are under observation. I have rechecked the probabilities of consummation and they are already dropping."

"Very good," said Gulliman, and broke connection.

He went back to the list with an uneasy feeling that perhaps he had been overpompous. ———But then, one had to be firm with these permanent civil-service personnel and make sure they didn't imagine they were running everything, including the Chairman. Particularly this Othman, who had been working with Multivac since both were considerably younger, and had a proprietary air that could be infuriating.

To Gulliman, this matter of crime was the political chance of a lifetime. So far, no Chairman had passed through his term without a murder taking place somewhere on Earth, some time. The previous Chairman had ended with a record of eight, three more (*more*, in fact) than under his predecessor.

Now Gulliman intended to have *none*. He was going to be, he had decided, the first Chairman without any murder at all anywhere on Earth during his term. After that, and the favorable publicity that would result——

He barely skimmed the rest of the report. He estimated that there were at least two thousand cases of prospective wife-beatings listed. Undoubtedly, not all would be stopped in time. Perhaps thirty per cent would be consummated. But the incidence was dropping and consummations were dropping even more quickly.

Multivac had added wife-beating to its list of predictable crimes only some five years earlier and the average man was not yet accustomed to the thought that if he planned to wallop his wife, it would be known in advance. As the conviction percolated through society, woman would first suffer fewer bruises and then, eventually, none.

Some husband-beatings were on the list, too, Gulliman noticed.

Ali Othman closed connections and stared at the screen from which Gulliman's jowled and balding head had departed. Then he looked across at his assistant, Rafe Leemy and said, "What do we do?"

"Don't ask me. *He*'s worried about just a lousy murder or two."

"It's an awful chance trying to handle this thing on our own. Still if we tell him, he'll have a first-class fit. These elective politicians have their skins to think of, so he's bound to get in our way and make things worse."

Leemy nodded his head and put a thick lower lip between his teeth. "Trouble is, though, what if we miss out? It would just about be the end of the world, you know."

"If we miss out, who cares what happens to us? We'll just be part of the general catastrophe." Then he said in a more lively manner, "But hell, the probability is only 12.3 per cent. On anything else, except maybe murder, we'd let the probabilities rise a bit before taking any action at all. There could still be spontaneous correction."

"I wouldn't count on it," said Leemy dryly.

"I don't intend to. I was just pointing the fact out. Still, at this probability, I suggest we confine ourselves to simple observation for the moment. No one could plan a crime like this alone; there must be accomplices."

"Multivac didn't name any."

"I know. Still——" His voice trailed off.

So they stared at the details of the one crime not included on the list handed out to Gulliman; the one crime much worse than first-degree murder; the one crime never before attempted in the history of Multivac; and wondered what to do.

Ben Manners considered himself the happiest sixteen-year-old in Baltimore. This was, perhaps, doubtful. But he was certainly one of the happiest, and one of the most excited.

At least, he was one of the handful admitted to the galleries of the stadium during the swearing in of the eighteen-year-olds. His older brother was going to be sworn in so his parents had applied for spectator's tickets and they had allowed Ben to do so, too. But when Multivac chose among all the applicants, it was Ben who got the ticket.

Two years later, Ben would be sworn in himself, but watching big brother Michael now was the next best thing.

His parents had dressed him (or supervised the dressing, at any rate) with all care, as representative of the family and sent him off with numerous messages for Michael, who had left days earlier for preliminary physical and neurological examinations.

The stadium was on the outskirts of town and Ben, just bursting with self-importance, was shown to his seat. Below him, now, were rows upon rows of hundreds upon hundreds of eighteen-year-olds (boys to the right, girls to the left), all from the second district of Baltimore. At various times in the year, similar meetings were going on all over the world, but this was Baltimore, this was the important one. Down there (somewhere) was Mike, Ben's own brother.

Ben scanned the tops of heads, thinking somehow he might recognize his brother. He didn't, of course, but then a man came out on the raised platform in front of all the crowd and Ben stopped looking to listen.

The man said, "Good afternoon, swearers and guests. I am Randolph T. Hoch, in charge of the Baltimore ceremonies this year. The swearers have met me several times now during the progress of the physical and neurological portions of this examination. Most of the task is done, but the most important matter is left. The swearer himself, his personality, must go into Multivac's records.

"Each year, this requires some explanation to the young people reaching adulthood. Until now" (he turned to the young people before him and his eyes went no more to the gallery) "you have not been adult; you have not been individuals in the eyes of Multivac, except where you were especially singled out as such by your parents or your government.

"Until now, when the time for the yearly up-dating of information came, it was your parents who filled in the necessary data on you. Now the time has come for you to take over that duty yourself. It is a great honor, a great responsibility. Your parents have told us what schooling you've had, what diseases, what habits; a great many things. But now you must tell us a great deal more; your innermost thoughts; your most secret deeds.

"This is hard to do the first time, embarrassing even, but it *must* be done. Once it is done, Multivac will have a complete analysis of all of you in its files. It will understand your actions and reactions. It will even be able to guess with fair accuracy at your future actions and reactions.

"In this way, Multivac will protect you. If you are in danger of accident, it will know. If someone plans harm to you, it will know. If *you* plan harm, it will know and you will be stopped in time so that it will not be necessary to punish you.

"With its knowledge of all of you, Multivac will be able to help Earth adjust its economy and its laws for the good of all. If you have a personal problem, you may come to Multivac with it and with its knowledge of all of you, Multivac will be able to help you.

"Now you will have many forms to fill out. Think carefully and answer all questions as accurately as you can. Do not hold back through shame or caution. No one will ever know your answers except Multivac unless it becomes necessary to learn the answers in order to protect you. And then only authorized officials of the government will know.

"It may occur to you to stretch the truth a bit here or there. Don't do this. We will find out if you do. All your answers put together form a pattern. If some answers are false, they will not fit the pattern and Multivac will discover them. If all your answers are false, there will be a distorted pattern of a type that Multivac will recognize. So you must tell the truth."

Eventually, it was all over, however; the form-filling; the ceremonies and speeches that followed. In the evening, Ben, standing tiptoe, finally spotted Michael, who was still carrying the robes he had worn in the "parade of the adults." They greeted one another with jubilation.

They shared a light supper and took the expressway home, alive and alight with the greatness of the day.

They were not prepared, then, for the sudden transition of the home-coming. It was a numbing shock to both of them to be stopped by a cold-faced young man in uniform outside their own front door; to have their papers inspected before they could enter their own house; to find their own parents sitting forlornly in the living room, the mark of tragedy on their faces.

Joseph Manners, looking much older than he had that morning, looked out of his puzzled, deep-sunken eyes at his sons (one with the robes of new adulthood still over his arm) and said, "I seem to be under house arrest."

Bernard Gulliman could not and did not read the entire report. He read only the summary and that was most gratifying, indeed.

A whole generation, it seemed, had grown up accustomed to the fact that Multivac could predict the commission of major crimes. They learned that Corrections agents would be on the scene before the crime could be committed. They found out that consummation of the crime led to inevitable punishment. Gradually, they were convinced that there was no way anyone could outsmart Multivac.

The result was, naturally, that even the intention of crime fell off. And as such intentions fell off and as Multivac's capacity was enlarged, minor crimes could be added to the list it would predict each morning, and these crimes, too, were now shrinking in incidence.

So Gulliman had ordered an analysis made (by Multivac naturally) of Multivac's capacity to turn its attention to the problem of predicting probabilities of disease incidence. Doctors might soon be alerted to individual patients who might grow diabetic in the course of the next year, or suffer an attack of tuberculosis or grow a cancer.

An ounce of prevention——

And the report was a favorable one!

After that, the roster of the day's possible crimes arrived and there was not a first-degree murder on the list.

Gulliman put in an intercom call to Ali Othman in high good humor. "Othman, how do the numbers of crimes in the daily lists of the past week average compared with those in my first week as Chairman?"

It had gone down, it turned out, by 8 per cent and Gulliman was happy indeed. No fault of his own, of course, but the electorate would not know that. He blessed his luck that he had come in at the right time, at the very climax of Multivac, when disease, too, could be placed under its all-embracing and protecting knowledge.

Gulliman would prosper by this.

Othman shrugged his shoulders. "Well, he's happy."

"When do we break the bubble?" said Leemy. "Putting Manners under observation just raised the probabilities and house arrest gave it another boost."

"Don't I know it?" said Othman peevishly. "What I don't know is why."

"Accomplices, maybe, like you said. With Manners in trouble, the rest have to strike at once or be lost."

"Just the other way around. With our hand on one, the rest would scatter for safety and disappear. Besides, why aren't the accomplices named by Multivac?"

"Well, then, do we tell Gulliman?"

"No, not yet. The probability is still only 17.3 per cent. Let's get a bit more drastic first."

Elizabeth Manners said to her younger son, "You go to your room, Ben."

"But what's it all about, Mom?" asked Ben, voice breaking at this strange ending to what had been a glorious day.

"Please!"

He left reluctantly, passing through the door to the stairway, walking up it noisily and down again quietly.

And Mike Manners, the older son, the new-minted adult and the hope of the family, said in a voice and tone that mirrored his brother's, "What's it all about?"

Joe Manners said, "As heaven is my witness, son, I don't know. I haven't done anything."

"Well, sure you haven't done anything." Mike looked at his small-boned, mild-mannered father in wonder. "They must be here because you're *thinking* of doing something."

"I'm not."

Mrs. Manners broke in angrily, "How can he be thinking of doing something worth all—all this." She cast her arm about, in a gesture toward the enclosing shell of government men about the house. "When I was a little girl, I remember the father of a friend of mine was working in a bank, and they once called him up and said to leave the money alone and he did. It was fifty thousand dollars. He hadn't really taken it. He was just thinking about taking it. They didn't keep those things as quiet in those days as they do now; the story got out. That's how I know about it.

"But I mean," she went on, rubbing her plump hands slowly together, "that was fifty thousand dollars; fifty—thousand—dollars. Yet all they did was call him; one phone call. What could your father be planning that would make it worth having a dozen men come down and close off the house?"

Joe Manners said, eyes filled with pain, "I am planning no crime, not even the smallest. I swear it."

Mike, filled with the conscious wisdom of a new adult, said, "Maybe it's something subconscious, Pop. Some resentment against your supervisor."

"So that I would want to kill him? No!"

"Won't they tell you what it is, Pop?"

His mother interrupted again, "No, they won't. We've asked. I said they were ruining our standing in the community just being here. The least they could do is tell us what it's all about so we could fight it, so we could explain."

"And they wouldn't?"

"They wouldn't."

Mike stood with his legs spread apart and his hands deep in his pockets. He said, troubled, "Gee, Mom, Multivac doesn't make mistakes."

His father pounded his fist helplessly on the arm of the sofa. "I tell you I'm not planning any crime."

The door opened without a knock and a man in uniform walked in with sharp, self-possessed stride. His face had a glazed, official appearance. He said, "Are you Joseph Manners?"

Joe Manners rose to his feet. "Yes. Now what is it you want of me?"

"Joseph Manners, I place you under arrest by order of the government," and curtly he showed his identification as a Corrections officer. "I must ask you to come with me."

"For what reason? What have I done?"

"I am not at liberty to discuss that."

"But I can't be arrested just for planning a crime even if I were doing that. To be arrested I must actually have *done* something. You can't arrest me otherwise. It's against the law."

The officer was impervious to the logic. "You will have to come with me."

Mrs. Manners shrieked and fell on the couch, weeping hysterically. Joseph Manners could not bring himself to violate the code drilled into him all his life by actually resisting an officer, but he hung back at least, forcing the Corrections officer to use muscular power to drag him forward.

And Manners called out as he went, "But tell me what it is. Just tell me. If I *knew*—— Is it murder? Am I supposed to be planning murder?"

The door closed behind him and Mike Manners, white-faced

and suddenly feeling not the least bit adult, stared first at the door, then at his weeping mother.

Ben Manners, behind the door and suddenly feeling quite adult, pressed his lips tightly together and thought he knew exactly what to do.

If Multivac took away, Multivac could also give. Ben had been at the ceremonies that very day. He had heard this man, Randolph Hoch, speak of Multivac and all that Multivac could do. It could direct the government and it could also unbend and help out some plain person who came to it for help.

Anyone could ask help of Multivac and anyone meant Ben. Neither his mother nor Mike were in any condition to stop him now, and he had some money left of the amount they had given him for his great outing that day. If afterward they found him gone and worried about it, that couldn't be helped. Right now, his first loyalty was to his father.

He ran out the back way and the officer at the door cast a glance at his papers and let him go.

Harold Quimby handled the complaints department of the Baltimore substation of Multivac. He considered himself to be a member of that branch of the civil service that was most important of all. In some ways, he may have been right, and those who heard him discuss the matter would have had to be made of iron not to feel impressed.

For one thing, Quimby would say, Multivac was essentially an invader of privacy. In the past fifty years, mankind had had to acknowledge that its thoughts and impulses were no longer secret, that it owned no inner recess where anything could be hidden. And mankind had to have something in return.

Of course, it got prosperity, peace, and safety, but that was abstract. Each man and woman needed something personal as his or her own reward for surrendering privacy, and each one got it. Within reach of every human being was a Multivac station with circuits into which he could freely enter his own problems and questions without control or hindrance, and from which, in a matter of minutes, he could receive answers.

At any given moment, five million individual circuits among the quadrillion or more within Multivac might be involved in this question-and-answer program. The answers might not always be certain, but they were the best available, and every questioner *knew* the answer to be the best available and had faith in it. That was what counted.

And now an anxious sixteen-year-old had moved slowly up the waiting line of men and women (each face in that line illuminated by a different mixture of hope with fear or anxiety or even anguish —always with hope predominating as the person stepped nearer and nearer to Multivac).

Without looking up, Quimby took the filled-out form being handed him and said, "Booth 5-B."

Ben said, "How do I ask the question, sir?"

Quimby looked up then, with a bit of surprise. Preadults did not generally make use of the service. He said kindly, "Have you ever done this before, son?"

"No, sir."

Quimby pointed to the model on his desk. "You use this. You see how it works? Just like a typewriter. Don't you try to write or print anything by hand. Just use the machine. Now you take booth 5-B, and if you need help, just press the red button and someone will come. Down that aisle, son, on the right."

He watched the youngster go down the aisle and out of view and smiled. No one was ever turned away from Multivac. Of course, there was always a certain percentage of trivia: people who asked personal questions about their neighbors or obscene questions about prominent personalities; college youths trying to outguess their professors or thinking it clever to stump Multivac by asking it Russell's class-of-all-classes paradox and so on.

Multivac could take care of all that. It needed no help.

Besides, each question and answer was filed and formed but another item in the fact assembly for each individual. Even the most trivial question and the most impertinent, insofar as it reflected the personality of the questioner, helped humanity by helping Multivac know about humanity.

Quimby turned his attention to the next person in line, a middle-aged woman, gaunt and angular, with the look of trouble in her eye.

Ali Othman strode the length of his office, his heels thumping desperately on the carpet. "The probability still goes up. It's 22.4 per cent now. Damnation! We have Joseph Manners under actual arrest and it still goes up." He was perspiring freely.

Leemy turned away from the telephone. "No confession yet. He's under Psychic Probing and there is no sign of crime. He may be telling the truth."

Othman said, "Is Multivac crazy then?"

Another phone sprang to life. Othman closed connections quickly, glad of the interruption. A Corrections officer's face came to life in the screen. The officer said, "Sir, are there any new directions as to Manners' family? Are they to be allowed to come and go as they have been?"

"What do you mean, as they have been?"

"The original instructions were for the house arrest of Joseph Manners. Nothing was said of the rest of the family, sir."

"Well, extend it to the rest of the family until you are informed otherwise."

"Sir, that is the point. The mother and older son are demanding information about the younger son. The younger son is gone and they claim he is in custody and wish to go to headquarters to inquire about it."

Othman frowned and said in almost a whisper, "Younger son? How young?"

"Sixteen, sir," said the officer.

"Sixteen and he's gone. Don't you know where?"

"He was allowed to leave, sir. There were no orders to hold him."

"Hold the line. Don't move." Othman put the line into suspension, then clutched at his coal-black hair with both hands and shrieked, "Fool! Fool! Fool!"

Leemy was startled. "What the hell?"

"The man has a sixteen-year-old son," choked out Othman. "A sixteen-year-old is not an adult and he is not filed independently in Multivac, but only as part of his father's file." He glared at Leemy. "Doesn't everyone know that until eighteen a youngster does not file his own reports with Multivac but that his father does it for him? Don't I know it? Don't you?"

"You mean Multivac didn't mean Joe Manners?" said Leemy.

"Multivac meant his minor son, and the youngster is gone, now. With officers three deep around the house, he calmly walks out and goes on you know what errand."

He whirled to the telephone circuit to which the Corrections officer still clung, the minute break having given Othman just time enough to collect himself and to assume a cool and self-possessed mien. (It would never have done to throw a fit before the eyes of the officer, however much good it did in purging his spleen.)

He said, "Officer, locate the younger son who has disappeared. Take every man you have, if necessary. Take every man available in the district, if necessary. I shall give the appropriate orders. You must find that boy at all costs."

"Yes, sir."

Connection was broken. Othman said, "Have another rundown on the probabilities, Leemy."

Five minutes later, Leemy said, "It's down to 19.6 per cent. It's *down*."

Othman drew a long breath. "We're on the right track at last."

Ben Manners sat in Booth 5-B and punched out slowly, "My name is Benjamin Manners, number MB–71833412. My father, Joseph Manners, has been arrested but we don't know what crime he is planning. Is there any way we can help him?"

He sat and waited. He might be only sixteen but he was old enough to know that somewhere those words were being whirled into the most complex structure ever conceived by man; that a trillion facts would blend and co-ordinate into a whole, and that from that whole, Multivac would abstract the best help.

The machine clicked and a card emerged. It had an answer on it, a long answer. It began, "Take the expressway to Washington, D.C. at once. Get off at the Connecticut Avenue stop. You will find a special exit, labeled "Multivac" with a guard. Inform the guard you are a special courier for Dr. Trumbull and he will let you enter.

"You will be in a corridor. Proceed along it till you reach a small door labeled 'Interior.' Enter and say to the men inside,

'Message for Doctor Trumbull.' You will be allowed to pass. Proceed on——"

It went on in this fashion. Ben could not see the application to his question, but he had complete faith in Multivac. He left at a run, heading for the expressway to Washington.

The Corrections officers traced Ben Manners to the Baltimore station an hour after he had left. A shocked Harold Quimby found himself flabbergasted at the number and importance of the men who had focused on him in the search for a sixteen-year-old.

"Yes, a boy," he said, "but I don't know where he went to after he was through here. I had no way of knowing that anyone was looking for him. We accept all comers here. Yes, I can get the record of the question and answer."

They looked at the record and televised it to Central Headquarters at once.

Othman read it through, turned up his eyes, and collapsed. They brought him to almost at once. He said to Leemy weakly, "Have them catch that boy. And have a copy of Multivac's answer made out for me. There's no way any more, no way out. I must see Gulliman now."

Bernard Gulliman had never seen Ali Othman as much as perturbed before, and watching the co-ordinator's wild eyes now sent a trickle of ice water down his spine.

He stammered, "What do you mean, Othman? What do you mean worse than murder?"

"Much worse than just murder."

Gulliman was quite pale. "Do you mean assassination of a high government official?" (It did cross his mind that he himself——).

Othman nodded. "Not just *a* government official. *The* government official."

"The *Secretary-General?*" said Gulliman in an appalled whisper.

"More than that, even. Much more. We deal with a plan to assassinate Multivac!"

"WHAT!"

"For the first time in the history of Multivac, the computer came up with the report that it itself was in danger."

"Why was I not at once informed?"

Othman half-truthed out of it. "The matter was so unprecedented, sir, that we explored the situation first before daring to put it on official record."

"But Multivac has been saved, of course? It's been saved?"

"The probabilities of harm have declined to under 4 per cent. I am waiting for the report now."

"Message for Dr. Trumbull," said Ben Manners to the man on the high stool, working carefully on what looked like the controls of a stratojet cruiser, enormously magnified.

"Sure, Jim," said the man. "Go ahead."

Ben looked at his instructions and hurried on. Eventually, he would find a tiny control lever which he was to shift to a DOWN position at a moment when a certain indicator spot would light up red.

He heard an agitated voice behind him, then another, and suddenly, two men had him by his elbows. His feet were lifted off the floor.

One man said, "Come with us, boy."

Ali Othman's face did not noticeably lighten at the news, even though Gulliman said with great relief, "If we have the boy, then Multivac is safe."

"For the moment."

Gulliman put a trembling hand to his forehead. "What a half hour I've had. Can you imagine what the destruction of Multivac for even a short time would mean. The government would have collapsed; the economy broken down. It would have meant devastation worse——" His head snapped up, "What do you mean *for the moment?*"

"The boy, this Ben Manners, had no intention of doing harm. He and his family must be released and compensation for false imprisonment given them. He was only following Multivac's instructions in order to help his father and it's done that. His father is free now."

"Do you mean Multivac ordered the boy to pull a lever under circumstances that would burn out enough circuits to require a month's repair work? You mean Multivac would suggest its own destruction for the comfort of one man?"

"It's worse than that, sir. Multivac not only gave those instructions but selected the Manners family in the first place because Ben Manners looked exactly like one of Dr. Trumbull's pages so that he could get into Multivac without being stopped."

"What do you mean the family was selected?"

"Well, the boy would have never gone to ask the question if his father had not been arrested. His father would never have been arrested if Multivac had not blamed him for planning the destruction of Multivac. Multivac's own action started the chain of events that almost led to Multivac's destruction."

"But there's no sense to that," Gulliman said in a pleading voice. He felt small and helpless and he was virtually on his knees, begging this Othman, this man who had spent nearly a lifetime with Multivac, to reassure him.

Othman did not do so. He said, "This is Multivac's first attempt along this line as far as I know. In some ways, it planned well. It chose the right family. It carefully did not distinguish between father and son to send us off the track. It was still an amateur at the game, though. It could not overcome its own instructions that led it to report the probability of its own destruction as increasing with every step we took down the wrong road. It could not avoid recording the answer it gave the youngster. With further practice, it will probably learn deceit. It will learn to hide certain facts, fail to record certain others. From now on, every instruction it gives may have the seeds in it of its own destruction. We will never know. And however careful we are, eventually Multivac will succeed. I think, Mr. Gulliman, you will be the last Chairman of this organization."

Gulliman pounded his desk in fury. "But why, why, why? Damn you, why? What is wrong with it? Can't it be fixed?"

"I don't think so," said Othman, in soft despair. "I've never thought about this before. I've never had the occasion to until this happened, but now that I think of it, it seems to me we have reached the end of the road because Multivac is too good. Multivac has grown so complicated, its reactions are no longer those of a machine, but those of a living thing."

"You're mad, but even so?"

"For fifty years and more we have been loading humanity's troubles on Multivac, on this living thing. We've asked it to care for us, all together and each individually. We've asked it to take all our secrets into itself; we've asked it to absorb our evil and guard us against it. Each of us brings his troubles to it, adding his bit to the burden. Now we are planning to load the burden of human disease on Multivac, too."

Othman paused a moment, then burst out, "Mr. Gulliman, Multivac bears all the troubles of the world on its shoulders and it is tired."

"Madness. Midsummer madness," muttered Gulliman.

"Then let me show you something. Let me put it to the test. May I have permission to use the Multivac circuit line here in your office?"

"Why?"

"To ask it a question no one has ever asked Multivac before?"

"Will you do it harm?" asked Gulliman in quick alarm.

"No. But it will tell us what we want to know."

The Chairman hesitated a trifle. Then he said, "Go ahead."

Othman used the instrument on Gulliman's desk. His fingers punched out the question with deft strokes: "Multivac, what do you yourself want more than anything else?"

The moment between question and answer lengthened unbearably, but neither Othman nor Gulliman breathed.

And there was a clicking and a card popped out. It was a small card. On it, in precise letters, was the answer:

"I want to die."

SPELL MY NAME WITH AN S

MARSHALL ZEBATINSKY FELT FOOLISH. He felt as though there were eyes staring through the grimy store-front glass and across the scarred wooden partition; eyes watching him. He felt no confidence in the old clothes he had resurrected or the turned-down brim of a hat he never otherwise wore or the glasses he had left in their case.

He felt foolish and it made the lines in his forehead deeper and his young-old face a little paler.

He would never be able to explain to anyone why a nuclear physicist such as himself should visit a numerologist. (Never, he thought. Never.) Hell, he could not explain it to himself except that he had let his wife talk him into it.

The numerologist sat behind an old desk that must have been secondhand when bought. No desk could get that old with only one owner. The same might almost be said of his clothes. He was little and dark and peered at Zebatinsky with little dark eyes that were brightly alive.

He said, "I have never had a physicist for a client before, Dr. Zebatinsky."

Zebatinsky flushed at once. "You understand this is confidential."

The numerologist smiled so that wrinkles creased about the corners of his mouth and the skin around his chin stretched. "All my dealings are confidential."

Zebatinsky said, "I think I ought to tell you one thing. I don't believe in numerology and I don't expect to begin believing in it. If that makes a difference, say so now."

"But why are you here, then?"

"My wife thinks you may have something, whatever it is. I promised her and I am here." He shrugged and the feeling of folly grew more acute.

"And what is it you are looking for? Money? Security? Long life? What?"

Zebatinsky sat for a long moment while the numerologist watched him quietly and made no move to hurry his client.

Zebatinsky thought: What do I say anyway? That I'm thirty-four and without a future?

He said, "I want success. I want recognition."

"A better job?"

"A *different* job. A different *kind* of job. Right now, I'm part of a team, working under orders. Teams! That's all government research is. You're a violinist lost in a symphony orchestra."

"And you want to solo."

"I want to get out of a team and into—into *me*." Zebatinsky felt carried away, almost lightheaded, just putting this into words to someone other than his wife. He said, "Twenty-five years ago, with my kind of training and my kind of ability, I would have gotten to work on the first nuclear power plants. Today I'd be running one of them or I'd be head of a pure research group at a university. But with my start these days where will I be twenty-five years from now? Nowhere. Still on the team. Still carrying my 2 per cent of the ball. I'm drowning in an anonymous crowd of nuclear physicists, and what I want is room on dry land if you see what I mean."

The numerologist nodded slowly. "You realize, Dr. Zebatinsky, that I don't guarantee success."

Zebatinsky, for all his lack of faith, felt a sharp bite of disappointment. "You don't? Then what the devil *do* you guarantee?"

"An improvement in the probabilities. My work is statistical in nature. Since you deal with atoms, I think you understand the laws of statistics."

"Do you?" asked the physicist sourly.

"I do, as a matter of fact. I am a mathematician and I work mathematically. I don't tell you this in order to raise my fee. That is standard. Fifty dollars. But since you are a scientist, you can appreciate the nature of my work better than my other clients. It is even a pleasure to be able to explain to you."

Zebatinsky said, "I'd rather you wouldn't, if you don't mind. It's no use telling me about the numerical values of letters, their mystic significance and that kind of thing. I don't consider that mathematics. Let's get to the point——"

The numerologist said, "Then you want me to help you provided I don't embarrass you by telling you the silly nonscientific basis of the way in which I helped you. Is that it?"

"All right. That's it."

"But you still work on the assumption that I am a numerologist, and I am not. I call myself that so that the police won't bother me and," (the little man chuckled dryly) "so that the psychiatrists won't either. I am a mathematician; an honest one."

Zebatinsky smiled.

The numerologist said, "I build computers. I study probable futures."

"What?"

"Does that sound worse than numerology to you? Why? Given enough data and a computer capable of sufficient number of operations in unit time, the future is predictable, at least in terms of probabilities. When you compute the motions of a missile in order to aim an anti-missile, isn't it the future you're predicting? The missile and anti-missile would not collide if the future were predicted incorrectly. I do the same thing. Since I work with a greater number of variables, my results are less accurate."

"You mean you'll predict *my* future?"

"Very approximately. Once I have done that, I will modify the data by changing your name and no other fact about you. I throw that modified datum into the operation-program. Then I try other modified names. I study each modified future and find one that contains a greater degree of recognition for you than the future that now lies ahead of you. Or no, let me put it another way. I will find you a future in which the probability of adequate recognition is higher than the probability of that in your present future."

"Why change my name?"

"That is the only change I ever make, for several reasons. Number one, it is a simple change. After all, if I make a great change or many changes, so many new variables enter that I can no longer interpret the result. My machine is still crude. Number two, it is a reasonable change. I can't change your height, can I, or the color of your eyes, or even your temperament. Number three, it is a significant change. Names mean a lot to people. Finally, number four, it is a common change that is done every day by various people."

Zebatinsky said, "What if you don't find a better future?"

"That is the risk you will have to take. You will be no worse off than now, my friend."

Zebatinsky stared at the little man uneasily, "I don't believe any of this. I'd sooner believe numerology."

The numerologist sighed. "I thought a person like yourself would feel more comfortable with the truth. I *want* to help you and there is much yet for you to do. If you believed me a numerologist, you would not follow through. I thought if I told you the truth you would let me help you."

Zebatinsky said, "If you can see the future——"

"Why am I not the richest man on earth? Is that it? But I am rich—in all I want. You want recognition and I want to be left alone. I do my work. No one bothers me. That makes me a billionaire. I need a little real money and this I get from people such as yourself. Helping people is nice and perhaps a psychiatrist would say it gives me a feeling of power and feeds my ego. Now—do you want me to help you?"

"How much did you say?"

"Fifty dollars. I will need a great deal of biographical information from you but I have prepared a form to guide you. It's a little long, I'm afraid. Still, if you can get it in the mail by the end of the week, I will have an answer for you by the——" (he put out his lower lip and frowned in mental calculation) "the twentieth of next month."

"Five weeks? So long?"

"I have other work, my friend, and other clients. If I were a fake, I could do it much more quickly. Is it agreed then?"

Zebatinsky rose. "Well, agreed. ——This is all confidential, now."

"Perfectly. You will have all your information back when I tell you what change to make and you have my word that I will never make any further use of any of it."

The nuclear physicist stopped at the door. "Aren't you afraid I might tell someone you're not a numerologist?"

The numerologist shook his head. "Who would believe you, my friend? Even supposing you were willing to admit to anyone that you've been here."

On the twentieth, Marshall Zebatinsky was at the paint-peeling door, glancing sideways at the shop front with the little card up against the glass reading "Numerology," dimmed and scarcely legible through the dust. He peered in, almost hoping that someone else would be there already so that he might have an excuse to tear up the wavering intention in his mind and go home.

He had tried wiping the thing out of his mind several times. He could never stick at filling out the necessary data for long. It was embarrassing to work at it. He felt incredibly silly filling out the names of his friends, the cost of his house, whether his wife had had any miscarriages, if so, when. He abandoned it.

But he couldn't stick at stopping altogether either. He returned to it each evening.

It was the thought of the computer that did it, perhaps; the thought of the infernal gall of the little man pretending he had a computer. The temptation to call the bluff, see what would happen, proved irresistible after all.

He finally sent off the completed data by ordinary mail, putting on nine cents worth of stamps without weighing the letter. If it comes back, he thought, I'll call it off.

It didn't come back.

He looked into the shop now and it was empty. Zebatinsky had no choice but to enter. A bell tinkled.

The old numerologist emerged from a curtained door. "Yes? ——Ah, Dr. Zebatinsky."

"You remember me?" Zebatinsky tried to smile.

"Oh, yes."

"What's the verdict?"

The numerologist moved one gnarled hand over the other. "Before that, sir, there's a little——"

"A little matter of the fee?"

"I have already done the work, sir. I have earned the money."

Zebatinsky raised no objection. He was prepared to pay. If he had come this far, it would be silly to turn back just because of the money.

He counted out five ten-dollar bills and shoved them across the counter. "Well?"

The numerologist counted the bills again slowly, then pushed them into a cash drawer in his desk.

He said, "Your case was very interesting. I would advise you to change your name to Sebatinsky."

"Seba—— How do you spell that?"

"S-e-b-a-t-i-n-s-k-y."

Zebatinsky stared indignantly. "You mean change the initial? Change the *Z* to an *S*? That's all?"

"It's enough. As long as the change is adequate, a small change is safer than a big one."

"But how could the change affect anything?"

"How could any name?" asked the numerologist softly. "I can't say. It may, somehow, and that's all I can say. Remember, I don't guarantee results. Of course, if you do not wish to make the change, leave things as they are. But in that case, I cannot refund the fee."

Zebatinsky said, "What do I do? Just tell everyone to spell my name with an *S?*"

"If you want my advice, consult a lawyer. Change your name legally. He can advise you on little things."

"How long will it all take? I mean for things to improve for me?"

"How can I tell? Maybe never. Maybe tomorrow."

"But you saw the future. You *claim* you see it."

"Not as in a crystal ball. No, no, Dr. Zebatinsky. All I get out of my computer is a set of coded figures. I can recite probabilities to you, but I saw no pictures."

Zebatinsky turned and walked rapidly out of the place. Fifty dollars to change a letter! Fifty dollars for Sebatinsky! Lord, what a name! Worse than Zebatinsky.

It took another month before he could make up his mind to see a lawyer, and then he finally went.

He told himself he could always change the name back.

Give it a chance, he told himself.

Hell, there was no law against it.

Henry Brand looked through the folder page by page, with the practiced eye of one who had been in Security for fourteen years. He didn't have to read every word. Anything peculiar would have leaped off the paper and punched him in the eye.

He said, "The man looks clean to me." Henry Brand looked clean, too; with a soft, rounded paunch and a pink and freshly scrubbed complexion. It was as though continuous contact with all sorts of human failings, from possible ignorance to possible treason, had compelled him into frequent washings.

Lieutenant Albert Quincy, who had brought him the folder, was young and filled with the responsibility of being Security officer at the Hanford Station. "But why Sebatinsky?" he demanded.

"Why not?"

"Because it doesn't make sense. Zebatinsky is a foreign name and I'd change it myself if I had it, but I'd change it to something Anglo-Saxon. If Zebatinsky had done that, it would make sense and I wouldn't give it a second thought. But why change a Z to an S? I think we must find out what his reasons were."

"Has anyone asked him directly?"

"Certainly. In ordinary conversation, of course. I was careful to arrange that. He won't say anything more than that he's tired of being last in the alphabet."

"That could be, couldn't it, Lieutenant?"

"It could, but why not change his name to Sands or Smith,

if he wants an *S?* Or if he's that tired of *Z,* why not go the whole way and change it to an *A?* Why not a name like—uh—Aarons?"

"Not Anglo-Saxon enough," muttered Brand. Then, "But there's nothing to pin against the man. No matter how queer a name-change may be, that alone can't be used against anyone."

Lieutenant Quincy looked markedly unhappy.

Brand said, "Tell me, Lieutenant, there must be something specific that bothers you. Something in your mind; some theory; some gimmick. What is it?"

The lieutenant frowned. His light eyebrows drew together and his lips tightened. "Well, damn it, sir, the man's a Russian."

Brand said, "He's not that. He's a third-generation American."

"I mean his name's Russian."

Brand's face lost some of its deceptive softness. "No, Lieutenant, wrong again. Polish."

The lieutenant pushed his hands out impatiently, palms up. "Same thing."

Brand, whose mother's maiden name had been Wiszewski, snapped, "Don't tell that to a Pole, Lieutenant." ——Then, more thoughtfully, "Or to a Russian either, I suppose."

"What I'm trying to say, sir," said the lieutenant, reddening, "is that the Poles and Russians are both on the other side of the Curtain."

"We all know that."

"And Zebatinsky or Sebatinsky, whatever you want to call him, may have relatives there."

"He's third generation. He might have second cousins there, I suppose. So what?"

"Nothing in itself. Lots of people may have distant relatives there. But Zebatinsky changed his name."

"Go on."

"Maybe he's trying to distract attention. Maybe a second cousin over there is getting too famous and our Zebatinsky is afraid that the relationship may spoil his own chances of advancement."

"Changing his name won't do any good. He'd still be a second cousin."

"Sure, but he wouldn't feel as though he were shoving the relationship in our face."

"Have *you* ever heard of any Zebatinsky on the other side?"

"No, sir."

"Then he can't be too famous. How would our Zebatinsky know about him?"

"He might keep in touch with his own relatives. That would be suspicious under the circumstances, he being a nuclear physicist."

Methodically, Brand went through the folder again. "This is awfully thin, Lieutenant. It's thin enough to be completely invisible."

"Can you offer any other explanation, sir, of why he ought to change his name in just this way?"

"No, I can't. I admit that."

"Then I think, sir, we ought to investigate. We ought to look for any men named Zebatinsky on the other side and see if we can draw a connection." The lieutenant's voice rose a trifle as a new thought occurred to him. "He might be changing his name to withdraw attention from *them;* I mean to protect them."

"He's doing just the opposite, I think."

"He doesn't realize that, maybe, but protecting them could be his motive."

Brand sighed. "All right, we'll tackle the Zebatinsky angle. ——But if nothing turns up, Lieutenant, we drop the matter. Leave the folder with me."

When the information finally reached Brand, he had all but forgotten the lieutenant and his theories. His first thought on receiving data that included a list of seventeen biographies of seventeen Russian and Polish citizens, all named Zebatinsky, was: What the devil is this?

Then he remembered, swore mildly, and began reading.

It started on the American side. Marshall Zebatinsky (fingerprints) had been born in Buffalo, New York (date, hospital statistics). His father had been born in Buffalo as well, his mother in Oswego, New York. His paternal grandparents had both been born in Bialystok, Poland (date of entry into the United States, dates of citizenship, photographs).

The seventeen Russian and Polish citizens named Zebatinsky were all descendants of people who, some half century earlier, had lived in or near Bialystok. Presumably, they could be relatives, but this was not explicitly stated in any particular case. (Vital statistics in East Europe during the aftermath of World War I were kept poorly, if at all.)

Brand passed through the individual life histories of the current Zebatinsky men and women (amazing how thoroughly intelligence did its work; probably the Russians' was as thorough). He stopped at one and his smooth forehead sprouted lines as his eyebrows shot upward. He put that one to one side and went on. Eventually, he stacked everything but that one and returned it to its envelope. Staring at that one, he tapped a neatly kept fingernail on the desk.

With a certain reluctance, he went to call on Dr. Paul Kristow of the Atomic Energy Commission.

Dr. Kristow listened to the matter with a stony expression. He lifted a little finger occasionally to dab at his bulbous nose and remove a nonexistent speck. His hair was iron gray, thinning and cut short. He might as well have been bald.

He said, "No, I never heard of any Russian Zebatinsky. But then, I never heard of the American one either."

"Well," Brand scratched at his hairline over one temple and said slowly, "I don't think there's anything to this, but I don't like to drop it too soon. I have a young lieutenant on my tail and you know what they can be like. I don't want to do anything that will drive him to a Congressional committee. Besides, the fact is that one of the Russian Zebatinsky fellows, Mikhail Andreyevich Zebatinsky, *is* a nuclear physicist. Are you sure you never heard of him?"

"Mikhail Andreyevich Zebatinsky? No—— No, I never did. Not that that proves anything."

"I could say it was coincidence, but you know that would be piling it a trifle high. One Zebatinsky here and one Zebatinsky there, both nuclear physicists, and the one here suddenly changes his name to Sebatinsky, and goes around anxious about it, too. He won't allow misspelling. He says, emphatically, 'Spell my name with an *S*.' It all just fits well enough to make my spy-conscious lieutenant begin to look a little too good. ——And another peculiar thing is that the Russian Zebatinsky dropped out of sight just about a year ago."

Dr. Kristow said stolidly, "Executed!"

"He might have been. Ordinarily, I would even assume so, though the Russians are not more foolish than we are and don't kill any nuclear physicist they can avoid killing. The thing is there's another reason why a nuclear physicist, of all people, might suddenly disappear. I don't have to tell you."

"Crash research; top secret. I take it that's what you mean. Do you believe that's it?"

"Put it together with everything else, add in the lieutenant's intuition, and I just begin to wonder."

"Give me that biography." Dr. Kristow reached for the sheet of paper and read it over twice. He shook his head. Then he said, "I'll check this in *Nuclear Abstracts.*"

Nuclear Abstracts lined one wall of Dr. Kristow's study in neat little boxes, each filled with its squares of microfilm.

The A.E.C. man used his projector on the indices while Brand watched with what patience he could muster.

Dr. Kristow muttered, "A Mikhail Zebatinsky authored or co-authored half a dozen papers in the Soviet journals in the last half dozen years. We'll get out the abstracts and maybe we can make something out of it. I doubt it."

A selector flipped out the appropriate squares. Dr. Kristow lined them up, ran them through the projector, and by degrees an expression of odd intentness crossed his face. He said, "That's odd."

Brand said, "What's odd?"

Dr. Kristow sat back. "I'd rather not say just yet. Can you get me a list of other nuclear physicists who have dropped out of sight in the Soviet Union in the last year?"

"You mean you see something?"

"Not really. Not if I were just looking at any one of these papers. It's just that looking at all of them and knowing that this man may be on a crash research program and, on top of that, having you putting suspicions in my head——" He shrugged. "It's nothing."

Brand said earnestly, "I wish you'd say what's on your mind. We may as well be foolish about this together."

"If you feel that way—— It's just possible this man may have been inching toward gamma-ray reflection."

"And the significance?"

"If a reflecting shield against gamma rays could be devised, individual shelters could be built to protect against fallout. It's fallout that's the real danger, you know. A hydrogen bomb might destroy a city but the fallout could slow-kill the population over a strip thousands of miles long and hundreds wide."

Brand said quickly, "Are we doing any work on this?"

"No."

"And if they get it and we don't, they can destroy the United States *in toto* at the cost of, say, ten cities, after they have their shelter program completed."

"That's far in the future. ——And, what are we getting in a hurrah about? All this is built on one man changing one letter in his name."

"All right, I'm insane," said Brand. "But I don't leave the matter at this point. Not at *this* point. I'll get you your list of disappearing nuclear physicists if I have to go to Moscow to get it."

He got the list. They went through all the research papers authored by any of them. They called a full meeting of the Commission, then of the nuclear brains of the nation. Dr. Kristow walked out of an all night session, finally, part of which the President himself had attended.

Brand met him. Both looked haggard and in need of sleep.

Brand said, "Well?"

Kristow nodded. "Most agree. Some are doubtful even yet, but most agree."

"How about you? Are you sure?"

"I'm far from sure, but let me put it this way. It's easier to believe that the Soviets are working on a gamma-ray shield than to believe that all the data we've uncovered has no interconnection."

"Has it been decided that we're to go on shield research, too?"

"Yes." Kristow's hand went back over his short, bristly hair, making a dry, whispery sound. "We're going to give it everything we've got. Knowing the papers written by the men who disappeared, we can get right on their heels. We may even beat them to it. ———Of course, they'll find out we're working on it."

"Let them," said Brand. "Let them. It will keep them from attacking. I don't see any percentage in selling ten of our cities just to get ten of theirs—if we're both protected and they're too dumb to know that."

"But not too soon. We don't want them finding out *too* soon. What about the American Zebatinsky-Sebatinsky?"

Brand looked solemn and shook his head. "There's nothing to connect him with any of this even yet. Hell, we've *looked*. I agree with you, of course. He's in a sensitive spot where he is now and we can't afford to keep him there even if he's in the clear."

"We can't kick him out just like that, either, or the Russians will start wondering."

"Do you have any suggestions?"

They were walking down the long corridor toward the distant elevator in the emptiness of four in the morning.

Dr. Kristow said, "I've looked into his work. He's a good man, better than most, and not happy in his job, either. He hasn't the temperament for teamwork."

"So?"

"But he is the type for an academic job. If we can arrange to have a large university offer him a chair in physics, I think he would take it gladly. There would be enough nonsensitive areas to keep him occupied; we would be able to keep him in close view; *and* it would be a natural development. The Russians might not start scratching their heads. What do you think?"

Brand nodded. "It's an idea. Even sounds good. I'll put it up to the chief."

They stepped into the elevator and Brand allowed himself to wonder about it all. What an ending to what had started with one letter of a name.

Marshall Sebatinsky could hardly talk. He said to his wife, "I swear I don't see how this happened. I wouldn't have thought they knew me from a meson detector. ——Good Lord, Sophie, Associate Professor of Physics at Princeton. Think of it."

Sophie said, "Do you suppose it was your talk at the A.P.S. meetings?"

"I don't see how. It was a thoroughly uninspired paper once everyone in the divison was done hacking at it." He snapped his fingers. "It must have been Princeton that was investigating me. That's it. You know all those forms I've been filling out in the last six months; those interviews they wouldn't explain. Honestly, I was beginning to think I was under suspicion as a subversive. ——It was Princeton investigating me. They're thorough."

"Maybe it was your name," said Sophie. "I mean the change."

"Watch me now. My professional life will be my own finally. I'll make my mark. Once I have a chance to do my work without——" He stopped and turned to look at his wife. "My name! You mean the S."

"You didn't get the offer till after you changed your name, did you?"

"Not till long after. No, that part's just coincidence. I've told you before Sophie, it was just a case of throwing out fifty dollars to please you. Lord, what a fool I've felt all these months insisting on that stupid S."

Sophie was instantly on the defensive. "I didn't make you do it, Marshall. I suggested it but I didn't nag you about it. Don't say I did. Besides, it did turn out well. I'm sure it was the name that did this."

Sebatinsky smiled indulgently. "Now that's superstition."

"I don't care what you call it, but you're not changing your name back."

"Well, no, I suppose not. I've had so much trouble getting them to spell my name with an S, that the thought of making everyone move back is more than I want to face. Maybe I ought to change my name to Jones, eh?" He laughed almost hysterically.

But Sophie didn't. "You leave it alone."

"Oh, all right, I'm just joking. ——Tell you what. I'll step down to that old fellow's place one of these days and tell him everything worked out and slip him another tenner. Will that satisfy you?"

He was exuberant enough to do so the next week. He assumed no disguise this time. He wore his glasses and his ordinary suit and was minus a hat.

He was even humming as he approached the store front and stepped to one side to allow a weary, sour-faced woman to maneuver her twin baby carriage past.

He put his hand on the door handle and his thumb on the iron latch. The latch didn't give to his thumb's downward pressure. The door was locked.

The dusty, dim card with "Numerologist" on it was gone, now that he looked. Another sign, printed and beginning to yellow and curl with the sunlight, said "To let."

Sebatinsky shrugged. That was that. He had tried to do the right thing.

*

Haround, happily divested of corporeal excrescence, capered happily and his energy vortices glowed a dim purple over cubic hypermiles. He said, "Have I won? Have I won?"

Mestack was withdrawn, his vortices almost a sphere of light in hyperspace. "I haven't calculated it yet."

"Well, go ahead. You won't change the results any by taking a long time. ——Wowf, it's a relief to get back into clean energy. It took me a microcycle of time as a corporeal body; a nearly used-up one, too. But it was worth it to show *you*."

Mestack said, "All right, I admit you stopped a nuclear war on the planet."

"Is that or is that not a Class A effect?"

"It is a Class A effect. Of course it is."

"All right. Now check and see if I didn't get that Class A effect with a Class F stimulus. I changed one letter of one name."

"What?"

"Oh, never mind. It's all there. I've worked it out for you."

Mestack said reluctantly, "I yield. A Class F stimulus."

"Then I *win*. Admit it."

"Neither one of us will win when the Watchman gets a look at this."

Haround, who had been an elderly numerologist on Earth and was still somewhat unsettled with relief at no longer being one, said, "You weren't worried about that when you made the bet."

"I didn't think you'd be fool enough to go through with it."

"Heat-waste! Besides, why worry? The Watchman will never detect a Class F stimulus."

"Maybe not, but he'll detect a Class A effect. Those corporeals will still be around after a dozen microcycles. The Watchman will notice that."

"The trouble with you, Mestack, is that you don't want to pay off. You're stalling."

"I'll pay. But just wait till the Watchman finds out we've been working on an unassigned problem and made an unallowed-for change. Of course, if we——" He paused.

Haround said, "All right, we'll change it back. He'll never know."

There was a crafty glow to Mestack's brightening energy pattern. "You'll need another Class F stimulus if you expect him not to notice."

Haround hesitated. "I can do it."

"I doubt it."

"I could."

"Would you be willing to bet on that, too?" Jubilation was creeping into Mestack's radiations.

"Sure," said the goaded Haround. "I'll put those corporeals right back where they were and the Watchman will never know the difference."

Mestack followed through his advantage. "Suspend the first bet, then. Triple the stakes on the second."

The mounting eagerness of the gamble caught at Haround, too. "All right, I'm game. Triple the stakes."

"Done, then!"

"Done."

THE LAST QUESTION

THE LAST QUESTION was asked for the first time, half in jest, on May 21, 2061, at a time when humanity first stepped into the light. The question came about as a result of a five-dollar bet over highballs, and it happened this way:

Alexander Adell and Bertram Lupov were two of the faithful attendants of Multivac. As well as any human beings could, they knew what lay behind the cold, clicking, flashing face——miles and miles of face——of that giant computer. They had at least a vague notion of the general plan of relays and circuits that had long since grown past the point where any single human could possibly have a firm grasp of the whole.

Multivac was self-adjusting and self-correcting. It had to be, for nothing human could adjust and correct it quickly enough or even adequately enough. ——So Adell and Lupov attended the monstrous giant only lightly and superficially, yet as well as any men could. They fed it data, adjusted questions to its needs and translated the answers that were issued. Certainly they, and all others like them, were fully entitled to share in the glory that was Multivac's.

For decades, Multivac had helped design the ships and plot the trajectories that enabled man to reach the Moon, Mars, and Venus, but past that, Earth's poor resources could not support the ships. Too much energy was needed for the long trips. Earth exploited its coal and uranium with increasing efficiency, but there was only so much of both.

But slowly Multivac learned enough to answer deeper questions more fundamentally, and on May 14, 2061, what had been theory, became fact.

The energy of the sun was stored, converted, and utilized directly on a planet-wide scale. All Earth turned off its burning coal, its fissioning uranium, and flipped the switch that connected all of it to a small station, one mile in diameter, circling the Earth at half the distance of the Moon. All Earth ran by invisible beams of sunpower.

Seven days had not sufficed to dim the glory of it and Adell and Lupov finally managed to escape from the public function, and to meet in quiet where no one would think of looking for them, in the deserted underground chambers, where portions of the mighty buried body of Multivac showed. Unattended, idling, sorting data with contented lazy clickings, Multivac, too, had earned its vacation and the boys appreciated that. They had no intention, originally, of disturbing it.

They had brought a bottle with them, and their only concern at the moment was to relax in the company of each other and the bottle.

"It's amazing when you think of it," said Adell. His broad face had lines of weariness in it, and he stirred his drink slowly with a glass rod, watching the cubes of ice slur clumsily about. "All the energy we can possibly ever use for free. Enough energy, if we wanted to draw on it, to melt all Earth into a big drop of impure liquid iron, and still never miss the energy so used. All the energy we could ever use, forever and forever and forever."

Lupov cocked his head sideways. He had a trick of doing that when he wanted to be contrary, and he wanted to be contrary now, partly because he had had to carry the ice and glassware. "Not forever," he said.

"Oh, hell, just about forever. Till the sun runs down, Bert."

"That's not forever."

"All right, then. Billions and billions of years. Twenty billion, maybe. Are you satisfied?"

Lupov put his fingers through his thinning hair as though to reassure himself that some was still left and sipped gently at his own drink. "Twenty billion years isn't forever."

"Well, it will last our time, won't it?"

"So would the coal and uranium."

"All right, but now we can hook up each individual spaceship to the Solar Station, and it can go to Pluto and back a million times without ever worrying about fuel. You can't do *that* on coal and uranium. Ask Multivac, if you don't believe me."

"I don't have to ask Multivac. I know that."

"Then stop running down what Multivac's done for us," said Adell, blazing up, "It did all right."

"Who says it didn't? What I say is that a sun won't last forever. That's all I'm saying. We're safe for twenty billion years, but then what?" Lupov pointed a slightly shaky finger at the other. "And don't say we'll switch to another sun."

There was silence for a while. Adell put his glass to his lips only occasionally, and Lupov's eyes slowly closed. They rested.

Then Lupov's eyes snapped open. "You're thinking we'll switch to another sun when ours is done, aren't you?"

"I'm not thinking."

"Sure you are. You're weak on logic, that's the trouble with you. You're like the guy in the story who was caught in a sudden shower and who ran to a grove of trees and got under one. He wasn't worried, you see, because he figured when one tree got wet through, he would just get under another one."

"I get it," said Adell. "Don't shout. When the sun is done, the other stars will be gone, too."

"Darn right they will," muttered Lupov. "It all had a beginning in the original cosmic explosion, whatever that was, and it'll all have an end when all the stars run down. Some run down faster than others. Hell, the giants won't last a hundred million years. The sun will last twenty billion years and maybe the dwarfs will last a hundred billion for all the good they are. But just give us a trillion years and everything will be dark. Entropy has to increase to maximum, that's all."

"I know all about entropy," said Adell, standing on his dignity.

"The hell you do."

"I know as much as you do."

"Then you know everything's got to run down someday."

"All right. Who says they won't?"

"You did, you poor sap. You said we had all the energy we needed, forever. You said 'forever.' "

It was Adell's turn to be contrary. "Maybe we can build things up again someday," he said.

"Never."

"Why not? Someday."

"Never."

"Ask Multivac."

"*You* ask Multivac. I dare you. Five dollars says it can't be done."

Adell was just drunk enough to try, just sober enough to be able to phrase the necessary symbols and operations into a question which, in words, might have corresponded to this: Will mankind one day without the net expenditure of energy be able to restore the sun to its full youthfulness even after it had died of old age?

Or maybe it could be put more simply like this: How can the net amount of entropy of the universe be massively decreased?

Multivac fell dead and silent. The slow flashing of lights ceased, the distant sounds of clicking relays ended.

Then, just as the frightened technicians felt they could hold their breath no longer, there was a sudden springing to life of the teletype attached to that portion of Multivac. Five words were printed: INSUFFICIENT DATA FOR MEANINGFUL ANSWER.

"No bet," whispered Lupov. They left hurriedly.

By next morning, the two, plagued with throbbing head and cottony mouth, had forgotten the incident.

Jerrodd, Jerrodine, and Jerrodette I and II watched the starry picture in the visiplate change as the passage through hyperspace was completed in its non-time lapse. At once, the even powdering of stars gave way to the predominance of a single bright marble-disk, centered.

"That's X-23," said Jerrodd confidently. His thin hands clamped tightly behind his back and the knuckles whitened.

The little Jerrodettes, both girls, had experienced the hyperspace passage for the first time in their lives and were self-conscious over the momentary sensation of inside-outness. They buried their giggles and chased one another wildly about their mother, screaming, "We've reached X-23—we've reached X-23—we've——"

"Quiet, children," said Jerrodine sharply. "Are you sure, Jerrodd?"

"What is there to be but sure?" asked Jerrodd, glancing up at the bulge of featureless metal just under the ceiling. It ran the length of the room, disappearing through the wall at either end. It was as long as the ship.

Jerrodd scarcely knew a thing about the thick rod of metal except that it was called a Microvac, that one asked it questions if one wished; that if one did not it still had its task of guiding the ship to a preordered destination; of feeding on energies from the various Sub-galactic Power Stations; of computing the equations for the hyperspacial jumps.

Jerrodd and his family had only to wait and live in the comfortable residence quarters of the ship.

Someone had once told Jerrodd that the "ac" at the end of "Microvac" stood for "analog computer" in ancient English, but he was on the edge of forgetting even that.

Jerrodine's eyes were moist as she watched the visiplate. "I can't help it. I feel funny about leaving Earth."

"Why, for Pete's sake?" demanded Jerrodd. "We had nothing there. We'll have everything on X-23. You won't be alone. You won't be a pioneer. There are over a million people on the planet already. Good Lord, our great-grandchildren will be looking for new worlds because X-23 will be overcrowded." Then, after a reflective pause, "I tell you, it's a lucky thing the computers worked out interstellar travel the way the race is growing."

"I know, I know," said Jerrodine miserably.

Jerrodette I said promptly, "Our Microvac is the best Microvac in the world."

"I think so, too," said Jerrodd, tousling her hair.

It *was* a nice feeling to have a Microvac of your own and Jerrodd was glad he was part of his generation and no other. In his father's youth, the only computers had been tremendous machines taking up a hundred square miles of land. There was only one to a planet. Planetary ACs they were called. They had been growing in size steadily for a thousand years and then, all at once, came refinement. In place of transistors, had come molecular valves so that even the largest Planetary AC could be put into a space only half the volume of a spaceship.

Jerrodd felt uplifted, as he always did when he thought that his own personal Microvac was many times more complicated than the ancient and primitive Multivac that had first tamed the Sun, and almost as complicated as Earth's Planetary AC (the largest) that had first solved the problem of hyperspatial travel and had made trips to the stars possible.

"So many stars, so many planets," sighed Jerrodine, busy with her own thoughts. "I suppose families will be going out to new planets forever, the way we are now."

"Not forever," said Jerrodd, with a smile. "It will all stop someday, but not for billions of years. Many billions. Even the stars run down, you know. Entropy must increase."

"What's entropy, daddy?" shrilled Jerrodette II.

"Entropy, little sweet, is just a word which means the amount of running-down of the universe. Everything runs down, you know, like your little walkie-talkie robot, remember?"

"Can't you just put in a new power-unit, like with my robot?"

"The stars *are* the power-units, dear. Once they're gone, there are no more power-units."

Jerrodette I at once set up a howl. "Don't let them, daddy. Don't let the stars run down."

"Now look what you've done," whispered Jerrodine, exasperated.

"How was I to know it would frighten them?" Jerrodd whispered back.

"Ask the Microvac," wailed Jerrodette I. "Ask him how to turn the stars on again."

"Go ahead," said Jerrodine. "It will quiet them down." (Jerrodette II was beginning to cry, also.)

Jerrodd shrugged "Now, now, honeys. I'll ask Microvac. Don't worry, he'll tell us."

He asked the Microvac, adding quickly, "Print the answer."

Jerrodd cupped the strip of thin cellufilm and said cheerfully, "See now, the Microvac says it will take care of everything when the time comes so don't worry."

Jerrodine said, "And now, children, it's time for bed. We'll be in our new home soon."

Jerrodd read the words on the cellufilm again before destroying it: INSUFFICIENT DATA FOR MEANINGFUL ANSWER.

He shrugged and looked at the visiplate. X-23 was just ahead.

VJ-23X of Lameth stared into the black depths of the three-dimensional, small-scale map of the Galaxy and said, "Are we ridiculous, I wonder, in being so concerned about the matter?"

MQ-17J of Nicron shook his head. "I think not. You know the Galaxy will be filled in five years at the present rate of expansion."

Both seemed in their early twenties, both were tall and perfectly formed.

"Still," said VJ-23X, "I hesitate to submit a pessimistic report to the Galactic Council."

"I wouldn't consider any other kind of report. Stir them up a bit. We've got to stir them up."

VJ-23X sighed. "Space is infinite. A hundred billion Galaxies are there for the taking. More."

"A hundred billion is *not* infinite and it's getting less infinite all the time. Consider! Twenty thousand years ago, mankind first solved the problem of utilizing stellar energy, and a few centuries later, interstellar travel became possible. It took mankind a million years to fill one small world and then only fifteen thousand years to fill the rest of the Galaxy. Now the population doubles every ten years——"

VJ-23X interrupted. "We can thank immortality for that."

"Very well. Immortality exists and we have to take it into account. I admit it has its seamy side, this immortality. The Galactic AC has solved many problems for us, but in solving the problem of preventing old age and death, it has undone all its other solutions."

"Yet you wouldn't want to abandon life, I suppose."

"Not at all," snapped MQ-17J, softening it at once to, "Not yet. I'm by no means old enough. How old are you?"

"Two hundred twenty-three. And you?"

"I'm still under two hundred. ——But to get back to my point. Population doubles every ten years. Once this Galaxy is filled, we'll have filled another in ten years. Another ten years and we'll have filled two more. Another decade, four more. In a hundred years, we'll have filled a thousand Galaxies. In a thousand years, a million Galaxies. In ten thousand years, the entire known Universe. Then what?"

VJ-23X said, "As a side issue, there's a problem of transportation. I wonder how many sunpower units it will take to move Galaxies of individuals from one Galaxy to the next."

"A very good point. Already, mankind consumes two sunpower units per year."

"Most of it's wasted. After all, our own Galaxy alone pours out a thousand sunpower units a year and we only use two of those."

"Granted, but even with a hundred per cent efficiency, we only stave off the end. Our energy requirements are going up in a geometric progression even faster than our population. We'll run out of energy even sooner than we run out of Galaxies. A good point. A very good point."

"We'll just have to build new stars out of interstellar gas."

"Or out of dissipated heat?" asked MQ-17J, sarcastically.

"There may be some way to reverse entropy. We ought to ask the Galactic AC."

VJ-23X was not really serious, but MQ-17J pulled out his AC-contact from his pocket and placed it on the table before him.

"I've half a mind to," he said. "It's something the human race will have to face someday."

He stared somberly at his small AC-contact. It was only two inches cubed and nothing in itself, but it was connected through hyperspace with the great Galactic AC that served all mankind. Hyperspace considered, it was an integral part of the Galactic AC.

MQ-17J paused to wonder if someday in his immortal life he would get to see the Galactic AC. It was on a little world of its own, a spider webbing of force-beams holding the matter within which surges of sub-mesons took the place of the old clumsy molecular valves. Yet despite its sub-etheric workings, the Galactic AC was known to be a full thousand feet across.

MQ-17J asked suddenly of his AC-contact, "Can entropy ever be reversed?"

VJ-23X looked startled and said at once, "Oh, say, I didn't really mean to have you ask that."

"Why not?"

"We both know entropy can't be reversed. You can't turn smoke and ash back into a tree."

"Do you have trees on your world?" asked MQ-17J.

The sound of the Galactic AC startled them into silence. Its voice came thin and beautiful out of the small AC-contact on the desk. It said: THERE IS INSUFFICIENT DATA FOR A MEANINGFUL ANSWER.

VJ-23X said, "See!"

The two men thereupon returned to the question of the report they were to make to the Galactic Council.

Zee Prime's mind spanned the new Galaxy with a faint interest in the countless twists of stars that powdered it. He had never seen this one before. Would he ever see them all? So many of them, each with its load of humanity. ——But a load that was almost a dead weight. More and more, the real essence of men was to be found out here, in space.

Minds, not bodies! The immortal bodies remained back on the planets, in suspension over the eons. Sometimes they roused for material activity but that was growing rarer. Few new individuals were coming into existence to join the incredibly mighty throng, but what matter? There was little room in the Universe for new individuals.

Zee Prime was roused out of his reverie upon coming across the wispy tendrils of another mind.

"I am Zee Prime," said Zee Prime. "And you?"

"I am Dee Sub Wun. Your Galaxy?"

"We call it only the Galaxy. And you?"

"We call ours the same. All men call their Galaxy their Galaxy and nothing more. Why not?"

"True. Since all Galaxies are the same."

"Not all Galaxies. On one particular Galaxy the race of man must have originated. That makes it different."

Zee Prime said, "On which one?"

"I cannot say. The Universal AC would know."

"Shall we ask him? I am suddenly curious."

Zee Prime's perceptions broadened until the Galaxies themselves shrank and became a new, more diffuse powdering on a much larger background. So many hundreds of billions of them, all with their immortal beings, all carrying their load of intelligences with minds that drifted freely through space. And yet one of them was unique among them all in being the original Galaxy. One of them had, in its vague and distant past, a period when it was the only Galaxy populated by man.

Zee Prime was consumed with curiosity to see this Galaxy and he called out: "Universal AC! On which Galaxy did mankind originate?"

The Universal AC heard, for on every world and throughout space, it had its receptors ready, and each receptor lead through hyperspace to some unknown point where the Universal AC kept itself aloof.

Zee Prime knew of only one man whose thoughts had penetrated within sensing distance of Universal AC, and he reported only a shining globe, two feet across, difficult to see.

"But how can that be all of Universal AC?" Zee Prime had asked.

"Most of it," had been the answer, "is in hyperspace. In what form it is there I cannot imagine."

Nor could anyone, for the day had long since passed, Zee Prime knew, when any man had any part of the making of a Universal AC. Each Universal AC designed and constructed its successor. Each, during its existence of a million years or more accumulated the necessary data to build a better and more intricate, more capable successor in which its own store of data and individuality would be submerged.

The Universal AC interrupted Zee Prime's wandering thoughts, not with words, but with guidance. Zee Prime's mentality was guided into the dim sea of Galaxies and one in particular enlarged into stars.

A thought came, infinitely distant, but infinitely clear. "THIS IS THE ORIGINAL GALAXY OF MAN."

But it was the same after all, the same as any other, and Zee Prime stifled his disappointment.

Dee Sub Wun, whose mind had accompanied the other, said suddenly, "And is one of these stars the original star of Man?"

The Universal AC said, "MAN'S ORIGINAL STAR HAS GONE NOVA. IT IS A WHITE DWARF."

"Did the men upon it die?" asked Zee Prime, startled and without thinking.

The Universal AC said, "A NEW WORLD, AS IN SUCH CASES WAS CONSTRUCTED FOR THEIR PHYSICAL BODIES IN TIME."

"Yes, of course," said Zee Prime, but a sense of loss overwhelmed him even so. His mind released its hold on the original Galaxy of Man, let it spring back and lose itself among the blurred pin points. He never wanted to see it again.

Dee Sub Wun said, "What is wrong?"

"The stars are dying. The original star is dead."

"They must all die. Why not?"

"But when all energy is gone, our bodies will finally die, and you and I with them."

"It will take billions of years."

"I do not wish it to happen even after billions of years. Universal AC! How may stars be kept from dying?"

Dee Sub Wun said in amusement, "You're asking how entropy might be reversed in direction."

And the Universal AC answered: "THERE IS AS YET INSUFFICIENT DATA FOR A MEANINGFUL ANSWER."

Zee Prime's thoughts fled back to his own Galaxy. He gave no further thought to Dee Sub Wun, whose body might be waiting on a Galaxy a trillion light-years away, or on the star next to Zee Prime's own. It didn't matter.

Unhappily, Zee Prime began collecting interstellar hydrogen out of which to build a small star of his own. If the stars must someday die, at least some could yet be built.

Man considered with himself, for in a way, Man, mentally, was one. He consisted of a trillion, trillion, trillion ageless bodies, each in its place, each resting quiet and incorruptible, each cared for by perfect automatons, equally incorruptible, while the minds of all the bodies freely melted one into the other, indistinguishable.

Man said, "The Universe is dying."

Man looked about at the dimming Galaxies. The giant stars, spendthrifts, were gone long ago, back in the dimmest of the dim far past. Almost all stars were white dwarfs, fading to the end.

New stars had been built of the dust between the stars, some by natural processes, some by Man himself, and those were going, too. White dwarfs might yet be crashed together and of the mighty forces so released, new stars built, but only one star for every thousand white dwarfs destroyed, and those would come to an end, too.

Man said, "Carefully husbanded, as directed by the Cosmic AC, the energy that is even yet left in all the Universe will last for billions of years."

"But even so," said Man, "eventually it will all come to an end. However it may be husbanded, however stretched out, the energy once expended is gone and cannot be restored. Entropy must increase forever to the maximum."

Man said, "Can entropy not be reversed? Let us ask the Cosmic AC."

The Cosmic AC surrounded them but not in space. Not a fragment of it was in space. It was in hyperspace and made of something that was neither matter nor energy. The question of its size and nature no longer had meaning in any terms that Man could comprehend.

"Cosmic AC," said Man, "how may entropy be reversed?"

The Cosmic AC said, "THERE IS AS YET INSUFFICIENT DATA FOR A MEANINGFUL ANSWER."

Man said, "Collect additional data."

The Cosmic AC said, "I WILL DO SO. I HAVE BEEN DOING SO FOR A HUNDRED BILLION YEARS. MY PREDECESSORS AND I HAVE BEEN ASKED THIS QUESTION MANY TIMES. ALL THE DATA I HAVE REMAINS INSUFFICIENT."

"Will there come a time," said Man, "when data will be sufficient or is the problem insoluble in all conceivable circumstances?"

The Cosmic AC said, "NO PROBLEM IS INSOLUBLE IN ALL CONCEIVABLE CIRCUMSTANCES."

Man said, "When will you have enough data to answer the question?"

The Cosmic AC said, "THERE IS AS YET INSUFFICIENT DATA FOR A MEANINGFUL ANSWER."

"Will you keep working on it?" asked Man.

The Cosmic AC said, "I WILL."

Man said, "We shall wait."

The stars and Galaxies died and snuffed out, and space grew black after ten trillion years of running down.

One by one Man fused with AC, each physical body losing its mental identity in a manner that was somehow not a loss but a gain.

Man's last mind paused before fusion, looking over a space that included nothing but the dregs of one last dark star and nothing besides but incredibly thin matter, agitated randomly by the tag ends of heat wearing out, asymptotically, to the absolute zero.

Man said, "AC, is this the end? Can this chaos not be reversed into the Universe once more? Can that not be done?"

AC said, "THERE IS AS YET INSUFFICIENT DATA FOR A MEANINGFUL ANSWER."

Man's last mind fused and only AC existed—and that in hyperspace.

Matter and energy had ended and with it space and time. Even AC existed only for the sake of the one last question that it had never answered from the time a half-drunken computer ten trillion years before had asked the question of a computer that was to AC far less than was a man to Man.

All other questions had been answered, and until this last question was answered also, AC might not release his consciousness.

All collected data had come to a final end. Nothing was left to be collected.

But all collected data had yet to be completely correlated and put together in all possible relationships.

A timeless interval was spent in doing that.

And it came to pass that AC learned how to reverse the direction of entropy.

But there was now no man to whom AC might give the answer of the last question. No matter. The answer—by demonstration—would take care of that, too.

For another timeless interval, AC thought how best to do this. Carefully, AC organized the program.

The consciousness of AC encompassed all of what had once been a Universe and brooded over what was now Chaos. Step by step, it must be done.

And AC said, "LET THERE BE LIGHT!"

And there was light——

THE UGLY LITTLE BOY

EDITH FELLOWES smoothed her working smock as she always did before opening the elaborately locked door and stepping across the invisible dividing line between the *is* and the *is not*. She carried her notebook and her pen although she no longer took notes except when she felt the absolute need for some report.

This time she also carried a suitcase. ("Games for the boy," she had said, smiling, to the guard—who had long since stopped even thinking of questioning her and who waved her on.)

And, as always, the ugly little boy knew that she had entered and came running to her, crying, "Miss Fellowes—— Miss Fellowes——" in his soft, slurring way.

"Timmie," she said, and passed her hand over the shaggy, brown hair on his misshapen little head. "What's wrong?"

He said, "Will Jerry be back to play again? I'm sorry about what happened."

"Never mind that now, Timmie. Is that why you've been crying?"

He looked away. "Not just about that, Miss Fellowes. I dreamed again."

Copyright 1958, by Galaxy Publishing Corporation (first appeared in Galaxy Magazine, September 1958. Original title: Lastborn).

"The same dream?" Miss Fellowes' lips set. Of course, the Jerry affair would bring back the dream.

He nodded. His too large teeth showed as he tried to smile and the lips of his forward-thrusting mouth stretched wide. "When will I be big enough to go out there, Miss Fellowes?"

"Soon," she said softly, feeling her heart break. "Soon."

Miss Fellowes let him take her hand and enjoyed the warm touch of the thick dry skin of his palm. He led her through the three rooms that made up the whole of Stasis Section One—comfortable enough, yes, but an eternal prison for the ugly little boy all the seven (was it seven?) years of his life.

He led her to the one window, looking out onto a scrubby woodland section of the world of *is* (now hidden by night), where a fence and painted instructions allowed no men to wander without permission.

He pressed his nose against the window. "Out there, Miss Fellowes?"

"Better places. Nicer places," she said sadly as she looked at his poor little imprisoned face outlined in profile against the window. The forehead retreated flatly and his hair lay down in tufts upon it. The back of his skull bulged and seemed to make the head overheavy so that it sagged and bent forward, forcing the whole body into a stoop. Already, bony ridges were beginning to bulge the skin above his eyes. His wide mouth thrust forward more prominently than did his wide and flattened nose and he had no chin to speak of, only a jawbone that curved smoothly down and back. He was small for his years and his stumpy legs were bowed.

He was a very ugly little boy and Edith Fellowes loved him dearly.

Her own face was behind his line of vision, so she allowed her lips the luxury of a tremor.

They would *not* kill him. She would do anything to prevent it. Anything. She opened the suitcase and began taking out the clothes it contained.

Edith Fellowes had crossed the threshold of Stasis, Inc. for the first time just a little over three years before. She hadn't, at that time, the slightest idea as to what Stasis meant or what the place did. No one did then, except those who worked there. In fact, it was only the day after she arrived that the news broke upon the world.

At the time, it was just that they had advertised for a woman with knowledge of physiology, experience with clinical chemistry, and a love for children. Edith Fellowes had been a nurse in a maternity ward and believed she fulfilled those qualifications.

Gerald Hoskins, whose name plate on the desk included a Ph.D. after the name, scratched his cheek with his thumb and looked at her steadily.

Miss Fellowes automatically stiffened and felt her face (with its slightly asymmetric nose and its a-trifle-too-heavy eyebrows) twitch.

He's no dreamboat himself, she thought resentfully. He's getting fat and bald and he's got a sullen mouth. ——But the salary mentioned had been considerably higher than she had expected, so she waited.

Hoskins said, "Now do you really love children?"

"I wouldn't say I did if I didn't."

"Or do you just love pretty children? Nice chubby children with cute little button-noses and gurgly ways?"

Miss Fellowes said, "Children are children, Dr. Hoskins, and the ones that aren't pretty are just the ones who may happen to need help most."

"Then suppose we take you on——"

"You mean you're offering me the job now?"

He smiled briefly, and for a moment, his broad face had an absentminded charm about it. He said, "I make quick decisions. So far the offer is tentative, however. I may make as quick a decision to let you go. Are you ready to take the chance?"

Miss Fellowes clutched at her purse and calculated just as swiftly as she could, then ignored calculations and followed impulse. "All right."

"Fine. We're going to form the Stasis tonight and I think you had better be there to take over at once. That will be at 8 P.M. and I'd appreciate it if you could be here at 7:30."

"But what——"

"Fine. Fine. That will be all now." On signal, a smiling secretary came in to usher her out.

Miss Fellowes stared back at Dr. Hoskins' closed door for a moment. What was Stasis? What had this large barn of a building—with its badged employees, its makeshift corridors, and its unmistakable air of engineering—to do with children?

She wondered if she should go back that evening or stay away and teach that arrogant man a lesson. But she knew she would be back if only out of sheer frustration. She would have to find out about the children.

She came back at 7:30 and did not have to announce herself. One after another, men and women seemed to know her and to know her function. She found herself all but placed on skids as she was moved inward.

Dr. Hoskins was there, but he only looked at her distantly and murmured, "Miss Fellowes."

He did not even suggest that she take a seat, but she drew one calmly up to the railing and sat down.

They were on a balcony, looking down into a large pit, filled with instruments that looked like a cross between the control panel of a spaceship and the working face of a computer. On one side were partitions that seemed to make up an unceilinged apartment, a giant dollhouse into the rooms of which she could look from above.

She could see an electronic cooker and a freeze-space unit in one room and a washroom arrangement off another. And surely the object she made out in another room could only be part of a bed, a small bed.

Hoskins was speaking to another man and, with Miss Fellowes, they made up the total occupancy of the balcony. Hoskins did not offer to introduce the other man, and Miss Fellowes eyed him surreptitiously. He was thin and quite fine-looking in a middle-aged way. He had a small mustache and keen eyes that seemed to busy themselves with everything.

He was saying, "I won't pretend for one moment that I understand all this, Dr. Hoskins; I mean, except as a layman, a reasonably intelligent layman, may be expected to understand it. Still, if there's one part I understand less than another, it's this matter of selectivity. You can only reach out so far; that seems sensible; things get dimmer the further you go; it takes more energy. ——But then, you can only reach out so near. That's the puzzling part."

"I can make it seem less paradoxical, Deveney, if you will allow me to use an analogy."

(Miss Fellowes placed the new man the moment she heard his name, and despite herself was impressed. This was obviously Candide Deveney, the science writer of the Telenews, who was notoriously at the scene of every major scientific break-through. She even recognized his face as one she saw on the news-plate when the landing on Mars had been announced. ——So Dr. Hoskins must have something important here.

"By all means use an analogy," said Deveney ruefully, "if you think it will help."

"Well, then, you can't read a book with ordinary-sized print if it is held six feet from your eyes, but you can read it if you hold it one foot from your eyes. So far, the closer the better. If you bring the book to within one inch of your eyes, however, you've lost it again. There is such a thing as being too close, you see."

"Hmm," said Deveney.

"Or take another example. Your right shoulder is about thirty inches from the tip of your right forefinger and you can place your right forefinger on your right shoulder. Your right elbow is only half the distance from the tip of your right forefinger; it should by all ordinary logic be easier to reach, and yet you cannot place your right finger on your right elbow. Again, there is such a thing as being too close."

Deveney said, "May I use these analogies in my story?"

"Well, of course. Only too glad. I've been waiting long enough for someone like you to have a story. I'll give you anything else you want. It is time, finally, that we want the world looking over our shoulder. They'll see something."

(Miss Fellowes found herself admiring his calm certainty despite herself. There was strength there.)

Deveney said, "How far out will you reach?"

"Forty thousand years."

Miss Fellowes drew in her breath sharply.

Years?

There was tension in the air. The men at the controls scarcely moved. One man at a microphone spoke into it in a soft monotone, in short phrases that made no sense to Miss Fellowes.

Deveney, leaning over the balcony railing with an intent stare, said, "Will we see anything, Dr. Hoskins?"

"What? No. Nothing till the job is done. We detect indirectly, something on the principle of radar, except that we use mesons rather than radiation. Mesons reach backward under the proper conditions. Some are reflected and we must analyze the reflections."

"That sounds difficult."

Hoskins smiled again, briefly as always. "It is the end product of fifty years of research; forty years of it before I entered the field. ——Yes, it's difficult."

The man at the microphone raised one hand.

Hoskins said, "We've had the fix on one particular moment in time for weeks; breaking it, remaking it after calculating our own movements in time; making certain that we could handle time-flow with sufficient precision. This must work now."

But his forehead glistened.

Edith Fellowes found herself out of her seat and at the balcony railing, but there was nothing to see.

The man at the microphone said quietly, "Now."

There was a space of silence sufficient for one breath and then the sound of a terrified little boy's scream from the dollhouse rooms. Terror! Piercing terror!

Miss Fellowes' head twisted in the direction of the cry. A child was involved. She had forgotten.

And Hoskins' fist pounded on the railing and he said in a tight voice, trembling with triumph, *"Did* it."

Miss Fellowes was urged down the short, spiral flight of steps by the hard press of Hoskins' palm between her shoulder blades. He did not speak to her.

The men who had been at the controls were standing about now, smiling, smoking, watching the three as they entered on the main floor. A very soft buzz sounded from the direction of the doll-house.

Hoskins said to Deveney, "It's perfectly safe to enter Stasis. I've done it a thousand times. There's a queer sensation which is momentary and means nothing."

He stepped through an open door in mute demonstration, and Deveney, smiling stiffly and drawing an obviously deep breath, followed him.

Hoskins said, "Miss Fellowes! Please!" He crooked his forefinger impatiently.

Miss Fellowes nodded and stepped stiffly through. It was as though a ripple went through her, an internal tickle.

But once inside all seemed normal. There was the smell of the fresh wood of the dollhouse and—of—of soil somehow.

There was silence now, no voice at least, but there was the dry shuffling of feet, a scrabbling as of a hand over wood—then a low moan.

"Where is it?" asked Miss Fellowes in distress. Didn't these fool men *care?*

The boy was in the bedroom; at least the room with the bed in it.

It was standing naked, with its small, dirt-smeared chest heaving raggedly. A bushel of dirt and coarse grass spread over the floor at his bare brown feet. The smell of soil came from it and a touch of something fetid.

Hoskins followed her horrified glance and said with annoyance, "You can't pluck a boy cleanly out of time, Miss Fellowes. We had to take some of the surroundings with it for safety. Or would you have preferred to have it arrive here minus a leg or with only half a head?"

"Please!" said Miss Fellowes, in an agony of revulsion. "Are we just to stand here? The poor child is frightened. And it's *filthy.*"

She was quite correct. It was smeared with encrusted dirt and grease and had a scratch on its thigh that looked red and sore.

As Hoskins approached him, the boy, who seemed to be something over three years in age, hunched low and backed away rapidly. He lifted his upper lip and snarled in a hissing fashion like a cat. With a rapid gesture, Hoskins seized both the child's arms and lifted him, writhing and screaming, from the floor.

Miss Fellowes said, "Hold him, now. He needs a warm bath first. He needs to be cleaned. Have you the equipment? If so, have it brought here, and I'll need to have help in handling him just at first. Then, too, for heaven's sake, have all this trash and filth removed."

She was giving the orders now and she felt perfectly good about that. And because now she was an efficient nurse, rather than a confused spectator, she looked at the child with a clinical eye— and hesitated for one shocked moment. She saw past the dirt and shrieking, past the thrashing of limbs and useless twisting. She saw the boy himself.

It was the ugliest little boy she had ever seen. It was horribly ugly from misshapen head to bandy legs.

She got the boy cleaned with three men helping her and with others milling about in their efforts to clean the room. She worked in silence and with a sense of outrage, annoyed by the continued strugglings and outcries of the boy and by the undignified drenchings of soapy water to which she was subjected.

Dr. Hoskins had hinted that the child would not be pretty, but that was far from stating that it would be repulsively deformed. And there was a stench about the boy that soap and water was only alleviating little by little.

She had the strong desire to thrust the boy, soaped as he was, into Hoskins' arms and walk out; but there was the pride of profession. She had accepted an assignment after all. ——And there would be the look in his eyes. A cold look that would read: Only pretty children, Miss Fellowes?

He was standing apart from them, watching coolly from a distance with a half-smile on his face when he caught her eyes, as though amused at her outrage.

She decided she would wait a while before quitting. To do so now would only demean her.

Then, when the boy was a bearable pink and smelled of scented soap, she felt better anyway. His cries changed to whimpers of exhaustion as he watched carefully, eyes moving in quick frightened suspicion from one to another of those in the room. His cleanness accentuated his thin nakedness as he shivered with cold after his bath.

Miss Fellowes said sharply, "Bring me a nightgown for the child!"

A nightgown appeared at once. It was as though everything were ready and yet nothing were ready unless she gave orders; as though they were deliberately leaving this in her charge without help, to test her.

The newsman, Deveney, approached and said, "I'll hold him, Miss. You won't get it on yourself."

"Thank you," said Miss Fellowes. And it was a battle indeed, but the nightgown went on, and when the boy made as though to rip it off, she slapped his hand sharply.

The boy reddened, but did not cry. He stared at her and the splayed fingers of one hand moved slowly across the flannel of the nightgown, feeling the strangeness of it.

Miss Fellowes thought desperately: Well, what next?

Everyone seemed in suspended animation, waiting for her—even the ugly little boy.

Miss Fellowes said sharply, "Have you provided food? Milk?"

They had. A mobile unit was wheeled in, with its refrigeration compartment containing three quarts of milk, with a warming unit and a supply of fortifications in the form of vitamin drops, copper-cobalt-iron syrup and others she had no time to be concerned with. There was a variety of canned self-warming junior foods.

She used milk, simply milk, to begin with. The radar unit heated the milk to a set temperature in a matter of ten seconds and clicked off, and she put some in a saucer. She had a certainty about the boy's savagery. He wouldn't know how to handle a cup.

Miss Fellowes nodded and said to the boy, "Drink. Drink." She made a gesture as though to raise the milk to her mouth. The boy's eyes followed but he made no move.

Suddenly, the nurse resorted to direct measures. She seized the boy's upper arm in one hand and dipped the other in the milk. She dashed the milk across his lips, so that it dripped down cheeks and receding chin.

For a moment, the child uttered a high-pitched cry, then his tongue moved over his wetted lips. Miss Fellowes stepped back.

The boy approached the saucer, bent toward it, then looked up and behind sharply as though expecting a crouching enemy; bent again and licked at the milk eagerly, like a cat. He made a slurping noise. He did not use his hands to lift the saucer.

Miss Fellowes allowed a bit of the revulsion she felt show on her face. She couldn't help it.

Deveney caught that, perhaps. He said, "Does the nurse know, Dr. Hoskins?"

"Know what?" demanded Miss Fellowes.

Deveney hesitated, but Hoskins (again that look of detached amusement on his face) said, "Well, tell her."

Deveney addressed Miss Fellowes. "You may not suspect it, Miss, but you happen to be the first civilized woman in history ever to be taking care of a Neanderthal youngster."

She turned on Hoskins with a kind of controlled ferocity. "You might have told me, Doctor."

"Why? What difference does it make?"

"You said a child."

"Isn't that a child? Have you ever had a puppy or a kitten, Miss Fellowes? Are those closer to the human? If that were a baby chimpanzee, would you be repelled? You're a nurse, Miss Fellowes. Your record places you in a maternity ward for three years. Have you ever refused to take care of a deformed infant?"

Miss Fellowes felt her case slipping away. She said, with much less decision, "You might have told me."

"And you would have refused the position? Well, do you refuse it now?" He gazed at her coolly, while Deveney watched from the other side of the room, and the Neanderthal child, having finished the milk and licked the plate, looked up at her with a wet face and wide, longing eyes.

The boy pointed to the milk and suddenly burst out in a short series of sounds repeated over and over; sounds made up of gutturals and elaborate tongue-clickings.

Miss Fellowes said, in surprise, "Why, he talks."

"Of course," said Hoskins. "Homo neanderthalensis is not a truly separate species, but rather a subspecies of Homo sapiens.

Why shouldn't he talk? He's probably asking for more milk."

Automatically, Miss Fellowes reached for the bottle of milk, but Hoskins seized her wrist. "Now, Miss Fellowes, before we go any further, are you staying on the job?"

Miss Fellowes shook free in annoyance, "Won't you feed him if I don't? I'll stay with him—for a while."

She poured the milk.

Hoskins said, "We are going to leave you with the boy, Miss Fellowes. This is the only door to Stasis Number One and it is elaborately locked and guarded. I'll want you to learn the details of the lock which will, of course, be keyed to your fingerprints as they are already keyed to mine. The spaces overhead" (he looked upward to the open ceilings of the dollhouse) "are also guarded and we will be warned if anything untoward takes place in here."

Miss Fellowes said indignantly, "You mean I'll be under view." She thought suddenly of her own survey of the room interiors from the balcony.

"No, no," said Hoskins seriously, "your privacy will be respected completely. The view will consist of electronic symbolism only, which only a computer will deal with. Now you will stay with him tonight, Miss Fellowes, and every night until further notice. You will be relieved during the day according to some schedule you will find convenient. We will allow you to arrange that."

Miss Fellowes looked about the dollhouse with a puzzled expression. "But why all this, Dr. Hoskins? Is the boy dangerous?"

"It's a matter of energy, Miss Fellowes. He must never be allowed to leave these rooms. Never. Not for an instant. Not for any reason. Not to save his life. Not even to save *your* life, Miss Fellowes. Is that clear?"

Miss Fellowes raised her chin. "I understand the orders, Dr. Hoskins, and the nursing profession is accustomed to placing its duties ahead of self-preservation."

"Good. You can always signal if you need anyone." And the two men left.

Miss Fellowes turned to the boy. He was watching her and there was still milk in the saucer. Laboriously, she tried to show him how to lift the saucer and place it to his lips. He resisted, but let her touch him without crying out.

Always, his frightened eyes were on her, watching, watching for the one false move. She found herself soothing him, trying to move her hand very slowly toward his hair, letting him see it every inch of the way, see there was no harm in it.

And she succeeded in stroking his hair for an instant.

She said, "I'm going to have to show you how to use the bathroom. Do you think you can learn?"

She spoke quietly, kindly, knowing he would not understand the words but hoping he would respond to the calmness of the tone.

The boy launched into a clicking phrase again.

She said, "May I take your hand?"

She held out hers and the boy looked at it. She left it outstretched and waited. The boy's own hand crept forward toward hers.

"That's right," she said.

It approached within an inch of hers and then the boy's courage failed him. He snatched it back.

"Well," said Miss Fellowes calmly, "we'll try again later. Would you like to sit down here?" She patted the mattress of the bed.

The hours passed slowly and progress was minute. She did not succeed either with bathroom or with the bed. In fact, after the child had given unmistakable signs of sleepiness he lay down on the bare ground and then, with a quick movement, rolled beneath the bed.

She bent to look at him and his eyes gleamed out at her as he tongue-clicked at her.

"All right," she said, "if you feel safer there, you sleep there."

She closed the door to the bedroom and retired to the cot that had been placed for her use in the largest room. At her insistence, a make-shift canopy had been stretched over it. She thought: Those stupid men will have to place a mirror in this room and a larger chest of drawers and a separate washroom if they expect me to spend nights here.

It was difficult to sleep. She found herself straining to hear possible sounds in the next room. He couldn't get out, could he? The walls were sheer and impossibly high but suppose the child could climb like a monkey? Well, Hoskins said there were observational devices watching through the ceiling.

Suddenly she thought: Can he be dangerous? Physically dangerous?

Surely, Hoskins couldn't have meant that. Surely, he would not have left her here alone, if——

She tried to laugh at herself. He was only a three- or four-year-old child. Still, she had not succeeded in cutting his nails. If he should attack her with nails and teeth while she slept——

Her breath came quickly. Oh, ridiculous, and yet——

She listened with painful attentiveness, and this time she heard the sound.

The boy was crying.

Not shrieking in fear or anger; not yelling or screaming. It was crying softly, and the cry was the heartbroken sobbing of a lonely, lonely child.

For the first time, Miss Fellowes thought with a pang: Poor thing!

Of course, it was a child; what did the shape of its head matter? It was a child that had been orphaned as no child had ever been orphaned before. Not only its mother and father were gone, but all its species. Snatched callously out of time, it was now the only creature of its kind in the world. The last. The only.

She felt pity for it strengthen, and with it shame at her own callousness. Tucking her own nightgown carefully about her calves (incongruously, she thought: Tomorrow I'll have to bring in a bathrobe) she got out of bed and went into the boy's room.

"Little boy," she called in a whisper. "Little boy."

She was about to reach under the bed, but she thought of a possible bite and did not. Instead, she turned on the night light and moved the bed.

The poor thing was huddled in the corner, knees up against his chin, looking up at her with blurred and apprehensive eyes.

In the dim light, she was not aware of his repulsiveness.

"Poor boy," she said, "poor boy." She felt him stiffen as she stroked his hair, then relax. "Poor boy. May I hold you?"

She sat down on the floor next to him and slowly and rhythmically stroked his hair, his cheek, his arm. Softly, she began to sing a slow and gentle song.

He lifted his head at that, staring at her mouth in the dimness, as though wondering at the sound.

She maneuvered him closer while he listened to her. Slowly, she pressed gently against the side of his head, until it rested on her shoulder. She put her arm under his thighs and with a smooth and unhurried motion lifted him into her lap.

She continued singing, the same simple verse over and over, while she rocked back and forth, back and forth.

He stopped crying, and after a while the smooth burr of his breathing showed he was asleep.

With infinite care, she pushed his bed back against the wall and laid him down. She covered him and stared down. His face looked so peaceful and little-boy as he slept. It didn't matter so much that it was so ugly. Really.

She began to tiptoe out, then thought: If he wakes up?

She came back, battled irresolutely with herself, then sighed and slowly got into bed with the child.

It was too small for her. She was cramped and uneasy at the lack of canopy, but the child's hand crept into hers and, somehow, she fell asleep in that position.

She awoke with a start and a wild impulse to scream. The latter she just managed to suppress into a gurgle. The boy was looking at her, wide-eyed. It took her a long moment to remember getting into bed with him, and now, slowly, without unfixing her eyes from his, she stretched one leg carefully and let it touch the floor, then the other one.

She cast a quick and apprehensive glance toward the open ceiling, then tensed her muscles for quick disengagement.

But at that moment, the boy's stubby fingers reached out and touched her lips. He said something.

She shrank at the touch. He was terribly ugly in the light of day.

The boy spoke again. He opened his own mouth and gestured with his hand as though something were coming out.

Miss Fellowes guessed at the meaning and said tremulously, "Do you want me to sing?"

The boy said nothing but stared at her mouth.

In a voice slightly off key with tension, Miss Fellowes began the little song she had sung the night before and the ugly little boy smiled. He swayed clumsily in rough time to the music and made a little gurgly sound that might have been the beginnings of a laugh.

Miss Fellowes sighed inwardly. Music hath charms to soothe the savage breast. It might help——

She said, "You wait. Let me get myself fixed up. It will just take a minute. Then I'll make breakfast for you."

She worked rapidly, conscious of the lack of ceiling at all times. The boy remained in bed, watching her when she was in view. She smiled at him at those times and waved. At the end, he waved back, and she found herself being charmed by that.

Finally, she said, "Would you like oatmeal with milk?" It took a moment to prepare, and then she beckoned to him.

Whether he understood the gesture or followed the aroma, Miss Fellowes did not know, but he got out of bed.

She tried to show him how to use a spoon but he shrank away from it in fright. (Time enough, she thought.) She compromised on insisting that he lift the bowl in his hands. He did it clumsily enough and it was incredibly messy but most of it did get into him.

She tried the drinking milk in a glass this time, and the little boy whined when he found the opening too small for him to get his face into conveniently. She held his hand, forcing it around the glass, making him tip it, forcing his mouth to the rim.

Again a mess but again most went into him, and she was used to messes.

The washroom, to her surprise and relief, was a less frustrating matter. He understood what it was she expected him to do.

She found herself patting his head, saying, "Good boy. Smart boy."

And to Miss Fellowes' exceeding pleasure, the boy smiled at that.

She thought: When he smiles, he's quite bearable. Really.

Later in the day, the gentlemen of the press arrived.

She held the boy in her arms and he clung to her wildly while across the open door they set cameras to work. The commotion frightened the boy and he began to cry, but it was ten minutes before Miss Fellowes was allowed to retreat and put the boy in the next room.

She emerged again, flushed with indignation, walked out of the apartment (for the first time in eighteen hours) and closed the door behind her. "I think you've had enough. It will take me a while to quiet him. Go away."

"Sure, sure," said the gentleman from the *Times-Herald*. "But is that really a Neanderthal or is this some kind of gag?"

"I assure you," said Hoskins' voice, suddenly, from the background, "that this is no gag. The child is authentic Homo neanderthalensis."

"Is it a boy or a girl?"

"Boy," said Miss Fellowes briefly.

"Ape-boy," said the gentleman from the *News*. "That's what we've got here. Ape-boy. How does he act, Nurse?"

"He acts exactly like a little boy," snapped Miss Fellowes, annoyed into the defensive, "and he is not an ape-boy. His name is—is Timothy, Timmie—and he is perfectly normal in his behavior."

She had chosen the name Timothy at a venture. It was the first that had occurred to her.

"Timmie the Ape-boy," said the gentleman from the *News* and, as it turned out, Timmie the Ape-boy was the name under which the child became known to the world.

The gentleman from the *Globe* turned to Hoskins and said, "Doc, what do you expect to do with the ape-boy?"

Hoskins shrugged. "My original plan was completed when I proved it possible to bring him here. However, the anthropologists will be very interested, I imagine, and the physiologists. We have here, after all, a creature which is at the edge of being human. We should learn a great deal about ourselves and our ancestry from him."

"How long will you keep him?"

"Until such a time as we need the space more than we need him. Quite a while, perhaps."

The gentleman from the *News* said, "Can you bring it out into the open so we can set up sub-etheric equipment and put on a real show?"

"I'm sorry, but the child cannot be removed from Stasis."

"Exactly what is Stasis?"

"Ah." Hoskins permitted himself one of his short smiles. "That would take a great deal of explanation, gentlemen. In Stasis, time as we know it doesn't exist. Those rooms are inside an invisible bubble that is not exactly part of our Universe. That is why the child could be plucked out of time as it was."

"Well, wait now," said the gentleman from the *News* discontentedly, "what are you giving us? The nurse goes into the room and out of it."

"And so can any of you," said Hoskins matter-of-factly. "You would be moving parallel to the lines of temporal force and no great energy gain or loss would be involved. The child, however, was taken from the far past. It moved across the lines and gained temporal potential. To move it into the Universe and into our own time would absorb enough energy to burn out every line in the place and probably blank out all power in the city of Washington. We had to store trash brought with him on the premises and will have to remove it little by little."

The newsmen were writing down sentences busily as Hoskins spoke to them. They did not understand and they were sure their readers would not, but it sounded scientific and that was what counted.

The gentleman from the *Times-Herald* said, "Would you be available for an all-circuit interview tonight?"

"I think so," said Hoskins at once, and they all moved off.

Miss Fellowes looked after them. She understood all this about Stasis and temporal force as little as the newsmen but she managed to get this much. Timmie's imprisonment (she found herself suddenly thinking of the little boy as Timmie) was a real one and not one imposed by the arbitrary fiat of Hoskins. Apparently, it was impossible to let him out of Stasis at all, ever.

Poor child. Poor child.

She was suddenly aware of his crying and she hastened in to console him.

Miss Fellowes did not have a chance to see Hoskins on the all-circuit hookup, and though his interview was beamed to every part of the world and even to the outpost on the Moon, it did not penetrate the apartment in which Miss Fellowes and the ugly little boy lived.

But he was down the next morning, radiant and joyful.

Miss Fellowes said, "Did the interview go well?"

"Extremely. And how is—Timmie?"

Miss Fellowes found herself pleased at the use of the name. "Doing quite well. Now come out here, Timmie, the nice gentleman will not hurt you."

But Timmie stayed in the other room, with a lock of his matted hair showing behind the barrier of the door and, occasionally, the corner of an eye.

"Actually," said Miss Fellowes, "he is settling down amazingly. He is quite intelligent."

"Are you surprised?"

She hesitated just a moment, then said, "Yes, I am. I suppose I thought he was an ape-boy."

"Well, ape-boy or not, he's done a great deal for us. He's put Stasis, Inc. on the map. We're in, Miss Fellowes, we're in." It was as though he had to express his triumph to someone, even if only to Miss Fellowes.

"Oh?" She let him talk.

He put his hands in his pockets and said, "We've been working on a shoestring for ten years, scrounging funds a penny at a time wherever we could. We had to shoot the works on one big show. It was everything, or nothing. And when I say the works, I mean it. This attempt to bring in a Neanderthal took every cent we could borrow or steal, and some of it *was* stolen—funds for other projects, used for this one without permission. If that experiment hadn't succeeded, I'd have been through."

Miss Fellowes said abruptly, "Is that why there are no ceilings?"

"Eh?" Hoskins looked up.

"Was there no money for ceilings?"

"Oh. Well, that wasn't the only reason. We didn't really know in advance how old the Neanderthal might be exactly. We can detect only dimly in time, and he might have been large and savage. It was possible we might have had to deal with him from a distance, like a caged animal."

"But since that hasn't turned out to be so, I suppose you can build a ceiling now."

"Now, yes. We have plenty of money, now. Funds have been promised from every source. This is all wonderful, Miss Fellowes." His broad face gleamed with a smile that lasted and when he left, even his back seemed to be smiling.

Miss Fellowes thought: He's quite a nice man when he's off guard and forgets about being scientific.

She wondered for an idle moment if he was married, then dismissed the thought in self-embarrassment.

"Timmie," she called. "Come here, Timmie."

In the months that passed, Miss Fellowes felt herself grow to be an integral part of Stasis, Inc. She was given a small office of her own with her name on the door, an office quite close to the dollhouse (as she never stopped calling Timmie's Stasis bubble). She was given a substantial raise. The dollhouse was covered by a ceiling; its furnishings were elaborated and improved; a second washroom was added—and even so, she gained an apartment of her own on the institute grounds and, on occasion, did not stay with Timmie during the night. An intercom was set up between the dollhouse and her apartment and Timmie learned how to use it.

Miss Fellowes got used to Timmie. She even grew less conscious of his ugliness. One day she found herself staring at an ordinary boy in the street and finding something bulgy and unattractive in his high domed forehead and jutting chin. She had to shake herself to break the spell.

It was more pleasant to grow used to Hoskins' occasional visits. It was obvious he welcomed escape from his increasingly harried role as head of Stasis, Inc., and that he took a sentimental interest in the child who had started it all, but it seemed to Miss Fellowes that he also enjoyed talking to her.

(She had learned some facts about Hoskins, too. He had invented the method of analyzing the reflection of the past-penetrating mesonic beam; he had invented the method of establishing Stasis; his coldness was only an effort to hide a kindly nature; and, oh yes, he *was* married.)

What Miss Fellowes could *not* get used to was the fact that she was engaged in a scientific experiment. Despite all she could do, she found herself getting personally involved to the point of quarreling with the physiologists.

On one occasion, Hoskins came down and found her in the midst of a hot urge to kill. They had no right; they had no *right*—— Even if he *was* a Neanderthal, he still wasn't an animal.

She was staring after them in a blind fury; staring out the open door and listening to Timmie's sobbing, when she noticed Hoskins standing before her. He might have been there for minutes.

He said, "May I come in?"

She nodded curtly, then hurried to Timmie, who clung to her, curling his little bandy legs—still thin, so thin—about her.

Hoskins watched, then said gravely, "He seems quite unhappy."

Miss Fellowes said, "I don't blame him. They're at him every day now with their blood samples and their probings. They keep him on synthetic diets that I wouldn't feed a pig."

"It's the sort of thing they can't try on a human, you know."

"And they can't try it on Timmie, either. Dr. Hoskins, I insist. You told me it was Timmie's coming that put Stasis, Inc. on the map. If you have any gratitude for that at all, you've *got* to keep them away from the poor thing at least until he's old enough to understand a little more. After he's had a bad session with them, he has nightmares, he can't sleep. Now I warn you," (she reached a sudden peak of fury) "I'm not letting them in here any more."

(She realized that she had screamed that, but she couldn't help it.)

She said more quietly, "I know he's Neanderthal but there's a great deal we don't appreciate about Neanderthals. I've read up on them. They had a culture of their own. Some of the greatest human inventions arose in Neanderthal times. The domestication of animals, for instance; the wheel; various techniques in grinding stone. They even had spiritual yearnings. They buried their dead and buried possessions with the body, showing they believed in a life after death. It amounts to the fact that they invented religion. Doesn't that mean Timmie has a right to human treatment?"

She patted the little boy gently on his buttocks and sent him off into his playroom. As the door was opened, Hoskins smiled briefly at the display of toys that could be seen.

Miss Fellowes said defensively, "The poor child deserves his toys. It's all he has and he earns them with what he goes through."

"No, no. No objections, I assure you. I was just thinking how you've changed since the first day, when you were quite angry I had foisted a Neanderthal on you."

Miss Fellowes said in a low voice, "I suppose I didn't——" and faded off.

Hoskins changed the subject, "How old would you say he is, Miss Fellowes?"

She said, "I can't say, since we don't know how Neanderthals develop. In size, he'd only be three but Neanderthals are smaller generally and with all the tampering they do with him, he probably isn't growing. The way he's learning English, though, I'd say he was well over four."

"Really? I haven't noticed anything about learning English in the reports."

"He won't speak to anyone but me. For now, anyway. He's terribly afraid of others, and no wonder. But he can ask for an article of food; he can indicate any need practically; and he understands almost anything I say. Of course," (she watched him shrewdly, trying to estimate if this was the time), "his development may not continue."

"Why not?"

"Any child needs stimulation and this one lives a life of solitary confinement. I do what I can, but I'm not with him all the time and I'm not all he needs. What I mean, Dr. Hoskins, is that he needs another boy to play with."

Hoskins nodded slowly. "Unfortunately, there's only one of him, isn't there? Poor child."

Miss Fellowes warmed to him at once. She said, "You do like Timmie, don't you?" It was so nice to have someone else feel like that.

"Oh, yes," said Hoskins, and with his guard down, she could see the weariness in his eyes.

Miss Fellowes dropped her plans to push the matter at once. She said, with real concern, "You look worn out, Dr. Hoskins."

"Do I, Miss Fellowes? I'll have to practice looking more lifelike then."

"I suppose Stasis, Inc. is very busy and that that keeps you very busy."

Hoskins shrugged. "You suppose right. It's a matter of animal, vegetable, and mineral in equal parts, Miss Fellowes. But then, I suppose you haven't ever seen our displays."

"Actually, I haven't. ——But it's not because I'm not interested. It's just that I've been so busy."

"Well, you're not all that busy right now," he said with impulsive decision. "I'll call for you tomorrow at eleven and give you a personal tour. How's that?"

She smiled happily. "I'd love it."

He nodded and smiled in his turn and left.

Miss Fellowes hummed at intervals for the rest of the day. Really —to think so was ridiculous, of course—but really, it was almost like—like making a date.

He was quite on time the next day, smiling and pleasant. She had replaced her nurse's uniform with a dress. One of conservative cut, to be sure, but she hadn't felt so feminine in years.

He complimented her on her appearance with staid formality and she accepted with equally formal grace. It was really a perfect prelude, she thought. And then the additional thought came, prelude to what?

She shut that off by hastening to say good-by to Timmie and to assure him she would be back soon. She made sure he knew all about what and where lunch was.

Hoskins took her into the new wing, into which she had never yet gone. It still had the odor of newess about it and the sound of construction, softly heard, was indication enough that it was still being extended.

"Animal, vegetable, and mineral," said Hoskins, as he had the day before. "Animal right there; our most spectacular exhibits."

The space was divided into many rooms, each a separate Stasis bubble. Hoskins brought her to the view-glass of one and she looked in. What she saw impressed her first as a scaled, tailed chicken. Skittering on two thin legs it ran from wall to wall with its delicate birdlike head, surmounted by a bony keel like the comb of a rooster, looking this way and that. The paws on its small forelimbs clenched and unclenched constantly.

Hoskins said, "It's our dinosaur. We've had it for months. I don't know when we'll be able to let go of it."

"Dinosaur?"

"Did you expect a giant?"

She dimpled. "One does, I suppose. I know some of them are small."

"A small one is all we aimed for, believe me. Generally, it's under investigation, but this seems to be an open hour. Some interesting things have been discovered. For instance, it is not entirely cold-blooded. It has an imperfect method of maintaining internal temperatures higher than that of its environment. Unfortunately, it's a male. Ever since we brought it in we've been trying to get a fix on another that may be female, but we've had no luck yet."

"Why female?"

He looked at her quizzically. "So that we might have a fighting chance to obtain fertile eggs, and baby dinosaurs."

"Of course."

He led her to the trilobite section. "That's Professor Dwayne of Washington University," he said. "He's a nuclear chemist. If I recall correctly, he's taking an isotope ratio on the oxygen of the water."

"Why?"

"It's primeval water; at least half a billion years old. The isotope ratio gives the temperature of the ocean at that time. He himself happens to ignore the trilobites, but others are chiefly concerned in dissecting them. They're the lucky ones because all they need are scalpels and microscopes. Dwayne has to set up a mass spectrograph each time he conducts an experiment."

"Why's that? Can't he——"

"No, he can't. He can't take anything out of the room as far as can be helped."

There were samples of primordial plant life too and chunks of rock formations. Those were the vegetable and mineral. And every specimen had its investigator. It was like a museum; a museum brought to life and serving as a superactive center of research.

"And you have to supervise all of this, Dr. Hoskins?"

"Only indirectly, Miss Fellowes. I have subordinates, thank heaven. My own interest is entirely in the theoretical aspects of the matter: the nature of Time, the technique of mesonic inter-temporal detection and so on. I would exchange all this for a method of detecting objects closer in Time than ten thousand years ago. If we could get into historical times——"

He was interrupted by a commotion at one of the distant booths, a thin voice raised querulously. He frowned, muttered hastily, "Excuse me," and hastened off.

Miss Fellowes followed as best she could without actually running.

An elderly man, thinly-bearded and red-faced, was saying, "I had vital aspects of my investigations to complete. Don't you understand that?"

A uniformed technician with the interwoven SI monogram (for Stasis, Inc.) on his lab coat, said, "Dr. Hoskins, it was arranged with Professor Ademewski at the beginning that the specimen could only remain here two weeks."

"I did not know then how long my investigations would take. I'm not a prophet," said Ademewski heatedly.

Dr. Hoskins said, "You understand, Professor, we have limited space; we must keep specimens rotating. That piece of chalcopyrite must go back; there are men waiting for the next specimen."

"Why can't I have it for myself, then? Let me take it out of there."

"You know you can't have it."

"A piece of chalcopyrite; a miserable five-kilogram piece? Why not?"

"We can't afford the energy expense!" said Hoskins brusquely. "You know that."

The technician interrupted. "The point is, Dr. Hoskins, that he tried to remove the rock against the rules and I almost punctured Stasis while he was in there, not knowing he was in there."

There was a short silence and Dr. Hoskins turned on the investigator with a cold formality. "Is that so, Professor?"

Professor Ademewski coughed. "I saw no harm———"

Hoskins reached up to a hand-pull dangling just within reach, outside the specimen room in question. He pulled it.

Miss Fellowes, who had been peering in, looking at the totally undistinguished sample of rock that occasioned the dispute, drew in her breath sharply as its existence flickered out. The room was empty.

Hoskins said, "Professor, your permit to investigate matters in Stasis will be permanently voided. I am sorry."

"But wait———"

"I am sorry. You have violated one of the stringent rules."

"I will appeal to the International Association———"

"Appeal away. In a case like this, you will find I can't be overruled."

He turned away deliberately, leaving the professor still protesting and said to Miss Fellowes (his face still white with anger), "Would you care to have lunch with me, Miss Fellowes?"

He took her into the small administration alcove of the cafeteria. He greeted others and introduced Miss Fellowes with complete ease, although she herself felt painfully self-conscious.

What must they think, she thought, and tried desperately to appear businesslike.

She said, "Do you have that kind of trouble often, Dr. Hoskins? I mean like that you just had with the professor?" She took her fork in hand and began eating.

"No," said Hoskins forcefully. "That was the first time. Of course I'm always having to argue men out of removing specimens but this is the first time one actually tried to *do* it."

"I remember you once talked about the energy it would consume."

"That's right. Of course, we've tried to take it into account. Accidents will happen and so we've got special power sources designed to stand the drain of accidental removal from Stasis, but that doesn't mean we want to see a year's supply of energy gone in half a second—or can afford to without having our plans of expansion delayed for years. ——Besides, imagine the professor's being in the room while Stasis was about to be punctured."

"What would have happened to him if it had been?"

"Well, we've experimented with inanimate objects and with mice and they've disappeared. Presumably they've traveled back in time; carried along, so to speak, by the pull of the object simultaneously snapping back into its natural time. For that reason, we have to anchor objects within Stasis that we don't want to move and that's a complicated procedure. The professor would not have been anchored and he would have gone back to the Pliocene at the moment when we abstracted the rock—plus, of course, the two weeks it had remained here in the present."

"How dreadful it would have been."

"Not on account of the professor, I assure you. If he were fool enough to do what he did, it would serve him right. But imagine the effect it would have on the public if the fact came out. All people would need is to become aware of the dangers involved and funds could be choked off like that." He snapped his fingers and played moodily with his food.

Miss Fellowes said, "Couldn't you get him back? The way you got the rock in the first place?"

"No, because once an object is returned, the original fix is lost unless we deliberately plan to retain it and there was no reason to do that in this case. There never is. Finding the professor again would mean relocating a specific fix and that would be like dropping a line into the oceanic abyss for the purpose of dredging up a particular fish. —My God, when I think of the precautions we take to prevent accidents, it makes me mad. We have every individual Stasis unit set up with its own puncturing device—we have to, since each unit has its separate fix and must be collapsible independently. The point is, though, none of the puncturing devices is ever activated until the last minute. And then we deliberately make activation impossible except by the pull of a rope carefully led outside the Stasis. The pull is a gross mechanical motion that requires a strong effort, not something that is likely to be done accidentally."

Miss Fellowes said, "But doesn't it—change history to move something in and out of Time?"

Hoskins shrugged. "Theoretically, yes; actually, except in unusual cases, no. We move objects out of Stasis all the time. Air molecules. Bacteria. Dust. About 10 per cent of our energy consumption goes to make up micro-losses of that nature. But moving even large objects in Time sets up changes that damp out. Take that chalcopyrite from the Pliocene. Because of its absence for two weeks some insect didn't find the shelter it might have found and is killed. That could initiate a whole series of changes, but the mathematics of Stasis indicates that this is a converging series. The amount of change diminishes with time and then things are as before."

"You mean, reality heals itself?"

"In a manner of speaking. Abstract a human from Time or send one back, and you make a larger wound. If the individual is an ordinary one, that wound still heals itself. Of course, there are a great many people who write to us each day and want us to bring Abraham Lincoln into the present, or Mohammed, or Lenin. *That* can't be done, of course. Even if we could find them, the change in reality in moving one of the history molders would be too great to be healed. There are ways of calculating when a change is likely to be too great and we avoid even approaching that limit."

Miss Fellowes said, "Then, Timmie——"

"No, he presents no problem in that direction. Reality is safe. But——" He gave her a quick, sharp glance, then went on, "But never mind. Yesterday you said Timmie needed companionship."

"Yes," Miss Fellowes smiled her delight. "I didn't think you paid that any attention."

"Of course I did. I'm fond of the child. I appreciate your feelings for him and I was concerned enough to want to explain to you. Now I have; you've seen what we do; you've gotten some insight into the difficulties involved; so you know why, with the best will in the world, we can't supply companionship for Timmie."

"You can't?" said Miss Fellowes, with sudden dismay.

"But I've just explained. We couldn't possibly expect to find another Neanderthal his age without incredible luck, and if we could, it wouldn't be fair to multiply risks by having another human being in Stasis."

Miss Fellowes put down her spoon and said energetically, "But, Dr. Hoskins, that is not at all what I meant. I don't want you to bring another Neanderthal into the present. I know that's impossible. But it isn't impossible to bring another child to play with Timmie."

Hoskins stared at her in concern. "A *human* child?"

"*Another* child," said Miss Fellowes, completely hostile now. "Timmie is human."

"I couldn't dream of such a thing."

"Why not? Why couldn't you? What is wrong with the notion? You pulled that child out of Time and made him an eternal prisoner. Don't you owe him something? Dr. Hoskins, if there is any man who, in this world, is that child's father in every sense but the biological, it is you. Why can't you do this little thing for him?"

Hoskins said, "His *father?*" He rose, somewhat unsteadily, to his feet. "Miss Fellowes, I think I'll take you back now, if you don't mind."

They returned to the dollhouse in a complete silence that neither broke.

It was a long time after that before she saw Hoskins again, except for an occasional glimpse in passing. She was sorry about that at times; then, at other times, when Timmie was more than usually woebegone or when he spent silent hours at the window with its prospect of little more than nothing, she thought, fiercely: Stupid man.

Timmie's speech grew better and more precise each day. It never entirely lost a certain soft, slurriness that Miss Fellowes found rather endearing. In times of excitement, he fell back into tongue-clicking but those times were becoming fewer. He must be forgetting the days before he came into the present—except for dreams.

As he grew older, the physiologists grew less interested and the psychologists more so. Miss Fellowes was not sure that she did not like the new group even less than the first. The needles were gone; the injections and withdrawals of fluid; the special diets. But now Timmie was made to overcome barriers to reach food and water. He had to lift panels, move bars, reach for cords. And the mild electric shocks made him cry and drove Miss Fellowes to distraction.

She did not wish to appeal to Hoskins; she did not wish to have to go to him; for each time she thought of him, she thought of his face over the luncheon table that last time. Her eyes moistened and she thought: Stupid, *stupid* man.

And then one day Hoskins' voice sounded unexpectedly, calling into the dollhouse, "Miss Fellowes."

She came out coldly, smoothing her nurse's uniform, then stopped in confusion at finding herself in the presence of a pale woman, slender and of middle height. The woman's fair hair and complexion gave her an appearance of fragility. Standing behind her and clutching at her skirt was a round-faced, large-eyed child of four.

Hoskins said, "Dear, this is Miss Fellowes, the nurse in charge of the boy. Miss Fellowes, this is my wife."

(Was this his wife? She was not as Miss Fellowes had imagined her to be. But then, why not? A man like Hoskins would choose a weak thing to be his foil. If that was what he wanted——)

She forced a matter-of-fact greeting. "Good afternoon, Mrs. Hoskins. Is this your—your little boy?"

(*That* was a surprise. She had thought of Hoskins as a husband, but not as a father, except, of course—— She suddenly caught Hoskins' grave eyes and flushed.)

Hoskins said, "Yes, this is my boy, Jerry. Say hello to Miss Fellowes, Jerry."

(Had he stressed the word "this" just a bit? Was he saying *this* was his son and not——)

Jerry receded a bit further into the folds of the maternal skirt and muttered his hello. Mrs. Hoskins' eyes were searching over Miss Fellowes' shoulders, peering into the room, looking for something.

Hoskins said, "Well, let's go in. Come, dear. There's a trifling discomfort at the threshold, but it passes."

Miss Fellowes said, "Do you want Jerry to come in, too?"

"Of course. He is to be Timmie's playmate. You said that Timmie needed a playmate. Or have you forgotten?"

"But——" She looked at him with a colossal, surprised wonder. "*Your* boy?"

He said peevishly, "Well, who's boy, then? Isn't this what you want? Come on in, dear. Come on in."

Mrs. Hoskins lifted Jerry into her arms with a distinct effort and, hesitantly, stepped over the threshold. Jerry squirmed as she did so, disliking the sensation.

Mrs. Hoskins said in a thin voice, "Is the creature here? I don't see him."

Miss Fellowes called, "Timmie. Come out."

Timmie peered around the edge of the door, staring up at the little boy who was visiting him. The muscles in Mrs. Hoskins' arms tensed visibly.

She said to her husband, "Gerald, are you sure it's safe?"

Miss Fellowes said at once, "If you mean is Timmie safe, why, of course he is. He's a gentle little boy."

"But he's a sa—savage."

(The ape-boy stories in the newspapers!) Miss Fellowes said emphatically, "He is not a savage. He is just as quiet and reasonable as you can possibly expect a five-and-a-half-year-old to be. It is very generous of you, Mrs. Hoskins, to agree to allow your boy to play with Timmie but please have no fears about it."

Mrs. Hoskins said with mild heat, "I'm not sure that I agree."

"We've had it out, dear," said Hoskins. "Let's not bring up the matter for new argument. Put Jerry down."

Mrs. Hoskins did so and the boy backed against her, staring at the pair of eyes which were staring back at him from the next room.

"Come here, Timmie," said Miss Fellowes. "Don't be afraid."

Slowly, Timmie stepped into the room. Hoskins bent to disengage Jerry's fingers from his mother's skirt. "Step back, dear. Give the children a chance."

The youngsters faced one another. Although the younger, Jerry was nevertheless an inch taller, and in the presence of his straightness and his high-held, well-proportioned head, Timmie's grotesqueries were suddenly almost as pronounced as they had been in the first days.

Miss Fellowes' lips quivered.

It was the little Neanderthal who spoke first, in childish treble. "What's your name?" And Timmie thrust his face suddenly forward as though to inspect the other's features more closely.

Startled, Jerry reponded with a vigorous shove that sent Timmie tumbling. Both began crying loudly and Mrs. Hoskins snatched up her child, while Miss Fellowes, flushed with repressed anger, lifted Timmie and comforted him.

Mrs. Hoskins said, "They just instinctively don't like one another."

"No more instinctively," said her husband wearily, "than any two children dislike each other. Now put Jerry down and let him get used to the situation. In fact, we had better leave. Miss Fellowes can bring Jerry to my office after a while and I'll have him taken home."

The two children spent the next hour very aware of each other. Jerry cried for his mother, struck out at Miss Fellowes and, finally, allowed himself to be comforted with a lollipop. Timmie sucked at another, and at the end of an hour, Miss Fellowes had them playing with the same set of blocks, though at opposite ends of the room.

She found herself almost maudlinly grateful to Hoskins when she brought Jerry to him.

She searched for ways to thank him but his very formality was a rebuff. Perhaps he could not forgive her for making him feel like a cruel father. Perhaps the bringing of his own child was an attempt, after all, to prove himself both a kind father to Timmie and, also, not his father at all. Both at the same time!

So all she could say was, "Thank you. Thank you very much."

And all he could say was, "It's all right. Don't mention it."

It became a settled routine. Twice a week, Jerry was brought in for an hour's play, later extended to two hour's play. The children learned each other's names and ways and played together.

And yet, after the first rush of gratitude, Miss Fellowes found herself disliking Jerry. He was larger and heavier and in all things dominant, forcing Timmie into a completely secondary role. All that reconciled her to the situation was the fact that, despite difficulties, Timmie looked forward with more and more delight to the periodic appearances of his playfellow.

It was all he had, she mourned to herself.

And once, as she watched them, she thought: Hoskins' two children, one by his wife and one by Stasis.

While she herself——

Heavens, she thought, putting her fists to her temples and feeling ashamed: I'm jealous!

"Miss Fellowes," said Timmie (carefully, she had never allowed him to call her anything else) "when will I go to school?"

She looked down at those eager brown eyes turned up to hers and passed her hand softly through his thick, curly hair. It was the most disheveled portion of his appearance, for she cut his hair herself while he sat restlessly under the scissors. She did not ask for professional help, for the very clumsiness of the cut served to mask the retreating fore part of the skull and the bulging hinder part.

She said, "Where did you hear about school?"

"Jerry goes to school. Kin-der-gar-ten." He said it carefully. "There are lots of places he goes. Outside. When can I go outside, Miss Fellowes?"

A small pain centered in Miss Fellowes' heart. Of course, she saw, there would be no way of avoiding the inevitability of Timmie's hearing more and more of the outer world he could never enter.

She said, with an attempt at gaiety, "Why, whatever would you do in kindergarten, Timmie?"

"Jerry says they play games, they have picture tapes. He says there are lots of children. He says—he says——" A thought, then a triumphant upholding of both small hands with the fingers splayed apart. "He says this many."

Miss Fellowes said, "Would you like picture tapes? I can get you picture tapes. Very nice ones. And music tapes, too."

So that Timmie was temporarily comforted.

He pored over the picture tapes in Jerry's absence and Miss Fellowes read to him out of ordinary books by the hours.

There was so much to explain in even the simplest story, so

much that was outside the perspective of his three rooms. Timmie took to having his dreams more often now that the outside was being introduced to him.

They were always the same, about the outside. He tried haltingly to describe them to Miss Fellowes. In his dreams, he was outside, an empty outside, but very large, with children and queer indescribable objects half-digested in his thought out of bookish descriptions half-understood, or out of distant Neanderthal memories half-recalled.

But the children and objects ignored him and though he was in the world, he was never part of it, but was as alone as though he were in his own room—and would wake up crying.

Miss Fellowes tried to laugh at the dreams, but there were nights in her own apartment when she cried, too.

One day, as Miss Fellowes read, Timmie put his hand under her chin and lifted it gently so that her eyes left the book and met his.

He said, "How do you know what to say, Miss Fellowes?"

She said, "You see these marks? They tell me what to say. These marks make words."

He stared at them long and curiously, taking the book out of her hands. "Some of these marks are the same."

She laughed with pleasure at this sign of his shrewdness and said, "So they are. Would you like to have me show you how to make the marks?"

"All right. That would be a nice game."

It did not occur to her that he could learn to read. Up to the very moment that he read a book to her, it did not occur to her that he could learn to read.

Then, weeks later, the enormity of what had been done struck her. Timmie sat in her lap, following word by word the printing in a child's book, reading to her. He was reading to her!

She struggled to her feet in amazement and said, "Now Timmie, I'll be back later. I want to see Dr. Hoskins."

Excited nearly to frenzy, it seemed to her she might have an answer to Timmie's unhappiness. If Timmie could not leave to enter the world, the world must be brought into those three rooms to Timmie—the whole world in books and film and sound. He must be educated to his full capacity. So much the world owed him.

She found Hoskins in a mood that was oddly analogous to her own; a kind of triumph and glory. His offices were unusually busy, and for a moment, she thought she would not get to see him, as she stood abashed in the anteroom.

But he saw her, and a smile spread over his broad face. "Miss Fellowes, come here."

He spoke rapidly into the intercom, then shut· it off. "Have you heard? ——No, of course, you couldn't have. We've done it. We've actually done it. We have intertemporal detection at close range."

"You mean," she tried to detach her thought from her own good news for a moment, "that you can get a person from historical times into the present?"

"That's just what I mean. We have a fix on a fourteenth-century individual right now. Imagine. *Imagine!* If you could only know how glad I'll be to shift from the eternal concentration on the Mesozoic, replace the paleontologists with the historians—— But there's something you wish to say to me, eh? Well, go ahead; go ahead. You find me in a good mood. Anything you want you can have."

Miss Fellowes smiled. "I'm glad. Because I wonder if we might not establish a system of instruction for Timmie?"

"Instruction? In what?"

"Well, in everything. A school. So that he might learn."

"But *can* he learn?"

"Certainly, he *is* learning. He can read. I've taught him so much myself."

Hoskins sat there, seeming suddenly depressed. "I don't know, Miss Fellowes."

She said, "You just said that anything I wanted——"

"I know and I should not have. You see, Miss Fellowes, I'm sure you must realize that we cannot maintain the Timmie experiment forever."

She stared at him with sudden horror, not really understanding what he had said. How did he mean "cannot maintain"? With an agonizing flash of recollection, she recalled Professor Ademewski and his mineral specimen that was taken away after two weeks. She said, "But you're talking about a boy. Not about a rock———"

Dr. Hoskins said uneasily, "Even a boy can't be given undue importance, Miss Fellowes. Now that we expect individuals out of historical time, we will need Stasis space, all we can get."

She didn't grasp it. "But you can't. Timmie—Timmie———"

"Now, Miss Fellowes, please don't upset yourself. Timmie won't go right away; perhaps not for months. Meanwhile we'll do what we can."

She was still staring at him.

"Let me get you something, Miss Fellowes."

"No," she whispered. "I don't need anything." She arose in a kind of nightmare and left.

Timmie, she thought, you will *not* die. You will *not* die.

It was all very well to hold tensely to the thought that Timmie must not die, but how was that to be arranged? In the first weeks, Miss Fellowes clung only to the hope that the attempt to bring forward a man from the fourteenth century would fail completely. Hoskins' theories might be wrong or his practice defective. Then things could go on as before.

Certainly, that was not the hope of the rest of the world and, irrationally, Miss Fellowes hated the world for it. "Project Middle Ages" reached a climax of white-hot publicity. The press and the public had hungered for something like this. Stasis, Inc. had lacked the necessary sensation for a long time now. A new rock or another ancient fish failed to stir them. But *this* was *it*.

A historical human; an adult speaking a known language; someone who could open a new page of history to the scholar.

Zero-time was coming and this time it was not a question of three onlookers from a balcony. This time there would be a world-wide audience. This time the technicians of Stasis, Inc. would play their role before nearly all of mankind.

Miss Fellowes was herself all but savage with waiting. When young Jerry Hoskins showed up for his scheduled playtime with

Timmie, she scarcely recognized him. He was not the one she was waiting for.

(The secretary who brought him left hurriedly after the barest nod for Miss Fellowes. She was rushing for a good place from which to watch the climax of Project Middle Ages. ——And so ought Miss Fellowes with far better reason, she thought bitterly, if only that stupid girl would arrive.)

Jerry Hoskins sidled toward her, embarrassed. "Miss Fellowes?" He took the reproduction of a news-strip out of his pocket.

"Yes? What is it, Jerry?"

"Is this a picture of Timmie?"

Miss Fellowes stared at him, then snatched the strip from Jerry's hand. The excitement of Project Middle Ages had brought about a pale revival of interest in Timmie on the part of the press.

Jerry watched her narrowly, then said, "It says Timmie is an ape-boy. What does that mean?"

Miss Fellowes caught the youngster's wrist and repressed the impulse to shake him. "Never say that, Jerry. Never, do you understand? It is a nasty word and you mustn't use it."

Jerry struggled out of her grip, frightened.

Miss Fellowes tore up the news-strip with a vicious twist of the wrist. "Now go inside and play with Timmie. He's got a new book to show you."

And then, finally, the girl appeared. Miss Fellowes did not know her. None of the usual stand-ins she had used when business took her elsewhere was available now, not with Project Middle Ages at climax, but Hoskins' secretary had promised to find *someone* and this must be the girl.

Miss Fellowes tried to keep querulousness out of her voice. "Are you the girl assigned to Stasis Section One?"

"Yes, I'm Mandy Terris. You're Miss Fellowes, aren't you?"

"That's right."

"I'm sorry I'm late. There's just so much excitement."

"I know. Now I want you——"

Mandy said, "You'll be watching, I suppose." Her thin, vacuously pretty face filled with envy.

"Never mind that. Now I want you to come inside and meet Timmie and Jerry. They will be playing for the next two hours so they'll be giving you no trouble. They've got milk handy and plenty of toys. In fact, it will be better if you leave them alone as much as possible. Now I'll show you where everything is located and ——"

"Is it Timmie that's the ape-b——"

"Timmie is the Stasis subject," said Miss Fellowes firmly.

"I mean, he's the one who's not supposed to get out, is that right?"

"Yes. Now, come in. There isn't much time."

And when she finally left, Mandy Terris called after her shrilly, "I hope you get a good seat and, golly, I sure hope it works."

Miss Fellowes did not trust herself to make a reasonable response. She hurried on without looking back.

But the delay meant she did *not* get a good seat. She got no nearer than the wall-viewing-plate in the assembly hall. Bitterly, she regretted that. If she could have been on the spot; if she could somehow have reached out for some sensitive portion of the instrumentations; if she were in some way able to wreck the experiment——

She found the strength to beat down her madness. Simple destruction would have done no good. They would have rebuilt and reconstructed and made the effort again. And she would never be allowed to return to Timmie.

Nothing would help. Nothing but that the experiment itself fail; that it break down irretrievably.

So she waited through the countdown, watching every move on the giant screen, scanning the faces of the technicians as the focus shifted from one to the other, watching for the look of worry and uncertainty that would mark something going unexpectedly wrong; watching, watching——

There was no such look. The count reached zero, and very quietly, very unassumingly, the experiment succeeded!

In the new Stasis that had been established there stood a bearded, stoop-shouldered peasant of indeterminate age, in ragged dirty clothing and wooden shoes, staring in dull horror at the sudden mad change that had flung itself over him.

And while the world went mad with jubilation, Miss Fellowes

228

stood frozen in sorrow, jostled and pushed, all but trampled; surrounded by triumph while bowed down with defeat.

And when the loud-speaker called her name with strident force, it sounded it three times before she responded.

"Miss Fellowes. Miss Fellowes. You are wanted in Stasis Section One immediately. Miss Fellowes. Miss Fell——"

"Let me through!" she cried breathlessly, while the loud-speaker continued its repetitions without pause. She forced her way through the crowds with wild energy, beating at it, striking out with closed fists, flailing, moving toward the door in a nightmare slowness.

Mandy Terris was in tears. "I don't know how it happened. I just went down to the edge of the corridor to watch a pocket-viewing-plate they had put up. Just for a minute. And then before I could move or do anything——" She cried out in sudden accusation, "You said they would make no trouble; you *said* to leave them alone——"

Miss Fellowes, disheveled and trembling uncontrollably, glared at her. "Where's Timmie?"

A nurse was swabbing the arm of a wailing Jerry with disinfectant and another was preparing an anti-tetanus shot. There was blood on Jerry's clothes.

"He bit me, Miss Fellowes," Jerry cried in rage. "He *bit* me."

But Miss Fellowes didn't even see him.

"What did you do with Timmie?" she cried out.

"I locked him in the bathroom," said Mandy. "I just threw the little monster in there and locked him in."

Miss Fellowes ran into the dollhouse. She fumbled at the bathroom door. It took an eternity to get it open and to find the ugly little boy cowering in the corner.

"Don't whip me, Miss Fellowes," he whispered. His eyes were red. His lips were quivering. "I didn't mean to do it."

"Oh, Timmie, who told you about whips?" She caught him to her, hugging him wildly.

He said tremulously, "She said, with a long rope. She said you would hit me and hit me."

"You won't be. She was wicked to say so. But what happened? What happened?"

"He called me an ape-boy. He said I wasn't a real boy. He said I was an animal." Timmie dissolved in a flood of tears. "He said he wasn't going to play with a monkey anymore. I said I wasn't a monkey; I *wasn't* a monkey. He said I was all funny-looking. He said I was horrible ugly. He kept saying and saying and I bit him."

They were both crying now. Miss Fellowes sobbed, "But it isn't true. You know that, Timmie. You're a real boy. You're a dear real boy and the best boy in the world. And no one, *no* one will ever take you away from me."

It was easy to make up her mind, now; easy to know what to do. Only it had to be done quickly. Hoskins wouldn't wait much longer, with his own son mangled——

No, it would have to be done this night, *this* night; with the place four-fifths asleep and the remaining fifth intellectually drunk over Project Middle Ages.

It would be an unusual time for her to return but not an unheard of one. The guard knew her well and would not dream of questioning her. He would think nothing of her carrying a suitcase. She rehearsed the noncommittal phrase, "Games for the boy," and the calm smile.

Why shouldn't he believe that?

He did. When she entered the dollhouse again, Timmie was still awake, and she maintained a desperate normality to avoid frightening him. She talked about his dreams with him and listened to him ask wistfully after Jerry.

There would be few to see her afterward, none to question the bundle she would be carrying. Timmie would be very quiet and then it would be a *fait accompli*. It would be done and what would be the use of trying to undo it. They would leave her be. They would leave them both be.

She opened the suitcase, took out the overcoat, the woolen cap with the ear-flaps and the rest.

Timmie said, with the beginning of alarm, "Why are you putting all these clothes on me, Miss Fellowes?"

She said, "I am going to take you outside, Timmie. To where your dreams are."

"My dreams?" His face twisted in sudden yearning, yet fear was there, too.

"You won't be afraid. You'll be with me. You won't be afraid if you're with me, will you, Timmie?"

"No, Miss Fellowes." He buried his little misshapen head against her side, and under her enclosing arm she could feel his small heart thud.

It was midnight and she lifted him into her arms. She disconnected the alarm and opened the door softly.

And she screamed, for facing her across the open door was Hoskins!

There were two men with him and he stared at her, as astonished as she.

Miss Fellowes recovered first by a second and made a quick attempt to push past him; but even with the second's delay he had time. He caught her roughly and hurled her back against a chest of drawers. He waved the men in and confronted her, blocking the door.

"I didn't expect this. Are you completely insane?"

She had managed to interpose her shoulder so that it, rather than Timmie, had struck the chest. She said pleadingly, "What harm can it do if I take him, Dr. Hoskins? You can't put energy loss ahead of a human life?"

Firmly, Hoskins took Timmie out of her arms. "An energy loss this size would mean millions of dollars lost out of the pockets of investors. It would mean a terrible setback for Stasis, Inc. It would mean eventual publicity about a sentimental nurse destroying all that for the sake of an ape-boy."

"*Ape-boy!*" said Miss Fellowes, in helpless fury.

"That's what the reporters would call him," said Hoskins.

One of the men emerged now, looping a nylon rope through eyelets along the upper portion of the wall.

Miss Fellowes remembered the rope that Hoskins had pulled outside the room containing Professor Ademewski's rock specimen so long ago.

She cried out, "No!"

But Hoskins put Timmie down and gently removed the over-coat he was wearing. "You stay here, Timmie. Nothing will happen to you. We're just going outside for a moment. All right?"

Timmie, white and wordless, managed to nod.

Hoskins steered Miss Fellowes out of the dollhouse ahead of himself. For the moment, Miss Fellowes was beyond resistance. Dully, she noticed the hand-pull being adjusted outside the doll-house.

"I'm sorry, Miss Fellowes," said Hoskins. "I would have spared you this. I planned it for the night so that you would know only when it was over."

She said in a weary whisper, "Because your son was hurt. Because he tormented this child into striking out at him."

"No. Believe me. I understand about the incident today and I know it was Jerry's fault. But the story has leaked out. It would have to with the press surrounding us on this day of all days. I can't risk having a distorted story about negligence and savage Neanderthalers, so-called, distract from the success of Project Middle Ages. Timmie has to go soon anyway; he might as well go now and give the sensationalists as small a peg as possible on which to hang their trash."

"It's not like sending a rock back. You'll be killing a human being."

"Not killing. There'll be no sensation. He'll simply be a Neander-thal boy in a Neanderthal world. He will no longer be a prisoner and alien. He will have a chance at a free life."

"What chance? He's only seven years old, used to being taken care of, fed, clothed, sheltered. He will be alone. His tribe may not be at the point where he left them now that four years have passed. And if they were, they would not recognize him. He will have to take care of himself. How will he know how?"

Hoskins shook his head in hopeless negative. "Lord, Miss Fellowes, do you think we haven't thought of that? Do you think we would have brought in a child if it weren't that it was the first successful fix of a human or near-human we made and that we did not dare to take the chance of unfixing him and finding another fix as good? Why do you suppose we kept Timmie as long as we did, if it were not for our reluctance to send a child back into the past.

It's just"—his voice took on a desperate urgency—"that we can wait no longer. Timmie stands in the way of expansion! Timmie is a source of possible bad publicity; we are on the threshold of great things, and I'm sorry, Miss Fellowes, but we can't let Timmie block us. We cannot. We cannot. I'm sorry, Miss Fellowes."

"Well, then," said Miss Fellowes sadly. "Let me say good-by. Give me five minutes to say good-by. Spare me that much."

Hoskins hesitated. "Go ahead."

Timmie ran to her. For the last time he ran to her and for the last time Miss Fellowes clasped him in her arms.

For a moment, she hugged him blindly. She caught at a chair with the toe of one foot, moved it against the wall, sat down.

"Don't be afraid, Timmie."

"I'm not afraid if you're here, Miss Fellowes. Is that man mad at me, the man out there?"

"No, he isn't. He just doesn't understand about us. ——Timmie, do you know what a mother is?"

"Like Jerry's mother?"

"Did he tell you about his mother?"

"Sometimes. I think maybe a mother is a lady who takes care of you and who's very nice to you and who does good things."

"That's right. Have you ever wanted a mother, Timmie?"

Timmie pulled his head away from her so that he could look into her face. Slowly, he put his hand to her cheek and hair and stroked her, as long, long ago she had stroked him. He said, "Aren't you my mother?"

"Oh, Timmie."

"Are you angry because I asked?"

"No. Of course not."

"Because I know your name is Miss Fellowes, but—but sometimes, I call you 'Mother' inside. Is that all right?"

"Yes. Yes. It's all right. And I won't leave you any more and nothing will hurt you. I'll be with you to care for you always. Call me Mother, so I can hear you."

"Mother," said Timmie contentedly, leaning his cheek against hers.

She rose, and, still holding him, stepped up on the chair. The sudden beginning of a shout from outside went unheard and, with her free hand, she yanked with all her weight at the cord where it hung suspended between two eyelets.

And Stasis was punctured and the room was empty.

REJECTION SLIPS

a - Learned

Dear Asimov, all mental laws
Prove orthodoxy has its flaws.
Consider that eclectic clause
In Kant's philosophy that gnaws
With ceaseless anti-logic jaws
At all outworn and useless saws
That stick in modern mutant craws.
So here's your tale (with faint applause).
The words above show ample cause.

b - Gruff

Dear Ike, I was prepared
(And, boy, I really *cared*)
To swallow almost anything you wrote.
But, Ike, you're just plain shot,
Your writing's gone to pot,
There's nothing left but hack and mental bloat.
Take back this piece of junk;

It smelled; it reeked; it stunk;
Just glancing through it once was deadly rough.
But Ike, boy, by and by,
Just try another try.
I need some yarns and, kid, I love your stuff.

c - *Kindly*

Dear Isaac, friend of mine,
I thought your tale was fine.
Just frightful-
Ly delightful
And with merits all a-shine.
It meant a quite full
Night, full,
Friend, of tension
Then relief
And attended
With full measure
Of the pleasure
Of suspended
Disbelief.
It is triteful,
Scarcely rightful,
Almost spiteful
To declare
That some tiny faults are there.
Nothing much,
Perhaps a touch,
And over such
You shouldn't pine.
So let me say
Without delay,
My pal, my friend,
Your story's end
Has left me gay
And joyfully composed.

P. S.
Oh, yes,
I must confess
(With some distress)
Your story is regretfully enclosed.